I0609274

# A Cruising Conspiracy

## A Will and Betsy Black Adventure

*This book is dedicated to Allene Webb, Carolyn Groner, Nell Thomas, and Mary Bush. Four English teachers who were each a cornerstone of one of the top English departments ever assembled in a public school. Each teacher had a profound and lasting effect on me.*

*It is also dedicated to the Greenville High School class of 1965. Maybe we didn't change the world, but we gave it our best, gave it a hell of a try, and made our mark.*

*Go Hornets!*

ABSOLUTELY AMAZING eBOOKS

Manhanset House
Dering Harbor, New York 11965

bricktower@aol.com ■ tech@absolutelyamazingebooks.com
■ absolutelyamazingebooks.com

All rights reserved under the International and
Pan-American Copyright Conventions.
Printed in the United States
by J. T. Colby & Company, Inc. New York.
No part of this publication may be reproduced, stored in a retrieval system, or transmitted in any form or by any means, electronic, or otherwise, without the prior written permission of the copyright holder.
The Absolutely Amazing eBooks colophon is a trademark of
J. T. Colby & Company, Inc.

Library of Congress Cataloging-in-Publication Data
Beckwith, David and Nancy
A Cruising Conspiracy
p. cm.

1. FICTION / Mystery & Detective / Amateur Sleuth
2. FICTION / Mystery & Detective / General
3. FICTION / Thrillers / Suspense

ISBN: 978-1-955036-39-9, Trade Paper
Copyright © 2022, David Beckwith
Electronic compilation/ paperback edition
copyright © 2022 By Absolutely Amazing eBooks

# A Cruising Conspiracy

A Will and Betsy Black Adventure

David and Nancy Beckwith

ABSOLUTELY AMAZING eBOOKS

# CHAPTER 1

Will and Betsy Black sat at the bar in Joe's Stone Crab on Miami Beach as they waited for their friends, Dick and Beth Peterson, to join them for an early dinner. The bartender asked them for their drink order. Will told him they were waiting for another couple to join them, and then they each ordered a dirty martini.

Betsy took in the elegant, gleaming walnut-paneled bar as she sat in the wrought iron chair with her foot propped on the brass foot-rail. The chair's back had been embellished with a relief image of a pineapple. The bar had fluted columns behind it, and she could see her reflection in the gleaming etched-glass mirror.

"How about a munchie to go with our drinks?" Will suggested to his wife.

"A wonderful idea."

He asked the bartender for suggestions. The bartender gave them an hors d'oeuvre menu when he returned with their drinks.

"I personally like the oysters or crab cakes or conch fritters, but you can't go wrong no matter what you order," the tuxcedoed bartender replied. "Have you ever had fried asparagus?"

"Let's save some appetite for when the Petersons get here," Betsy said. "The fried asparagus sounds intriguing or maybe the crab cakes. We get conch fritters at home all the time."

"Where's that?"

"Key West."

"It'd give us a chance to see if they know how to make conch fritters on the mainland," Will quipped before turning back to the bartender, "but we'll try the fried asparagus."

"Excellent choice. I'll put in your order immediately."

Will raised his glass and said, "Hotty toddy! To you, my darling. Do you know what Frank Sinatra said about booze?"

"Tell me."

"Alcohol may be man's worst enemy, but the Bible says love your enemy."

"Hear, hear, my dear. Yes, candy may be dandy, but liquor is quicker."

They both took a sip.

Wilson Black, who normally went by Will, was the branch manager of the RST Securities office in Key West. RST was a full service, traditional securities firm and New York Stock Exchange member. He was originally from the Mississippi Delta and had begun his career in the financial services industry in Mobile, Alabama, where he had met Betsy, his wife and soul mate.

Betsy Black was the area manager for WB Bank in Key West. She and Will had met in Mobile and their careers had subsequently taken them to Vero Beach, Florida, where their daughter Lexie had been born. They had raised Lexie in Vero and had every intention of remaining there after she had graduated from the University of Miami. Lexie's career in website hosting management had taken her to Austin, Texas. WB then offered Betsy the area manager's job in Key West. This coincided with RST's desire to open a Keys branch. Having nothing to hold them in Vero Beach at that point, the Blacks moved to Monroe County.

"The Petersons ought to be here soon," Betsy observed.

"Yeah. They came in on the American flight scheduled to hit MIA at 3:20. I stressed with them how important it is to get to Joe's early if they don't want to wait for dinner for a couple of hours. I told them to try to get here as close to five as possible."

"Even if we have to wait, it'll be worth it. There's nothing like Joe's in Memphis."

"Yeah. I thought it'd be fun to show them a Miami institution. It'd be kind of like them taking us to the Rendezvous in Memphis for bar-b-que."

"Or Galatoires in New Orleans. Joe's is just a fun place to take an out-of-towner. Remember when we took them to the Ocean Grill in Vero? They were totally blown away."

"Sho' ain't no place like the Ocean Grill. That's for sure. My dear, you're making me think. We've certainly lived a charmed life, but it wouldn't have been anywhere near as charmed if you hadn't been there to share it with me."

"I love you too," Betsy said and squeezed Will's hand affectionately. "Lean over."

Will leaned towards Betsy and she lightly and lovingly kissed him on the cheek. He beamed.

Dick Peterson and Will had been friends since junior high school and had briefly roomed together in a dorm at Ole Miss. Dick had met his wife Beth there, and as he was preparing to go to Viet Nam as an Army officer, the lovebirds had married. After getting his MBA after his discharge, Dick and Beth had settled in Memphis and raised their daughter Bethany there. Dick became an executive with NAPA; Beth became a speech pathologist.

"One more toast ... this time to two weeks of fun in the sun," Will said and saluted his wife once again.

"Every day with you is fun in the sun. As the saying goes, 'even a bad day in the Keys is an irie day'."

"Amen, my dear. Well, let's just say instead, fun in a different sun."

Will and Dick's Greenville Mississippi high school class had voted on taking a fifteen-day cruise for the class's fortieth reunion rather than just convene in Greenville as they had done for previous reunions. Will was looking forward to spending some quality time with his former classmates.

Will and Betsy clinked their glasses a third time.

"To us."

About that time, the Petersons walked in the door.

"And here are our guests," Will said as they both stood to greet their friends. "You're just in time before this place starts getting busy."

After everyone had hugged and the initial greetings were done, Will caught the maître D' and told him they would like a table. He then settled up with the bartender and asked him if he would instruct the waiter to bring the fried asparagus he had previously ordered to their table.

When they got settled at their table, a waiter took Dick and Beth's drink orders and handed menus to everyone.

"So, what's good in here?" Dick asked.

"Here we are in Joe's Stone Crab, the second highest grossing restaurant in the U.S. and the largest user of stone crabs in Florida, and you ask what's good?" Will teased with a twinkle in his eye. "I think they're known for their ribs."

Both Dick and Beth laughed.

"Touché. You know, you haven't changed a bit," Dick replied and handed him a napkin. "Will, you need wipe your mouth. There's a little bullshit around it."

"Actually, besides stone crabs, Joe's is known for its fried chicken," Will said and pretended to wipe his mouth.

"Oh, go on! You missed some of the BS with that napkin."

"You don't believe me?"

Will waved to the waiter.

"Sir, would you bring some fried chicken to the table along with our asparagus?"

"Of course, sir. They will complement each other nicely."

"So, we have two weeks of tropical splendor in front of us," Beth said. "It's going to be welcome after the winter we just had in Memphis. Are you guys looking forward to spending time with your old classmates?"

"Actually, I am," Will said. "I grew up with many of them and went to school with them from kindergarten on up. Many of us started at Miss Maude Bryan's kindergarten off of Broadway Street in Greenville."

"That's a lot of water under the bridge. I don't go back that far, but I go back far enough."

"Junior high, wasn't it? That's still a long time."

"You betcha."

Betsy and Beth winked at each other. Dick and Will began to reminisce. The girls had heard all of these war stories before on multiple occasions, but they politely listened to them again mostly in silence, only breaking in when they wanted to clarify part of a story they had previously heard or if the boys' memories deviated away from the way they had heard these exploits previously. The fried chicken and asparagus came, and everyone agreed that both were excellent. They all ordered stone crab.

As they were eating their meals, Will saw what looked like a familiar face across the room.

"Dick, look over your shoulder. Speaking of classmates, isn't that Suzzie and Billy Cobb over there?"

Dick glanced back and said, "I believe you're right. When we get through eating, we ought to go over and say hello."

Suzzie and Billy seemed to be in an earnest discussion. Both were frowning. He was gesturing. As they talked, each of them raised their voices. Billy chugged down a drink in a rocks glass and ordered two more. He then chugged both of them down and banged the glass down on the table. He was about to order another round, but Suzzie told the waitress to cancel the order.

They overheard Suzzie say, "Billy, you're getting drunk. Now, enough is enough."

"If I'm going to the poor house, I might as well do it drunk."

"If you order one more drink, I'm leaving right now."

Billy pulled car keys from his pocket and dangled them in front of her.

"You gonna walk? I've got the keys to the rental car."

"I'm not going to drive with you drunk. I'll catch a cab, Billy. I swear I will. Is this what I have to look forward to for the next two weeks on the ship, watching you get drunk every day? If that's the case, I'll just go on back to Tampa."

"If I have to look at that asshole Dickie-do Dunne for the next two weeks, you ain't wrong."

"Billy, Stop it. People are beginning to look at us. We're here to have fun. Let the past be the past. Let it die. I have. If I can put the past behind me, you oughta be able to do so as well."

"His day will come. I *do* know people who know how to even scores."

"Enough! One more word, and you can go on this cruise by yourself."

About that time, the Cobb's waiter brought out their meal. Billy just picked at his.

"I'm not hungry. I'm going to the men's room."

"If I'd been drinking as much as you have, I wouldn't be hungry either."

Billy pushed his chair back, and a walking stick propped against the table clattered to the floor.

"I wish you'd find something else to do with that damned walking stick," he said. "Here, get this mutha out of my way. I'm going to break my neck on it some day."

"Don't blame my walking stick for your carelessness ... or your condition."

Will whispered to Dick, "I don't remember her needing a walking stick. I wonder how come."

Dick shrugged and then quietly replied, "I don't think this would be a good time to say hi."

"Yeah," Will agreed. "Especially since high seems to be a major issue."

# CHAPTER 2

The Petersons had a room at the Wingate Hotel. Since Will and Betsy had taken the airport shuttle to Fort Lauderdale instead of driving their own car, they had gotten a room at another hotel near the airport. They caught a cab to the Wingate so they could have breakfast with their friends. From there, the group planned to go together to Port Everglades to board the ship.

After going through the breakfast buffet, the foursome got a table.

"I haven't seen most of our old classmates since our last reunion ten years ago," Dick commented.

"I was having a hard time recognizing some of them then," Will said.

"Well, everyone can't be expected to age as gracefully as we have."

Beth rolled her eyes at Betsy and said, "And we've got to spend two weeks with these two together."

"I better get my feet off the floor before the bull-crap tide reaches my ankles. These are new shoes. I'd suggest you do the same," Betsy replied.

"Do you know what soul mates are?" Dick said.

"No, but I will in a sec."

"People with the mutual understanding that no one else will put up with their shit."

"Touché," Betsy said. "I guess this makes us even ... for the moment."

"Changing the subject," Will said. "The only stop on this trip I've ever been to is Puerta Villarta, and I was only there once before Betsy and I got married. That was one of the things I found so intriguing about this cruise. It's got stops on it that we've talked about but have never done."

"You're one stop ahead of either one of us," Beth said.

"And ain't it a kick that Tom Hamilton is playing on the ship," Will said.

"Yeah, I never dreamed when he was playing football for Greenville High that he'd become a nationally known rock star. Well, that was one of the reasons the committee booked this cruise."

"Who'd a thunk it. He sure as hell wouldn't ever have become a star playing football. As good as our team was, he wasn't even offered a college scholarship."

Their former classmate Tom Hamilton had a band called Ross Revere and His Rebel Rousers. It was originally comprised mostly of friends of his from the Delta. He had become a star in the '70's when a song he wrote and sang entitled "Magnolias and Memories and You" had rocketed to the number one position on Billboard's charts. The band had then charted again with their cover versions of the classic rock tunes, "Jim Dandy" and "Money (That's What I Want)." Nowadays they played in Atlantic City, in Vegas, and on packaged oldies tours.

"People always get a kick out of me telling them that I went to school with Ross Revere."

"You still hear 'Magnolias and Memories' on the classic rock stations. I think Tom lives in L.A. now."

"And can you get over Rusty Herring working on the same cruise as Tom?" Will asked.

"I wonder what the odds are of that ever happening again."

"You remember, all the way through high school Rusty always said he wanted to be a writer. Remember when Mr. Groner appointed him to be editor of the PICA our senior year? He dropped off the football team take the position. Then he worked on The Daily Mississippian staff at Ole Miss."

"Well, by God, he made it. 'The Rape' hit the New York Times bestseller list and just stayed there for what seemed forever. And then it became a hit movie on top of that."

"Yeah. The jackpot. Ka-ching, Ka-ching."

"Rusty turned out to be a one-hit wonder, but I guess if you've only got one bestseller in you 'The Rape' would be a good one to have. Let's face it. Harper Lee was a one-hit wonder with 'To Kill a Mockingbird'."

"I wonder why he chose to write under the pseudonym of Bo Baker?"

"Almost like he had something to hide."

"Rusty? Never! No way!"

"One of the things the critics complimented him on was how shockingly realistic the book was."

"He's going to be doing on-board talks on literary topics. You guys wanna go?"

"Absolutely," Betsy said. "Do you know what he'll be talking about?"

"Don't have a clue, but I'm sure he's got his spiel down pat by now."

"Guys, these next two weeks ought to be really be fun. I'm glad the homecoming committee proposed the cruise idea," Will said.

"I'm looking forward to seeing the rest of our classmates as much as I am our two celebs," Dick replied.

"I second that. Are you guys checked out so we can call a cab and start working our way to the Regency Crown? Laissez les bon temps rouler!"

# CHAPTER 3

The cab with the Petersons and the Blacks arrived at the Port Everglades terminal. Vehicles of every description filled the industrial looking entrance in every direction as far as any of them could see.

"This terminal shore ain't nuttin' to look at," Beth commented.

"But it gets the job done," Will said. "Do you realize that this is the third most busy cruise ship port in the world. Hell, they process more than four million passengers a year through this place."

"That's more people than watch Alabama football games every year," Dick joked.

"Not if you include television," Betsy said.

"Now ... if we could figure out how to make a penny on each person ...," Will began.

"A penny ... if they'd be good for a penny, go for a nickel," Betsy said. "Dream in the big leagues if you want to dream."

"Sorry, I guess I was too busy dreaming of you, my darling."

"Riiight! I wish. OK, folks. Ready, set, go. Let the fun officially begin. Have you ever seen so many people in your life?"

"Are we having fun yet?" Beth asked.

"Mama, are we there yet?" Dick answered.

"Mama, can I have a Bahama Mama yet?" Will chipped in.

"No, no, and no. Let's do it to it."

"Ladies first. I'll pay the cabbie, Dick, and you and I can settle up later."

They checked their luggage at the door and entered the terminal. The inside appeared to be as large as a football field. People scurried everywhere with their carry-ons.

"Woof! Woof! Who let the dogs out?" Will quipped in a sing-song voice. "I'm sure glad we've ridden Regency enough times to be Platinum level customers in their Presidents Club. At least that line is shorter than the normal one."

A Regency employee looked at their boarding passes and pointed each couple towards the correct line.

"Yeah. Kind of like traveling business class instead of economy cattle-car," Will said and pointed. "Betsy, let's get in line. Follow me."

As they all stood in line waiting for their carry-ons to go through the scanner, Will saw a familiar face waiting for another scanning machine.

"Isn't that Dickie-do Dunne?"

Dickie-do was gesturing to the security officer. His carry-on had failed to scan because it had exposed two bottles of rum Dickie-do had tried to smuggle on board.

He was clearly upset, but his contraband booze was confiscated anyway.

"Some people never learn," Dick said. "He was always trying to see what he could get away with when we were growing up."

"I remember."

After being processed in, the Petersons and the Blacks headed for the hallway that would take them onto the ship's gangplank. A photographer took one picture of the four of them together and then another one of each couple separately.

"Now that we've got an official picture as proof, I really feel like this adventure is underway," Betsy commented.

As they came aboard, a waitress served each of them a glass of complimentary champagne.

Will raised his glass. "Now this adventure is indisputably underway., what you guys wanna do first?'

"How about lunch?" Dick said.

"Works for me. Wanna hunt up a real meal or just have pizza on the deck?"

"We can do pizza if you can."

They walked up on the main deck and saw Jerry Quackenbush sitting there finishing a piece of pepperoni pizza. He was surrounded by empty paper plates and empty plastic beer cups. Jerry was a big, brutish-looking guy with a double chin who had turned from muscle to fat now that he was middle-aged. He wore a greasy, dirty Caterpillar baseball cap. He was obviously not accustomed to wearing shorts or leisure wear since his legs were lily white. On his feet were well-worn work boots and white socks. When he finished eating, he got some Red Man chewing tobacco out of his pocket and bit off a plug with his stained teeth.

Will said in a low voice to Betsy, "Jerry was our left tackle in high school. He made all-state because he was such a badass. But he never had it upstairs."

Will tapped his forehead for emphasis.

"He sure looks like a redneck."

"Uh-huh. You can tell my dear? Your powers of observation never cease to amaze me."

Betsy smiled and said, "The reason the bank pays me so much money is that I'm such a good judge of character."

"That tobacco looks disgusting," Beth said.

"Don't knock it 'til you've tried it," Will teased back. "With a little practice, I bet you could learn to spit with the best of them."

Betsy gave him a dirty enough-is-enough look.

"Anyway, ... to finish Jerry's profile assessment ... as I was about to say before your callous but accurate comments concerning his level of sophistication ... Mississippi State drafted him, but he couldn't make his grades. Didn't even make it through his freshman year. I think he works construction nowadays."

Jerry noticed them and waved. He spit into his cup and the burped a beer burp. Without getting up, he stuck out a meaty hand when they approached his table. Betsy immediately noticed his chipped, dirty fingernails. His chunky, plain common-law wife, Judy, sat with him.

"I'll be gol-damned," he said, not bothering to introduce Judy. "If it ain't Will Black and Dick Peterson. After all these years, you guys still buds today? How they hangin', boys?"

"Can't complain. You're right, Jerry. It's good to keep in touch with your old friends."

"Yeah. One of the reasons I'm taking this trip is so I can see some of our old football team. We raised mucho hell in the old days. They weren't pussies like so many the other people in our class. And I'm damned ready and overdue to pick up where we left off. Set down and have a beer wi' me."

"Maybe later. We need to go to the bursar's office, and then maybe we'll come back and grab a slice of pizza. Looks like you're just finishing up anyway. But we'll have plenty of time for talking. After all, we've got two weeks to catch up."

"Hell yeh."

As they walked away, Betsy said, "Thanks, dear, for getting us out of that one."

Beth nodded in agreement and said, "I guess I wasn't in the mood for pizza after all. Let's try the buffet."

# CHAPTER 4

When they had gotten out of earshot of Jerry Quackenbush, Beth asked, “So where do you really want to go now?”

“Like you said, the buffet’s a safe option. After that, why don’t we just walk around the ship and get familiar with it,” Will suggested. “Our bags won’t be delivered to our staterooms until sometime later this afternoon.”

“I guess you know the shops won’t open until we’re at sea,” Dick said.

“I think I’ll live. We’ve got two weeks to shop, but right now I’m sure we can find plenty of other ways to entertain ourselves.”

About midafternoon, they heard an announcement that bags had been delivered to their deck and decided to part ways to go unpack and unwind until the opening function of the reunion that night.

“What are you going to wear?” Beth asked Betsy.

“Oh, just a nice sundress and dressy sandals.”

Dick and Will agreed that neither of them would wear a sports jacket and just go in an open-collar dress shirt. Since they were both on the same deck, they decided to touch base later and agreed to meet at the Black’s room at 5:45 so they could go down together.

The Petersons showed back up right on time.

“This is gonna be interesting,” Will observed to Betsy. “I’ll try to remember to introduce you to people, but if I’m kind of vague, it’s because I’m having a brain fart.”

“They should all have name tags on.”

"Good thing. I'd a been up shit creek at the last reunion otherwise. Some of those people looked nothing like what I remembered."

"Sorry I missed it. If you'll remember my mother was in the hospital, and I went to see her while you went to the reunion alone."

"I remember. ... And I sure missed you that weekend."

"No more than I missed you, my sweet. Experiences are so much better when you can share them with someone you love. Well, we'll make up for that lost weekend this time around."

"Let's not dwell on old memories. We've got some new ones to make."

"Friends, let those new memories begin," Dick said as they approached the meeting room.

A table had been set up just inside the doorway. Will and Dick shook hands with some classmates as they waited to get to the front of the sign-in line. The women running the check-in oohed and aahed over each person as they handed out the name tags and checked each new arrival off their master list.

"How'd you like to have that job for two hours?" Beth whispered to Betsy.

"Nooo, thank you. I'm waiting for someone's makeup to crack from the strain of all that smiling."

When they walked into the room, a banner proclaimed, "Welcome to The GHS 40$^{th}$ Reunion – Class of '65." They stopped to get their bearings before venturing in farther. An hors d'oeuvre table dominated the middle of the room. Makeshift bars had been set up along two walls. Each bar was tended by a tuxcedoed Regency employee. Against a third wall, their classmate Tom Hamilton and another guitarist entertained the group with his acoustic guitar from a makeshift stage. Tom seemed to be doing about as much chatting with various classmates as he did entertain. He saw Will and waved.

Like Tom, the guitarist accompanying him looked clean cut. While both wore their hair a little collegiately on the long side, each looked neatly trimmed. Both wore shorts, Panama hats, and flipflops. Whereas Tom's t-shirt said Rebel Rousers, his friend's t-shirt said Landsharks. Will guessed that the man's height to be probably a little over six feet and that he was in the early stages of being middle aged. He didn't see any visible tattoos.

"Let me say hello to Tom and then I guess we'll get a drink and then start to mingle," Will said in a low tone to Dick. "I'll meet you at that bar over there."

He pointed to his left. Dick and Will both asked their wives what they wanted, and Will told Betsy that he wanted say hello to Tom first.

A group of their old classmates were engaged in a boisterous conversation. Some looked like they were already starting to get in the bag. They were ignoring their bored-looking wives who were at a table a few feet away.

"Will, don't you abandon me or forget to introduce me," Betsy said. "I don't know all these people."

"Don't worry. I won't be long."

Beth gave Dick a look that sent the same message.

Will worked his way across the room to where Tom was playing. Tom greeted him enthusiastically when he got there.

"Long time no see," Will said.

"You know how it is. I don't get back to Mississippi very often anymore."

"That makes two of us. My wife and I live in the Keys."

"Lucky you."

"Is this one of your bandmates?"

Will turned to the other musician and said, "My name is Will Black."

"DV ... DV Craig. No, I'm not a Rebel Rouser. Just an itinerant guitar picker. Tom and I are friends. We've worked a lot of the same gigs and have done some session work together. I'm here just doing him a favor since my wife, Cee Cee, and I just happened to be on this cruise. Well, that's not quite the truth. One reason we signed up was because Tom had told me he was working it. You know how it is. Give us pickers a chance to pick, and we're not going to pass up the opportunity."

"Listen to him. Will, don't let DV pull that itinerant guitar picker line on you. He's more than that. He was part of the travelling group for the Beach Boys and considered to be part of the Wrecking Crew," Tom said.

"Best I remember you're considered to be a Wrecking Crew session man as well."

"Only when they're hard up."

"Don't let Tom hand you that line," DV said. "He's very much a member in good standing."

"I'll let you guys get back to doing what you do best. I hope we all get to visit and bend an elbow together over the next couple of weeks. Tom, great to see you. DV, it was pleasure to meet you. Let me go get my wife a drink before she thinks I abandoned her."

Will had to shake each classmate's hand as he tried to elbow his way to the bar and place his orders. Dick was waiting. He then held the drinks out in front of him shoulder-high to keep from spilling them as he worked his way back towards Betsy. Dick followed closely in the path Will was clearing. They handed the drinks to their wives.

Betsy nodded towards the women at one of the tables and said quietly, "Listen."

"Look at all that makeup Lois Ann has on. Bet she's covering up lines you could trip and fall in."

"If you'll remember, she always did have an acne problem."

"I remember."

"And look how fat Mary Kate is. Her hour-glass figure looks more like a beer barrel nowadays."

"I used to envy her big tits. Now they look like they're almost down to her waist."

"I hope she doesn't bend over. If she does – timber!"

"And look at that dowdy outfit Sara's got on."

"Bet she paid at least five bucks for it at Goodwill."

"Well, I see we're picking up right where we left off," Will said. "That bunch ran together in high school. Thought their shit didn't stink because they were all debutantes. They'd been hanging together since they were sub-debs. They were catty then, and things ain't changed. Continually sharpening their claws on someone to this day. Always thought they were better than anyone else because their fathers had money and they belonged to the country club. I always just tried to get along and stay off their shit list since you couldn't win with them if they got it in for you."

"Meeoow! Scratch! Scratch!" Dick said.

"My dear, your own claws are showing," Beth reminded him. "Let's work our way to the other side of the room. Maybe listen to your classmate play his guitar."

"When he was playing football, we sure never dreamed Tom would become a famous singer and songwriter. I wonder if it went to his head."

"I'm sure it had to, to a certain extent. Lord, you know he had to meet his share of parasite hanger-oners and yes-men. But overall, I think he's still a pretty decent guy."

"Holy shit! Is that Cunningham? He ain't got a hair on his head."

Betsy pointed with her drink back towards the table of women they had just walked away from and said, "Will, now don't you start like them."

"I'm sorry. You're right – but he still ain't got a hair on his head."

"Look who he's cozying up to," Dick said. "Isn't that Martha Hague he's got his arm around?"

"Aren't they both married?"

"Uh huh, and last I heard, not to each other."

Progress was slow as they worked their way towards Tom Hamilton. Every few steps, either Will or Dick had to stop and make small talk with someone wanting to say hello. Back near the front door, they heard Rusty Herring's voice holding court and telling people how his life had changed after his book, "The Rape", had become not only a best-seller but then became a movie as well. He dropped names liberally of the celebrities he now claimed as friends.

Billy Cobb sat at a table alone, quietly getting drunk. His wife Suzzie seethed.

"He looks just like he did at Joe's Stone Crab," Will said to Dick. "Shit-faced."

"That boy definitely appears to have a drinking problem. I'm surprised Suzzy puts up with him."

About that time, their senior class president, jumped enthusiastically onto the low, portable platform Tom was using for a stage and took over the microphone. He took a quick sip of the drink in his hand before beginning to speak. Tom quietly exited the stage and slipped out of the room. Rusty Herring did as well.

"Welcome! It's sure good to see all my classmates and friends. Are you ready for two weeks of fun? Darn, it's good to see all of you. I haven't seen most of you since our 20th in Greenville since I was unable to come to our 30th. I sure missed not being able to attend that one, but the timing was off. I was getting a divorce from my second wife and about to go into rehab. But it was worth it. Now I'm clean, and I have found the Lord."

"I understand Jamie's the preacher at some primitive Baptist church in Waynesville, Georgia."

Jamie rambled on telling everyone more than they wanted to know about his personal life including his time in a commune. People began to roll their eyes at whoever was standing near to them.

Dick whispered to Will, "I could have gone the whole two weeks without having to listen to that drivel."

"I agree. A person's personal life really ought to stay personal."

Betsy overheard the exchange and said, "That's your class president?"

"That's good old Jamie Kingston. He's a doozy ain't he?"

"Lord help us if that's the best leadership y'all could come up with."

"Nobody ran against him."

"A pity."

"Sometimes I think we have equally challenging leadership issues nowadays on every level."

"Don't get me started."

Jamie continued. "And now we have special surprise for you. You're in for a treat. I have the pleasure of presenting fresh off their groundbreaking initial tour – our own – our inimitable state champion Hornets – THE – HORNY – HORRN -- ETTES."

"Horny Hornettes?" Betsy whispered. "A hardshell Baptist preacher talking about horny?"

"What can I say? Our sports teams were called the Greenville High School Hornets," Will whispered back.

"And now for the starting lineup ... or should I say starring lineup ...

"First, J.R. Junior Juniors Jr."

A man entered the room with a Magic-Markered capital "H" printed on a piece of construction board. He wore a low-cut slinky, black, floor-length dress and an Elvira wig. The crowd began to laugh. It was Jimbo Littleton who had been the linebacker on their high school football team. As he walked, he slinked dramatically, running his black-gloved hands up and down his gown and playfully pinching some of the faces of the men present as he worked his way to the front where he attempted to sing an off-key rendition of the first line of "I Put A Spell On You."

"And now we have ... Creme de la Creme .... "

Tom Hamilton, the class's professional musician came dancing into the room carrying another piece of poster board with a big "O" on it. Tom was wearing a 1960's retro mod mini dress. It had huge black and white squares on both the top and bottom. He also wore white, knee-high boots that were made from either patent leather or shiny plastic. He started out doing the Stroll, which morphed into the Hully Gully, and finally he ended up doing the Jerk. He tried to unsuccessfully to recruit members of the class to be his partner as he worked his way to the front.

Will whispered to Betsy, "Tom was our halfback."

Following Tom was Rusty Herring.

Jamie announced, "I present to you ... Nyquillas Dillwad."

Rusty entered wearing a "Pink Ladies" jacket over a poodle skirt. He was wearing black and white spectators with white socks. He had on a pig-tailed, bleach-blonde wig.

Beth whispered to Dick, "I guess I shouldn't be surprised that "Grease" found its way into this skit – if that's what you want to call it."

Dick whispered back, "Rusty was our wide receiver."

Next to come in the door was Dickie-do Dunne, the Hornets' former tight end.

Dickie-do wore an off-the-shoulder polka-dotted Daisy Mae blouse blown out of proportion by some balloons that barely stayed in place as they jiggled and a Dolly Parton wig. A big "N" was on the poster board he carried. When he got to the front, he took the mike and sang in a sing-song fashion like "Dragnet", "They call me Morse Code, but it's pronounced dit – di-dit-dit – di-dit-dit-dit ---- dit."

Betsy rolled her eyes at Will.

"But we're not finished yet. I present to you Bismo Funyuns. Paul Walcox, the team's former quarterback, entered carrying an "E" and wearing a cheerleader costume. He stopped and did the "two-bits, four-bits" cheer on his way to the front.

Next through the door was Jerry Quackenbush, who they had run into on the deck earlier that day. He carried a "T". Jerry wore a shorty nighty and had blacked out his front teeth. The nighty looked especially ridiculous as his hairy, white legs protruded from beneath it. He still wore the same scuffed work boots

"Jest call me Fartrell Cluggins."

He cupped his hand under his hairy underarm and squeezed his arm down hard, making a loud imitation fart. The crowd roared, so he did it again.

"And last ... but certainly not least ... our own Splendiferous Finch who goes by the alias of Willard McFarley."

Will whispered to Betsy, "McFarley was our fullback until he was thrown off the team for training violations."

Willard entered in a Wonder Woman costume carrying an "S".

"Just call me Blunder Woman."

Each participant stuck his letter in a stiff-arm fashion out in front of him and yelled "GO" in a cheerleader fashion. Then each individually screamed the letter he was holding.

H – O –R – N – E -- T – S

Tom picked up his guitar, and the group attempted to sing "With A Little Help From My Friends." This was followed by "Still the One" before toasting each other with beers they pulled from a conveniently placed ice chest.

Beth and Betsy both looked at their husbands and said simultaneously, "I don't know what to say."

"Don't look at me," Will said. "I think someone must've seen 'Revenge of the Nerds'."

"More than once," Dick added. "I wonder what they'll do to top this performance."

"I don't see how anyone can help but," Will said with a laugh. "This has got to be a low-brow point for the reunion."

"I wouldn't be so sure," Dick concluded as he spread his stance and leaned back in an exaggerated manner. "As Chubby Checker said in 'Limbo Rock', with this bunch it may be 'how low can you go?'"

# CHAPTER 5

The following morning Will and Betsy walked up on deck as they waited for the Petersons to join them for the Horizon Court breakfast buffet. They found two unoccupied chaise lounges to sit in while they waited. Resplendent, glorious light shone through wispy clouds signifying a new day. The clouds gradually evaporated and were replaced by fluffy, soft ones that then parted to reveal the beautiful, blue sky underneath. It was a mesmerizing scene. As simple as it looked, the sky seemed to hold every one of their thoughts, dreams and secrets as it stretched out infinitely over their heads. The vastness was all powerful and yet affectionate. It seemed like it could not only swallow you whole but could also hold you lovingly as it whispered words of comfort.

"I guess I'll never take tropical skies for granted," Betsy said.

"Yeah, it *is* amazing and almost magical. Somehow makes you feel insignificant, doesn't it? As you watch the clouds go by, you feel like the sky may be trying to communicate with you."

"And the clouds *can* also be moody. Right now, they're speaking softly to us in a whisper, but as we both know, when it starts lightning and thundering, they can yell at the top of their lungs as well."

"Only ignorant people say, 'I don't see what the big deal is. It's only the sky'. Ready for breakfast? I see Dick and Beth coming."

"What a marvelous day," Beth said as they walked up.

"We were just talking about the sky and the clouds," Betsy said.

"And don't forget about that sea. How would you describe it – azure, cerulean, teal?"

"Do you know why the Caribbean's so blue?" Dick asked. "It's because the water molecules absorb wavelengths from the sun and reflect blue while the other colors are absorbed. Deeper waters have a deeper blue color while shallower water reflects the light and gives it a lighter color."

"Dick, enough is enough," Beth said. "Thank you for destroying our light, romantic mood with scientific facts."

They all laughed.

"And don't forget the algae's effect," Dick said, determined to get in the last word.

"Well, now that our romantic mood has been shot to shit," Will said. "Let's go to breakfast."

They got into the buffet line. Their old classmate Danny Pearce was in line ahead of them.

"Danny Pearce! Now this is a pleasant surprise," Will said, and he and Dick both shook Danny's hand. "I didn't see you at the reception last night. I didn't know you were on the ship."

"I didn't go."

"You missed an interesting show," Dick said. "You could have seen both our class president and some the members of our football team making fools of themselves."

Danny didn't respond. It was almost like he didn't care.

"Are you having breakfast by yourself this morning? I guess the wife is sleeping in. Why don't you join us at our table? Give us a chance to catch up."

All Danny said was, "OK. Sounds good."

When they got their food and found an empty table, Will asked, "So, how's life treated you?"

"OK, I guess."

"You married Misty Martin, didn't you? I remember y'all started dating while we were still in high school. She sleeping in this morning?"

Danny leaned back like Will was invading his personal space.

"She sleeps in every morning."

"I hope she doesn't have health problems. I look forward to seeing her again."

Danny looked at the floor and mumbled, "l lost Misty some time back."

"Man, I'm so sorry. That's rough. I .. didn't know."

"It's not the kind of thing you broadcast."

"Did you guys have any children?"

Danny's hand jiggled, sloshing some coffee out of his cup. He said nothing, just dabbed at it with a napkin.

After a delay, he responded, "No. Under the circumstances though, it was for the best."

"Do you mind me asking what she died of? Cancer? An accident?"

"I'd rather not talk about it. She suffered from depression."

There was silence around the table as each person thought about what to say next.

Dick broke in to change the subject.

"So, is this your first cruise?"

"No," Danny said and did not elaborate.

"So ... have you ever visited any of these places before?" Will said.

"Went to Puerta Vallarta."

"Looking forward to seeing it again?"

"Not especially. Our plane got fogged in as we were leaving, and we missed our connecting flight. The airline lost our luggage. The hotel gave our room away, and Misty had a panic attack as a result."

"I think we've all had a few trips we could classify as trips from hell," Will said, not knowing what else to say.

After rubbing his arm back and forth, Danny finally volunteered some information.

"I came on this trip because Suzzie Cobb said it'd be good for me."

"I'm glad to hear you're still in touch with Suzzie. She and Misty were really close in high school, weren't they? We saw Suzzie and Billy at Joe's Stone Crab the other night, but they were across the room, and we didn't get a chance to introduce Beth or Betsy to them."

Betsy gave Will that look that said, *I'm glad you didn't elaborate farther.*

They ate in silence, and everyone finished their breakfast.

"Anyone want more coffee?" Will asked.

"No."

"Well, we're going to wander around the ship and get to know it better," Dick said. "You're welcome to join us if you want to."

"Thanks for asking, but no thanks. I think I'll go back to my stateroom for a while."

Will stood to leave and said, "Well, it was sure nice seeing you again. We'll have plenty of time to talk and catch up over the next couple of weeks."

They went out onto the deck together and then went in separate directions.

"What was his nickname in your class, Mister Sunshine?" Betsy said.

"I think he should have been elected most likely to depress," Beth retorted.

“Did you notice how fidgety he was? You think he’s on some kind of meds?”

Will responded, “If he ain’t, he oughta be. He was about to give me the heebie-jeebies.”

“Holy, shit! I don’t remember Danny being that way in the old days,” Dick said. “Whatever happened to Misty must have really been tragic. He used to be an open person. Easy to talk to.”

“Kinda like his dad, Pat Pearce. If you’ll remember, Pat was mayor of Greenville for a while and a good mayor. Nice guy. Really tried to revitalize downtown. Everybody called him Popa. Brought his experience of being a small businessman into local politics.”

“Yeh, Popa-Lock. Well, Danny ain’t like his old papa now. Whatever it was with Misty, it seems to have changed Danny into a whole different person. And he sho’ didn’t want to talk about it. Under the circumstances, I didn’t want to push too hard,” Will added.

“I’m sure it’ll come out before this cruise is over. Her death can’t be that big of a secret.”

# CHAPTER 6

The Blacks and the Petersons walked down to the area of the ship containing the shops.

"So, you got any particular shop you wanta go in?" Will asked.

"Not really. Let's just look around and see what they have," Betsy said. "I don't see any reason to rush out and buy anything today on impulse. The cruise is just starting."

"Yeah," Dick said. "I'm sure they'll be running plenty of specials on stuff as the cruise progresses."

"They've got some pretty high-end merchandise here," Will said. "They're counting on the duty-free aspect to encourage people to spend that impulse money. Truth of the matter is I don't think you save a whole hell of a lot – probably mostly just sales tax. Reminds me. We were on a cruise ship during Hurricane Dennis, and the ship began to list from the pounding it was taking from the high waves. You should have seen the merchandise crashing off the shelves and hitting the floor and smashing. Things like the expensive crystal in that shop over there. I felt for the shop owners."

"Oh, I'm sure they were insured," Dick said.

"Still ...," Will replied. "We were in one of the dining rooms during the storm. It was wild to watch the waiters chasing the runaway food carts."

"Look," Beth said. "There's a Cartier shop. Let's go in and look."

"Look, that's all," her husband reminded her. "Don't even think about ...."

Beth gave him an exasperated look, and they entered the shop.

"Oh, my word," Will said. "There's Zelma McFarley. Let's go over and say hello."

Zelma was trying on a gold Cartier watch. It had a triple gold loop strap that wound around the wearer's wrist three times in a snakelike manner. As they walked up, she was staring at it mesmerized while the salesclerk looked on. Zelma waved her arm out in front of her with the watch on.

"That's the most gorgeous and unusual thing I think I've ever seen," she told the clerk.

She seemed almost like she was in a trance.

"All eighteen-carat gold. No other watch maker has anything like it," the clerk said. "It's a Cartier exclusive. You'll certainly get noticed when you walk into a room wearing this."

"I'd certainly be the envy of every woman at this reunion – I can see the jealous look in their eyes now," Zelma said and then muttered under her breath, "the catty bitches."

She continued to look at it longingly.

"How much?"

"Only thirty-three thousand. It's a deal at that price. If you bought it back home, you'd pay more – that is if you could even find one like it."

Will and Dick walked up to Zelma and said, "Hello, Zelma. It's great to see you. Let me introduce you to our wives. I don't think you've ever met either of them."

Zelma seemed to notice them for the first time.

"Well, Well. Will Black and Dick Peterson. I saw you were signed up for the cruise."

"We were at the reception last night. Willard made a cute Wonder ... or should I say Blunder Woman. Did he come up with the name Splendiferous Finch all by himself, or did you help him?"

Betsy broke in at this point and said, "I'm Betsy Black and this is Dick's wife Beth."

Zelma didn't seem to hear either Will's compliment or acknowledge Betsy's introduction but instead said, "Isn't this just the most exquisite watch you're ever seen?"

"It certainly is impressive."

"Where's Willard?" Will asked.

"Oh, I don't know. Probably wasting money in the casino if they're open. If not, I'm sure he'll be in there later."

She turned back around to the salesclerk and said, "Can you hold this for me?"

"We're not allowed to do that, ma'am. This is the only watch like this we have in the shop on this cruise. I'm sure someone is going to snap it up soon. But I *can* put it on your shipboard account."

"Oh, ... I'll take it. I know how to handle Willard."

Zelma had ceased to even know that the Blacks and Petersons were standing there so they said goodbye and left the shop.

"I can't imagine spending that kind of money without clearing it with you first," Betsy said.

"Same here, my dear. Why don't we do something cheap and go get some soft-serve ice cream on the deck. I'll fill you in on Zelma and Willard when we get there."

"I assume you noticed she was wearing a Jaeger-Le Coultre reversible watch," Beth said. "They aren't cheap. They were originally designed for British Army officers playing polo in India."

"My guess – probably a ten to fifteen-thousand-dollar bauble. That alligator band on it probably ran five hundred. But fifteen grand is one thing, but thirty plus grand is another."

"I'm glad you two don't have those expensive tastes," Dick said.

"Oh, we do. We just don't have the pocketbook," Betsy responded.

"After that display, makes me want to order tutti-fruiti," Beth said.

"Which display – Danny's or Zelma's?"

"Both!"

They found a table on the deck and each ordered their favorite ice cream flavor.

"Now that we're alone, let me tell you about the story of a man named Willard," Will sang to the tune of "The Beverly Hillbillies.

"A rich Delta farmer who kept his family fed," Dick chimed in.

"OK, OK! Will Flatt and Dick Scruggs," Beth said.

"Will's flat all right, "Betsy added.

"And Dick's certainly scruggly."

"Shall I continue with the story, or would you two rather hear us sing some more?"

"The story ... by all means."

"The McFarleys are an old Delta planting family. They live in McFarley, Mississippi – if that tells you anything. Been farming for several generations. I think Willard may be Willard the fourth. McFarley is a little-bitty place out past Wayside. I'd guess probably twenty – maybe twenty-five – thousand acres or so. Cotton and beans. Willard inherited it and owns it now. His parents were always doting on him when he was growing up since he was an only child, and he inevitably had more money than sense. Always into something. And of course, every time he'd get in trouble, they'd bail him out."

Dick broke in, “If you’ll remember, both the police chief and the high sheriff belonged to the Masonic Lodge with Willard’s daddy. ... And lodge brothers stick together like glue.”

“Yeah, in fact they were all in both the Blue Lodge and the Shrine,” Will said. “Of course, my dad and Dick’s pop were too.”

“Willard got out of a lot of scrapes ... He could be impulsive and downright mean at times ... you know, things like fighting, drinking, gambling, and racing. He and Billy Cobb and Jimbo Littleton ran together,” Dick said. “And their records always got expunged.”

“Surprise! Surprise! Surprise!”

“His parents bought him a GTO as soon as he was old enough to drive. And he always had a pocket full of money he never had to work for. He even got his pilot’s license when he was still a teenager and flew his dad’s plane.”

“And he must’ve played football,” Betsy said, “since he was in that skit last night.”

“He was our fullback until he got kicked off the team for repeated training violations. Coach Beech – another lodge member – wanted to keep him since the team was on a roll at the time, but Mr. Hall, our principal, wouldn’t let him. Probably the one-time Willard’s daddy didn’t get his way.”

Dick took up the story.

“After Willard got kicked off the team, he began to run with Zelma to get even with his folks since he knew they didn’t approve of her.”

“What was wrong with Zelma?”

“Oh, nothing. She just came from a poor family, and they thought she was white trash. This was his way of rebelling.”

“Well, she did have a reputation for being a little fast,” Will added. “But we never knew that for certain.”

"She wasn't a nun because she did get knocked up – or at least claimed she did. That's one reason Willard married her. That and to show his parents how independent he could be. Almost lost his inheritance because of it. Tried to prove he didn't need his family by breaking away for a while – started some kind of flying service or crop-dusting service or some such."

"Does he still do that?"

"Naw, he eventually made up with his folks. They decided not to disinherit him since he was their only child. Somebody told me he still does fly, however. I guess nowadays just for fun."

Betsy gave a brief whistle under her breath and shook her head.

"Lot of the gals in our class looked down on Zelma and probably still do today. Still regard her as a money-grubbing social climber."

"So that's why she's so hell-bent to impress them? Do they have a child?"

"They do now – more than one, I think. But that first one either turned out to be a false alarm or she had a miscarriage. I'm not sure which. Anyway, Willard and Zelma are still together today and live out on his parents' old place."

"Yep, still farming. The king and queen of McFarley, Mississippi," Dick agreed. "But per the rumor mill, up to his ass in past-due debt. Plus, supposedly he owes the IRS money."

"Figures. Banks like mine don't like to lend to people with tax problems," Betsy said.

"Hope he's had enough sense not to borrow from folks who'll hurt you if you can't pay them back."

"I hope so too, but I wouldn't bet the farm on it."

"Yuk, Yuk."

"Seriously. After what you just told me about Willard, sounds like something he might do," Betsy observed. "I've seen it before."

Later that day they ran into Zelma again. Her jaw was beginning to swell up, and her eyes looked puffy. When she saw them, she turned and went in the other direction without speaking.

"I wonder if Zelma and Willard had a – shall we say – uh, family discussion – over the watch," Dick said.

"If they did, she didn't take it back. She's still got it on."

# CHAPTER 7

"Want to walk the perimeter of the ship and get the kinks out?" Betsy asked Will the following morning.

"Sounds like a wonderful idea, my dear," Will agreed. "I could use both the exercise and the fresh air."

"Want me to see if Dick and Beth want to go?"

"I think I heard him say he was sleeping in this morning. I'd rather just spend some time with you anyway. He may be a friend, but you're still my bestest friend."

"Bestest?"

"Yeah, you know. As in good, better, best and bestest."

"You're my bestest friend too."

They went to the promenade deck and began their stroll. Other walkers all seemed to be walking counterclockwise so they fell in with the flow.

When they got to the ships bow, Betsy stopped to take in the blue horizon.

"My darling," she said with a sigh. "To some people the sky may seem vast and empty, but do you know what I see?"

"Tell me."

"I see a gigantic doorway to our dreams and to the adventure we're embarking on."

"Very well said. I can't think of a thing I'd add to that statement."

After a brief period of meditative silence, they continued walking around the ship. When they got to the stern, they saw Suzzie Cobb leaning on the rail looking wistfully out at the open ocean. She was watching the white-water churn from the ship's gigantic propellers, seemingly lost in thought. The wind blew through her loose hair as she leaned on her walking stick.

"Good morning, Suzzie," Will said. "Fantastic day, isn't it? Billy's not up here with you?"

"He's a slow starter in the mornings. Wasn't feeling well today. Got a headache. Actually, he doesn't feel especially spry most mornings. I'd rather come up here and have some time alone this time of day anyway."

"Well, some people are morning people, and some aren't. Suzzie, have you met my wife, Betsy?"

"Glad to meet you, Betsy. You're right. High-flying Billy's definitely a nighttime person. In fact, some of his nights begin in the afternoons."

"Well, life would be pretty dull if we were all the same."

"Life with Billy is never dull – challenging – but never dull."

"I couldn't help but notice you're using a walking stick. Did you hurt your leg?"

"Just a case of rheumatoid arthritis."

"Sorry to hear that. So, what have you done with yourself since our last reunion? Are you a worker bee or a homemaking bee?"

"Oh, a worker bee. I'm a computer technician in Tampa. Have my own company. Good thing too."

"I always knew you'd make a success of yourself. By the way, we're in Florida too – the Keys. Didn't Billy go to the Ole Miss law school? Is he practicing?"

"He went to Nova instead. As far as practicing, I guess that's a good name for it. It's not a general practice. He has a very specialized clientele."

"His own firm?"

"He's part of a larger firm."

"Bet he does well. Billy and Jimbo were always like brothers. Isn't Jimbo a lawyer too? Do they still keep up with each other?"

"Oh, yes. Plus, they have some mutual clients."

"I'm glad to hear that."

Suzzie was silent. She continued to stare at the horizon so Will decided to change the subject. Betsy decided it was best for her not to say anything.

"We had breakfast with Danny Pearce yesterday morning. I was sorry to hear that he lost Misty. He doesn't seem to have gotten over it. Didn't seem like the old effervescent Danny I remember from school. You and Misty were good friends, weren't you? By my recollection, y'all were cheer-leaders together. Danny told us you were the reason he decided to go on this cruise."

"Danny's had a tough time of it. You know Misty killed herself, don't you?"

"No? Misty? That's horrible."

"Well, it happened. She had depression problems the whole time they were married. I lost track of how many times she got treated for it. Danny's never gotten over it."

"Did she have depression problems in high school? Didn't she transfer out for a while and then come back?"

"Yeah, our junior year. Went back to Riverside for a while before returning for our senior year. That's about the time her depression issues began. Her parents kept it hush-hush until she graduated. That's why she went to Mississippi Southern in Hattiesburg so she could be treated at Forest General Hospital quietly when necessary."

"I never knew that."

"You weren't supposed to, and Danny doesn't like to talk about it."

"Thanks for giving me a heads up. I'll be sure to be extra nice to him. Well, we're going to finish our walk now. Great to see you. I'm sure we'll have plenty of opportunities to talk again over the next couple of weeks."

As Will and Betsy were turning to leave, Jimbo Littleton jogged up.

"Hi, guys. Wonderful day, isn't it?"

"We were just talking about that, Jimbo," Will said. "Or should I call you Jimbo Junior Junior Junior or whatever it was you called yourself in the cheerleader skit."

"J.R. Junior Juniors Jr. ... esquire ... at your service."

"Sounds like that makes you a junior to the fourth power instead of just a junior-junior. Junior, I'd like you to meet my wife, Betsy. I don't think you've ever met."

"With all those juniors, I bet your wife's a hit down at Junior League," Betsy said. "And black must be your color. Elvira herself never looked any more alluring in a black gown."

"And I guess Junior League made you their honorary mascot," Will added.

Everyone except Suzzie laughed. She just stared somberly.

"I can tell I'm going to like you, Betsy. Looks like Will picked out a girl with a keen sense of humor."

"So, what do you do when you're not in drag?" Betsy asked.

"Oh, nothing legal I'm afraid. ... I'm a lawyer."

"And what's Amanda doing nowadays?" Will asked. "Best I remember she was on the fast track a few years ago as an up-and-coming interior decorator. Didn't she contribute some articles to *Southern Living*?"

"Amanda's still on a fast track, but now instead of spending clients' money, she's trying to spend mine faster than I can make it."

He laughed and turned to Suzzie. Instead of ratifying Jimbo's statement, she continued to look uncomfortable.

Jimbo then said, “Amanda tells me she’s got a shopping trip set up with you and Zelma in Cartegena while Billy and I take care of a little business so we can pay for it.”

Suzzie suddenly announced, “They said something about it, but I’ve almost decided not to go.”

“I’m surprised. I thought you girls live to shop.”

“Maybe they do. Well, I need to get back and see if Billy’s up and around yet. Good to see all y’all.”

She abruptly turned and with no further goodbyes, began to walk aft on the promenade deck without looking back.

Will and Betsy finished their walk, returned to their stateroom, and showered before calling Dick and Beth. Betsy listened to Will’s end of the phone conversation.

“You guys up and around? You say you already had breakfast? Then run by our room. I’ve got something to tell you. Oh, you’ve got something to tell us too. I bet min is juicer than yours is. What you mean, you’re not so sure about that.”

When the Petersons arrived, Will rehashed his conversation with Suzzie Cobb.

“We were getting along great until Jimbo Littleton came up, and then it seemed like Suzzie couldn’t end it quick enough even though she apparently has an outing set up with Jimbo’s wife. I found the way she was acting to be kind of strange since according to her, Billy and Jimbo are still thick as thieves and even have some mutual clients. What do you think is going on?”

“Let me come back to that topic after I tell you my gossip. You done now?”

Will nodded and said, “Done.”

“Now ... let me tell you the rest of the story we learned at breakfast. And it may fill in some holes.”

“OK, Paul Harvey. I can’t wait. Shoot.”

Dick held up his fist with his index finger sticking out and wiggled his thumb back and forth like he was shooting a pistol.

"What Suzzie was telling you was being diplomatic about Billy having a very specialized practice. Word is he represents some pretty disreputable people – mostly drug dealers. And I don't mean little ones – I mean like – cartel."

"You're shitting me? Like Colombian?"

"I shit you not. People are saying that Billy's been dealing with some pretty dangerous individuals, and it may be coming home to roost."

Will and Betsy looked at each other – each thinking about some of their own past experiences which had involved Colombian cartels.

Dick continued.

"And apparently some of his attempts to represent these clients have brought him to the attention of the bar association which has led him to temporarily suspend his practice. We're talking possible disbarment procedures."

"Whoa! No wonder he drinks. You think that since Jimbo is also a lawyer and Billy has ... let's just call them, uh, law practice problems ... that Suzzie's either ashamed ... or embarrassed ... to be around him."

"Or afraid she might say something which could be used against Billy later if Jimbo had to testify?" Betsy added. "You know ... code of ethics or some such bull."

"I'm sure Billy's problems are no secret to other lawyers," Will said. "After all, the legal world *is* a small universe."

"Uh, huh. You could both possibly be on a right track. But I ain't done yet. People seem to think that he and Suzzie are living primarily off the proceeds of her parent's house that she inherited along with the income from her techie business."

"That explains some of Suzzie's cryptic comments."

Betsy broke in and said, "You guys do remember that this cruise's first stop in Cartegena, don't you? And then after that, we're also going to other countries that are meccas for drug dealers?"

"Surely old Billy isn't using this cruise for that kind of business purpose," Beth said.

"Or maybe to skip the country to avoid prosecution?" Betsy suggested.

"Well! Well! Well!" Will said. "I'm not gonna comment, but I *will* be keeping my eyes open."

"Poor Suzzie! Looks like Danny Pearce isn't the only classmate of ours who has a lot on his plate."

# CHAPTER 8

"I'm getting a little hungry," Will asked Betsy. "How about you?"

"I'm not starving, but I could eat some lunch."

"Wanna get something on the deck?"

"Nah, I'm not that hungry. A nice, cool salad at the Horizon Cafe buffet sounds better to me. Gimme a sec to freshen my makeup."

Will and Betsy caught the elevator to the Lido deck and strolled down to the Horizon Cafe. It was moderately busy, but they had no problem finding a table after going through the buffet line. Will went to get them both a glass of tea from the dispensary machine while Betsy held down their table.

When he returned, Betsy said, "Aren't those your classmates a few tables away?"

She nodded to her left.

"What's their names – Suzzy and Danny?"

Will discretely looked over his shoulder and said, "Sure is."

"I still haven't seen much of her husband since the style show – Billy, isn't it? He never seems to be with her."

"Danny's now deceased wife, Misty, was Suzzie's best friend for years. Betcha that's why they're having lunch together."

He glanced back over to Suzzie and Danny's table again. They seemed to be engaged in a serious discussion, seemingly totally oblivious to everyone else in the room.

"It's tragic that Misty killed herself. By the way, what does Danny do for a living?"

"His daddy had a gun shop and was also a locksmith. He was also Greenville's mayor for a while. I'm pretty sure Danny inherited the business. I think someone told me he's made it into a pawn shop as well."

"He certainly seems more comfortable talking to her than he was with us."

Danny said something they couldn't hear and afterwards looked tense. Suzzie reached across the table and squeezed both his hands with hers. This did not seem to calm him down. He simply stared down at her comforting hands. Then Suzzie said something in a low voice that they couldn't hear.

The only words they heard was "that night."

After a silent pause, Suzzie and Danny rose to leave and noticed the Blacks for the first time. Suzzie half-heartedly waved at them but didn't come over to speak. Danny never acknowledged their presence as the two walked out the door in the opposite direction from where the Blacks were sitting.

"I wonder what that was all about," Will said.

"If I had to guess, 'that night' probably referred to the night Danny's wife died. What else could it be?"

"I dunno. I guess we never will."

"Whatever it was, it's really none of our business."

"You're right. I just hate to see Danny like that. Suzie was right when she said Misty's death just tore him to shreds psychologically. And he doesn't seem to be able to move on. If you'd known the old Danny ... he was nothing like you see now."

******************************

Later that day, Will proposed an idea to Betsy.

"Wanna walk through the casino?"

"As long as that's all we do."

Will gave her that you-know-me-better-than-that look before responding.

"My dear, we both take calculated risks for a living. I insist on something that I have some control over. This random bullshit is just pissing your money away. Kind of like trading the minute fluctuations on the stock market. I can tell you what a trend is, but I know short term fluctuations are both above and below that trend line. They're random, and no one has any control over them."

"I couldn't have said it better myself. I guess in our own way each of us is a control freak. You study trends, and I study income statements and balance sheets. They rarely lie."

"Unless someone falsifies 'em."

"Just like people falsify or skew the numbers when they report earnings."

"Not to be trite, but remember the adage. 'Figures lie, and liars figure."

"Yes, they do, my dear, and that's why God made prisons. He who claims what isn't his'n, soon enough goes to prison."

"You're a poet but don't know it."

"And both my feet ... "

"Are Longfellows," they both said together, laughed and glanced around the room.

"Looks like some of your classmates have already found the casino."

"Yeh. That's Billy and Willard and Jimbo."

"Suzzie's Billy? He and Jimbo seem to be getting along better than Suzzy and Jimbo did when we ran into them both on the Promenade Deck," Betsy said.

"Well, they're both lawyers. And they are supposed to have some mutual clients. Maybe they're talking shop."

"So much for the theory that Suzzie was ducking Jimbo because of her husband's ... er ... legal dilemma with the bar association."

"It kind of looks like they're both talking to Willard ... and he doesn't look all too happy."

"It seems."

"As I told you before, Willard has been a loose cannon his whole life. His parents didn't do him any favors by putting up with his crap and bailing him out time after time. One thing I forgot to mention to you was how many times he flunked out of one college after another. His folks'd just find a way to get him in somewhere else. I don't think he ever graduated anywhere. He stayed in school so long that people started calling him the world's oldest living Kappa Alpha active. I wonder what kind of legal trouble he's gotten himself into now so that Jimbo and Billy have to be lecturing him."

"Whatever it is, he doesn't look like a happy camper. Look at how many empty glasses are on the table in front of him," Betsy said.

"Maybe that's one thing he and Billy have in common. They're both lushes."

"We know why Billy's a lush. I wonder what Willard's excuse is. Probably farm related."

"Who knows, but you just reminded me of an old saying."

"Another poem?"

"Naw, but more intuitive. ... Notice. I just used four syllables. ... If drinking interferes with your work, you're a heavy drinker. When work interferes with you drinking, you're an alcoholic."

"I love you, Wilson Black. You always seem to have a way with words. You're just a regular Wiley Wordsmith."

"Wordy Wiley Coyote at your service, ma'am."

"Now if you could only figure out how to spell all those words as well."

# CHAPTER 9

Will and Betsy sat on their stateroom patio enjoying the room service breakfast they had ordered.

"Kind of nice out here this time of day, isn't it," Will observed.

"Also, nice not to have to get dressed and put on makeup to go to breakfast," Betsy agreed.

"So what'cha wanna do this morning once we finally do get moving?" Will asked.

"Let's look at the Regency Rapper," Betsy said, referring to the ship's daily newsletter and see what our options are. Hmmm! There's an art auction at ten."

"Nope. We own enough hang-arounds."

"And a trivia contest at the same time."

"Nah! – Not unless you want to go."

"Doesn't do anything for me. Scavenger hunt? There's a battle of the sexes on the pool deck later this morning."

"What's that?"

"I think it's things like popping balloons against someone else's neck or trying to carry a pen with your butt cheeks without dropping it."

"I'll pass."

"Here's a marriage game – you know, to see how well do you know your soul mate."

"That could lead to major trouble, like 'Alice – bang, zoom –you're going to the moon.'"

"Yuk! Yuk! Hmmm! Mythbuster facts."

"Are you trying to say I'm a myth in my own mind?"

"No, Mytha Will. Mythbusters, like the Discovery Channel TV show. Adam Savage, one of the show's stars is doing a presentation in the Crooner's Lounge."

"Oh yeah! The show that tests hypotheses to see if they're true or not. That might be fun. Count me in if you wanta go. What time?"

"Ten. That's give us plenty of time to shower and get dressed."

Will and Betsy arrived at the Crooner's Lounge on deck 8 about a quarter to ten and were able to get a table by the window. The Crooner's Lounge was a small informal bar dedicated to the Rat Pack. There were blown-up pictures mostly in black and white of Frank Sinatra, Dean Martin, Sammy Davis Jr., and the rest of the Rat Pack on the walls. Some showed them performing; others just showed them partying. Most seemed to have been taken in Vegas during its heyday."

Will and Betsy settled into comfortable padded, armchairs and waited for the presentation to begin. A waiter came over to see if they wanted to order drinks while they waited.

"Want anything, darling?"

"A mimosa sounds good," Betsy replied.

Will handed the waiter their on-board plastic credit card.

"Well, I'll be damned," Will suddenly exclaimed. "I must be going crazy."

"Well, you do have an anxiety disorder, but relax, my dear. I haven't seen you do anything to make me panic about yet this morning."

"I think I just saw Adolfo Soltero."

"So, you're having delusions along with your anxiety disorder. Hmmm! Your condition may be more serious than I thought."

"I'm serious, my sweet. ... Serious as a stroke. Look over your shoulder."

"Holy ...!"

"Holy is not exactly the word I'd use with Al. His light doesn't come from holiness but from being blindingly polished."

Fate had had caused Will and Betsy's path to intersect with Adolfo Soltero's on multiple occasions in the past. Will and Betsy first encountered Al Soltero when the Blacks began to investigate the unexplained death of Dave Tressler, one of Will's Vero Beach security brokers, in the aftermath of Hurricane Clarice. They had discovered that Tressler had violated company policy and Federal securities laws by agreeing to sell macadamia nut limited partnerships for a company controlled by Soltero.

They had encountered Soltero once again after moving to the Keys when they unearthed the fact that Soltero was one of the front men for a Colombian cartel investment arm that turned out to be the Club Tropic real estate Ponzi scheme. In each case, while others got arrested and convicted, the Teflon Soltero always managed to avoid being formally implicated and charged.

"I know I shouldn't say this, but it's almost hard not to like that old shyster," Will said.

"Shhh! Keep your voice down, but you're right. He's one smooth operator. He's got to be one of the slickest and most polite rogues on Earth."

"And we thought he was just a Vero Beach phenomenon selling used cars. Shiit! I don't think I was ever quite as surprised as I was when I found out that he was the secret owner of that fenced compound in our Keys neighborhood as well. And he was using it to direct one of the biggest drug smuggling operations in the nation."

"He wasn't being sneaky secretive. ... He was just flying low ... under the radar screen. I'll never forget that unbelievable El Siboney paella dinner he treated us to after the United Way kickoff meeting at Mallory Square and what a delightful host he turned out to be. How many politicians do you think he owns?"

"You're making me wonder. What happened to County Commissioner Reverend LeRoy? Al had him wrapped up like a Christmas present, and then The Rev just disappeared ... like a puff of smoke."

"God! We could go on and on. The Sun Raye religious pyramid scheme ... Al's pump-and-dump bucket shop operation – 21st Century whatever it was. As I said, Soltero is *one* slick ...

"He definitely defines oily."

"... gentleman. And that's just with the stuff we know about. ... Hush up now! He's coming this way."

Adolfo Soltero saw Will and Betsy and his face broke out in an ear-to-ear seemingly sincere smile as he made a beeline for their table. His teeth almost flashed in the sun that was coming in the ship's window and contrasted with his tanned face. The Blacks both rose to greet him. Betsy detected the faint understated scent of Royal Mandarin cologne as he neared them.

"My horoscope said this would be a good day, but it was wrong. It's a fantastic day when I can run into one of my favorite power couples in the entire world. And to think it would happen here on a cruise ship of all places. Why is it that I just continue to age, Will, and you never do? You rat! You're keeping the fountain of youth to yourself instead of sharing. And Betsy Black! My favorite banker. My heavens! Not only as breathtakingly beautiful as always but brilliant as well – a virtuoso of all types of figures – a truly modern ideal of a Southern lady."

As usual, Al was impeccably dressed and freshly shaven. He wore an understated pastel linen guayabera shirt and had on ecru colored linen slacks. Both looked freshly pressed and were almost wrinkle free. His sock-less Gucci loafers didn't have scuff on them. He held an expensive looking Panama hat in his manicured left hand and had an elegant walking stick in his right. Al's hair gleamed from hair oil, and not one hair seemed to be out of place.

"Good to see you too, Al," Will said. "May I invite you to join us?"

"It would be an honor," Soltero said and pulled out Betsy's chair before he sat down himself.

He subtly nodded to his bodyguard, a swarthy brutish looking man, who had remained discretely in the background across the room. The man quietly found a table and spoke in a low voice to a waitress. Almost immediately, the waitress brought another mimosa and put it down in front of Al. Al did not seemed surprised and graciously thanked her.

"So, what brings you on a cruise to Central America?" Will asked. "You can fly down here anytime you want to."

"Yes, it is true, but even us overworked Colombian natives deserve a little downtime. I have several upcoming business meetings, so I decided to combine business with pleasure and enjoy the trip down this time before they begin. May I ask what brings you onto the Regency Crown?"

"We're here participating in my high school reunion. The class decided to combine the reunion with a trip through the Canal."

Will thought Al looked momentarily surprised. He seemed to be assessing matters before recovering and responding.

"What a delightful idea for a memorable reunion. I'd never have thought to use a cruise for that purpose. Have you been through the Canal before?"

"No. Or to any of the other stops on this cruise."

"Then you must let me show you the *real* Cartegena."

"We wouldn't want to put you out."

"I insist. It's not often I get to share the country I love with my American friends. I would love to introduce you to my favorite aunt."

"We're sort of traveling with another couple."

"Let's just make it delightful day for the three of us rather than trying to pack too many people in my car. I'm sure they will find plenty to do on their own."

Will looked at Betsy questioningly.

Al said, "I refuse to take no for an answer."

Betsy replied, "It'll be our pleasure to spend the day with you and your family. Thank you for asking us."

About that time, they heard the cruise director tapping on a microphone. He introduced Adam Savage who then gave the group an entertaining talk about the history of Mythbusters and told them about some of the show's highlights over the years.

When Savage finished, Al asked the Blacks for their cabin number and told them he would get back to them with the particulars of their upcoming day together. He then politely excused himself, saying he had other matters to attend to. Al walked across the room and his bodyguard quietly stood up and silently followed him out of Crooner's Lounge.

After Soltero left, Will looked at Betsy and said, "So what do you make of that?"

"As always with Al, I'm sure there's more reasons than relaxation and downtime that he's on this ship. I don't think he ever does anything that doesn't have a ... mostly nefarious ... purpose. The only coincidence in this whole thing is that we ended up on the same ship that he's on."

"Coincidence is God's way of being anonymous."

"What does that have to do with anything?"

"I dunno. I just like the way it sounded."

Betsy rolled her eyes and said, "Let's get out of here."

**********************

In the early afternoon, Will and Betsy strolled by the Crooner's Lounge again and saw Willard alone at a table. The bar was mostly empty that time of day. Willard downed a drink and ordered another, telling the waiter he was going to the men's room but would be back. As he stood, he staggered a bit but stabilized himself on the back of the chair until he got his equilibrium back.

"Looks like Willard is getting a head start on happy hour," Will commented.

"But he doesn't seem very happy to me."

Will nodded in agreement as they proceeded down the hall towards the Wheelhouse Lounge.

"Will. Quick. Look to your left."

Will did as she instructed and saw Adolfo Soltero. He was sitting at a remote table in the very far end of the lounge away from the bar. The bar was empty except for a few customers. Al's bodyguard sat a few tables away. Billy Cobb was on the same side of the table as Al, and they appeared to be talking to Jimbo Littleton. Al had a cup of coffee. Billy had a drink in his hand. An empty glass sat on the table.

"Do you see what I see?" Will asked Betsy.

"Uh huh. Why would Al be talking to Billy and Jimbo? How would he even know them? Surely, he's not one of Billy's disreputable clients."

"Shirley, my dear, I don't know, but I'd surely like to know. I don't want to go in the lounge and have him see us, but I'd *sure* love to stick around. Let's grab that empty couch in the hall across from the doorway and pretend to be reading something. We won't be able to hear that they're saying, but at least we can watch."

"And Al acted *so* surprised to find out there was a reunion on this cruise."

"Riiight! As I said, Al doesn't do anything that doesn't have a purpose. Damn, I wish I knew what was going on."

"I guess Al's only real surprise earlier was that you're part of this class reunion."

"Do you think that's why he invited us out? So, he can pick our brains about some of my classmates?"

"Wouldn't doubt it."

The conversation seemed to be getting more animated. Billy's voice rose as he gestured towards Jimbo. Soltero seemed content to let Billy lead the conversation but put his hand occasionally on Billy's arm as if the rein him in.

The Blacks thought they possibly heard Al say the word "commitment."

Betsy leaned over towards Will and whispered, "I think I just read Billy's lips, and it seemed like he may have said the word Willard."

"What? No way! You must have misunderstood. What would this bunch be doing that would involve Willard?"

"What would Al be doing with anyone in your class?"

"You think this could be legal shit?"

"More like illegal shit, what you want to bet."

"I don't think they're arguing politics. I guess that's why Suzzie seemed so uncomfortable with Jimbo up on the Promenade Deck. Do you think Jimbo's in bed with Billy and Al?"

"And Willard as well? Something's going on involving all of them. That's for certain. I don't think they're up there setting up a bridge foursome. What were we saying about coincidences?"

"My dear, let me tell you a story about coincidences. It involves three rich but ruthless parents with kids at the same school competing against other for one Ivy League scholarship. They don't always get along. Two of the kids get killed in accidents. The third kid goes to Harvard. Coincidence?"

"So, what's your point?"

"I don't buy coincidence theories as a rule. Where you may see coincidence, I see conspiracy."

About that time Jimbo stormed out of the Wheelhouse Lounge back in the directions of Crooner's, leaving Billy and Al to talk to each other. He noticed Will and Betsy and nodded recognition. He didn't pause to speak.

"I've got a hunch Jimbo's headed towards Crooner's for a reason."

"One way to find out," Betsy said.

When he got to Crooners, Jimbo went straight to Willard's table and began to explain something to him.

The only part of the conversation that Will and Betsy overheard was Willard's slurred response and Jimbo's reply as he walked out.

"Fuck him."

"Your funeral."

Willard ordered another drink.

Jimbo noticed Will and Betsy again. This time he didn't just continue to walk but came over.

"Every time I look up, I see you two."

'Small ship, I guess" Will responded.

"Sometimes too damned small. I thought for a moment I'd found your nose, and it was in my business."

# CHAPTER 10

The Regency Crown arrived at the port of Cartegena during the night. Will and Betsy met Al Soltero at the Crooner's Lounge at a prearranged time, and they departed the ship together. Al's nephew, Luis Alvarez, was waiting for them on the dock, and after Al made the introductions, he escorted them to as waiting black Mercedes.

After they got in the car, Soltero told them, "Luis is going to take us to Caregena's infamous peoples' market, the Mercado de Bazurto. It's only about a fifteen-minute ride. This place is the heart and soul for sophisticated local food professionals looking for the freshest fish and produce in the city – maybe even the country.

"You're not going to find Hawaiian-shirt-wearing Americans in socks and sandals here or colorful, cobblestone streets. And I'll warn you before we get there. Yes, it *is* dirty, and yes, it would be dangerous for you to come here unescorted by a knowledgeable local such as Luis or myself. It's full of pickpockets and other riffraff. Our guide will be Juan Felipe Camacho, who is one of the foremost chefs in all of Colombia. He owns Don Juan Restaurante. His legendary cooking is defined by both his expert technique and his love of the use Colombian ingredients."

"I'm impressed!" Will said. "How did you arrange this?"

"Let's just say that Juan is indebted to my family. We were there for him when he was first starting out."

Will and Betsy exchanged a knowing look.

Luis drove them down a nameless dirt road. There seemed to be an endless sprawling maze of dealers of all sorts under open tarps and rusting overhanging zinc roofs. Fruit dealers on one side had set up shop for the day and sat among baskets of oranges and stacks of pineapples. Others were still bagging generous portions of ripe strawberries. Across the way, fishermen spoke to customers in rapid Spanish as they animatedly pointed and negotiated next to plastic tarps piled high with large tuna, bright blue parrotfish, red snapper and other locally caught seafood. Butchers holding cleavers stood next to freshly slaughtered pork carcasses. Millions of flies buzzed around them. Machete-wielding farmers whacked coconuts. A donkey stood sullenly by the side of the road.

The place seemed to defy rhyme or reason. Legumes lay next to lingerie; fresh fish was displayed next to fake flowers. There was also plenty on the high gore scale – gray entrails and eyeballs that had been freshly plucked from unfortunate cows. The place had the feel of both an ongoing party and the aftermath of a riot as it assaulted Will and Betsy's senses.

After he had parked, Luis instructed his passengers to wait by the car while he located Chef Camacho. When he returned, he was accompanied by a slightly paunchy middle-aged man dressed in a stylish striped polo shirt. The two were engaged in a seemingly relaxed conversation.

Will stepped forward with his hand extended, almost stepping in a muddy puddle as he did so. Al grabbed his arm and pulled him back just in time.

"Watch where you where you walk, Will. I don't think you want to step in that," Soltero said. "I don't think you want a disgusting, gunky combination of mud, decomposing rubbish, and fish juice oozing between the toes of your sandals and splattering the back of your calf."

"You got that right," Will replied as he sidestepped back onto firmer ground.

"Mr. and Mrs. Black, it's always a pleasure to meet Adolfo's American friends. Welcome to Colombia," Camacho said in almost perfect English.

"Our pleasure," Betsy said. "And may I point out that you almost sound American yourself. What's your background?"

"Vancouver. As a young man, I signed up for a cooking course there to pass the time while I was in school and found out by accident that cooking was my calling in life."

"Juan's being modest," Al said. "He's a graduate of one of the world's great cooking schools in San Sebastian, Spain. They only take twenty candidates at any one time."

The mild-mannered Camacho looked embarrassed and changed the subject.

"Shall we begin? Follow me."

Luis excused himself and began talking to a local teenage boy. He then gave the kid some money before rejoining them.

"Uh! Just making sure our car doesn't get vandalized. Hired the kid to watch it until we get back."

As they walked along below concrete ceilings with jumbles of electrical mains hanging from open beams, Camacho began to point out exotic fruits and beloved fruit stands like was greeting old friends. He handed Betsy a sort of orange-like fruit with a paper-thin skin that revealed a clear milky pulp reminiscent of a lychee.

A thuggy looking person seemed to be eyeing Betsy's purse. Al nodded at Luis, who grabbed the man's arm and quietly twisted it behind his back. Will thought he heard a bone snap. After that, other equally disreputable looking individuals gave them a wide berth.

"Here at the Mercado de Bazurto I can find it all – tropical fruits from Cartegena, veggies from cold mountain places like Bogatá, and produce from Santa Marta, but today my main mission is to buy an ingredient that I can't buy anywhere else in the city. Locally we call it ponche; it's more formal name is capybera."

"What's that?" Will asked.

"The world's largest rodent. They can get as big as a German shepherd, but they have a stocky build like a beaver. Look kind of like a guinea pig."

"Sounds disgusting."

"South Americans have barbecued them since before Europeans arrived here. They're truly one of the original flavors of this part of the world."

Will and Betsy almost had trouble keeping up with Juan as he rushed from stall to stall occasionally disappearing momentarily behind slabs of deboned meat. The meat hung over metal bars and separated the stalls like privacy curtains.

Finally, on a counter behind a pile of chicken carcasses guarded by a stray dog, they heard him exclaim, "Eureka! Ponche!"

He had found his bounty. He excitedly told the butcher in Spanish to show him what he had for sale. The butcher brought out two quarter carcasses, and at Juan's instruction, he chopped a leg off of each.

"The leg is the most desirable portion of the ponche. All ponche comes from hunters. In some countries like Brazil, ponche is raised domestically, but here in Colombia those farms are still illegal. I can't wait to get this back to the restaurant."

When they got back out to the car, Betsy told Juan what an exciting experience the morning had been and how much they had learned.

"Let me put our cuisine in perspective before we part."

Juan asked Al for his hat and held it upside down before saying more.

"I wish you could stay in my country longer and let me introduce you more fully to our cuisine. Pretend Adolfo's hat is a cultural pot. At first the pot only contained indigenous people. Then after that, we added the Spanish. Then the Arabs came, bringing their spices and things like eggplant into the equation. The once homogeneous pot began to transform and 'voila' – what resulted is modern Colombian cuisine.

"I must leave you now, but I hope I will have the pleasure of meeting you again going forward. Adios, my new friends."

When they returned to the car, the teenager was still guarding it as if his life depended on it. Will wondered if that was the case.

"If the Mercado de Bazurto hasn't spoiled your appetite," Al said as they drove away, "I'll take you to a more refined Cartegenian landmark, and we can have a Colombian brunch with my Tìa Sophia. She's expecting us."

"Lead on, Maestro Soltero." Will said.

"Maestro?"

"What Will is trying to say is that as our host you have thus far taken us into your hands like a conductor," Betsy said.

"Yeah," Will agreed. "As in the host with the most."

Al laughed and said, "Luis, ... the Alfiz."

Luis drove them towards the port and into the older section of Cartegena as Al gave them an overview about the Alfiz Hotel.

"The Alfiz is about 300 years old. We call the architectural style "casa alta" which in English means high house. The first floor was originally used as a warehouse and shop, and the second was intended to be rooms. It's located in what was then Cartegena's most relevant quarter since this is where Spanish colonization began. It's been the home of such colorful owners as a French bootlegger and a British consul. You'll find you are within walking distance of many of the city's important buildings both historically and still today."

They drove up in front of a beautifully restored stucco building with high-arched, darkly stained doors that were beneath a long, stained balcony loaded with blooming plants.

"Welcome to the Alfiz."

Will and Betsy walked into a spacious high-ceilinged entryway that led to a small lobby and staircase with a small balcony overlooking it. Al then led them into a courtyard in the center of the house which had what had originally been a cistern in its middle. Now the room was being used as a cloistered dining room. A spiral staircase led upwards.

"How gorgeous," Betsy exclaimed. "Where does that staircase go?"

By this time Luis had parked the car and joined them in the courtyard.

"To the mirador on the roof. We Colombians enjoy rooftop dining when the weather permits," Luis responded.

A sophisticated looking Spanish lady came through a door at the back of the courtyard. Betsy could see that this was apparently where the kitchen was located. She could have been a stereotypical character out of an old movie. Her hair was in a bun, and she wore a long dress. She exuded a confidence that made her seem almost haughty and at the same time regal. Her eyes lit up when she saw Soltero.

"Mi sobrino, Adolfo. Bienvenido de tu vuelta. To he echado mucho de menos **(Welcome back, my nephew, Alolfo. How was your trip? I have missed you so much since you left.)**."

"Tia Sophia, I want you to meet my American friends from Florida, Will and Betsy Black."

He turned to the Blacks and said, "Will and Betsy, may I introduce Sophia López, the owner of the Alfiz."

After they finished the introductions, Will and Betsy told Sophia how impressed they were with the elegant hotel, and they all sat down to have brunch. They were not disappointed. A waiter brought them coffee and fresh juice followed by chagua, a milk and egg soup that contained scallions and cilantro. The final course was arepa de huevo, an arepa filled with egg. The conversation was relaxed and flowed easily. It quickly became apparent that Sophia and Luis were as socially adept as Al was.

Towards the end of the meal, Adolfo told Will and Betsy that unfortunately he had a business meeting to attend that morning and that Luis would take them on a stroll and show them the downtown area adjacent to the hotel.

"I'll see you back on the ship," Al said as he departed, kissing his aunt goodbye.

After thanking Sophia for her hospitality, Luis and the Blacks left soon afterward. Luis pointed out important landmarks as they walked. He showed them the house of royal officers, the Cabildo, the cathedral, and the Inquisition Palace before ending up at the Plaza Mayor and the Plaza del Mar.

As they walked along, the Blacks heard familiar voices. Amanda Littleton and Zelma McFarley babbled to each other. Each had shopping bags. Suzzie Cobb was there as well but didn't seem to be as excited as the other two. She carried only one small shopping bag that was sealed with tape.

When Amanda and Zelma saw Will and Betsy, they rushed over to greet them and tell them about some of their purchases. They obviously had been drinking while they shopped.

"What a small country this is," Amanda babbled. "First, we run into Suzzie, and now we run into you. We had to practically get out a whip to get Suzzie to join us. What've you guys been up to?"

"Oh, Señor Soltero on our ship has been our host for the day here in Cartagena. He's someone we've known for years both in Vero and the Keys. He's native Colombian."

"That was nice of him. I wonder what he wanted," Suzzie said almost in a monotone as she gritted her teeth.

"Sounds like you've really had a neat day like we have. We've found some of the coolest stuff. Suzzie won't show us what she bought," Amanda added.

"It's a surprise for Billy. If I told you what it is, it wouldn't be a surprise."

"Is this your friend?" Zelma asked.

"No, may I introduce our friend's nephew, Luis López?" Will said. "He is our guide downtown today."

"Funny," Amanda said. "I've heard Jimbo mention a Luis López, but I guess that's not such an unusual name in this part of the world."

"I think I may have heard that name as well," Zelma agreed.

"And your husband would be ...?" Luis asked.

"Jimbo Littleton. He's a lawyer. Suzzie's husband 's a lawyer too."

Luis only nodded and said, "Being an attorney is a very honorable profession."

He turned to Zelma saying, "And your husband is an attorney as well?"

"Naw! He's just a little ole dirt farmer from Mississippi – McFarley."

Luis's eyebrows arched when she said McFarley, but he said nothing.

"Little ole dirt farmer! An understatement if I ever heard one," Will said. "So, ladies, where are your hubbies? They let you girls out unchaperoned?"

"They all had some kind of meeting here in town. ... So here we are."

"They're working on vacation? Same meeting or separate ones?"

"Same one, I think. I dunno. Willard didn't say. Something about banking and money. What difference does it make?"

"Billy didn't either."

"Come on, guys. We haven't been in that shop over there yet. Don't be killjoys. Since you're here, you gotta come in with us and have fun too."

Betsy looked at Will. Will could practically read her mind. Banking? Money? Or maybe shylocking. Was Willard borrowing money or paying it back? Had he been using the plantation for collateral?

When they went into the jewelry shop, Zelma saw a pair of emerald earrings she felt like she had to have.

"Oooh! How much?"

The clerk quoted her a price.

"I gotta have them. After all, Colombia *is* where emeralds are really a bargain. I'll take them. How much did you say?"

Suzzie broke in and said, "Girl, are you sure you want to get these? Willard's probably going to be upset with you."

"Screw that tightwad Willard. They're an investment."

The clerk ran some numbers through a handheld calculator and held it up to show Zelma the final tally. Luis's eyebrows arched, momentarily betraying his thoughts as he read the numbers.

He quietly and politely asked the clerk in Spanish if he could speak to him in private in the store's office. The two went into the back room where Luis called Al's cell phone. Al spoke briefly to the clerk. When they emerged, the clerk was carrying one of Luis's business cards and looked visibly shaken.

"Excuse me, miss. I think my calculator mispriced the earrings that you're interested in. I think the battery may have been low. Based on today's emerald market, the price is somewhat lower. My apologies."

He then quoted her a price about 40% lower than he had before his conversations with Luis and Al. Luis nodded his approval, and Zelma gave the clerk her credit card.

Will and Betsy gave each other a "I'm-not-sure-what-just-happened-but-that-guy-looks-like-he-just-got-the-shit-scared-out-of-him" look.

Will whispered one phrase to Betsy, "The Soltero syndrome."

# CHAPTER 11

After the ship put back out to sea heading for their next stop in Panama, the Petersons and the Blacks decided to have a cocktail in the Crooner's Lounge before going to dinner. When they walked in, they could see that the gossipy ex-debutantes and their husbands had decided to do the same. Apparently, they too had just arrived since they were still waiting for their drink order. The wives were already so involved in an animated conversation that they didn't seem to notice when Will and Dick found a table near them. The husbands seemed to be talking golf. They were already involved in one conversation and the wives another.

Will and Dick gave the Philippine waiter their drink orders. Their ears perked up as they overheard their ex-classmates' conversation.

"I hear Zelma and Willard almost missed the boat."

"I heard she was out spending money like crazy on jewelry while he got drunk in some scummy bar and had a run-in with some local low-lifes."

"Where'd you hear that?"

"I have my sources."

The conversation at times seemed so disjointed that Will wondered if the women were even listening to each other as each tried to make sure she got her two cents put in.

"If I was married to Zelma, I'd get drunk too."

"Jewelry? Like they had the money for her to waste."

"Yeah. I think they owe everybody in the Delta."

"I heard they're delinquent on their taxes."

"Don't you think Zelma looks old?"

"I always did think she looked old for her age ... and cheap. Never could see what Willard saw in her."

One of the women made a circle with her thumb and index finger and poked the other index finger back and forth through it. The others laughed. Their husbands seemed to have totally tuned them out as they now talked about the upcoming college football season.

"That bunch is something else," Betsy commented in a low voice.

"I'm just not sure what," Beth said.

"I am," answered Will. "B – I-- T – C – H."

"Does that stand for beautiful, intelligent, talented, cute and hilarious?" Dick asked.

"I shore wasn't thinking it meant beautiful individuals that cause hard-ons," Will said.

"Y'all are as bad as they are. Seriously, you two clowns. Something bad must have happened to Willard after we left Zelma at the jewelry shop," Betsy said. "Will, why don't you call Suzzie's room and find out what really happened."

Will found a house phone and called the Cobbs' stateroom. No one answered.

"Why don't we go up to the Promenade Deck in the morning? That's where we ran into Suzzie before. She said she likes to go up there most days."

"Or maybe we'll run into Jimbo. He goes up there in the mornings as well to jog."

"I'd be careful there," Betsy reminded Will. "He seemed kind of touchy the last time we saw him."

"In the meantime, I need to wash up before dinner," Beth said.

"But you just took a shower," Dick replied.

"After listening to that catty crowd, I feel dirty all over again. Let's take this drink with us and finish it in the Wheelhouse Bar."

"Good idea."

When they walked into the Wheelhouse Bar, they saw Al Soltero enter with Jimbo, get a table, and order drinks. Al's massive bodyguard took a chair at the bar but ordered nothing. Jimbo seemed agitated.

"So, I want to know the truth. Did you have anything to do with it?" Jimbo said, his voice rising as his hands gestured.

The bodyguard almost got up, but Al motioned to him to stay where he was.

"I'm sorry it occurred, but things sometimes happen in this part of the world. You know – wrong place at the wrong time. Americans are especially vulnerable since they are perceived as having money, and the local people have nothing. You do realize, my friend, that the most dangerous people in the world are those with nothing to lose. The per capita income for a whole family in Colombia is only a little over sixteen hundred American dollars a year."

"You're so full of shit."

"Now, now. Rudeness will not undo what was done. As I said, you have my sympathy, and if I can do anything to right the unfortunate incident ..."

"I know, just let you know what you can do," Jimbo said in a sarcastic voice.

"I'm sorry to have to remind you, but it was probably bound to happen sooner or later. The man was not as careful as he should have been about keeping his word. This, shall we say ... laxity ... violates an almost inviolable protocol in my associates' world. You could be of great service to everyone involved if you reminded him of this."

"Thanks for the advice."

"And do I need to remind you that stars die all the time? Some explode. Some cave in on themselves and become black holes. Other stars get sucked up inside of them for just getting too close. A person should choose his alliances wisely, or he may be condemned for someone else's sins. Now if you will excuse me, I have other matters to attend to," Al said in a calm voice.

Al rose to leave, leaving Jimbo sitting at the table. Al's bodyguard followed him out.

**********************

When Will and Betsy went up to the Promenade Deck the following morning both Suzzie and Amanda were present. They seemed to be in the middle of a serious discussion.

"We overheard a conversation in the Crooner's Lounge last night that sounded like Willard McFarley may have gotten hurt yesterday while we were all ashore."

"You heard right," Amanda said. "He got beaten up pretty bad. Billy and Jimbo got him back on the ship though anyway."

"Do you know what happened?"

"Not completely. Billy and Jimbo don't seem to want to talk about it. All three of them went to some meeting together. I guess Willard wanted them to go because they're both lawyers."

"Do you know who Willard was meeting with?"

"I think it was a local banker. I think the name they used was Alfonse Sauterno or something like that."

"Surely this didn't happen at a banking meeting."

"I really don't know. I think it must have happened on the street after the meeting was over."

"A mugging? Did someone try to kidnap him? I understand that sometimes happens down here."

"As I said, I really don't know. Billy and Jimbo don't seem to know either. At least that's what they're telling us."

"They were all three still together when this happened?"

"Yes."

"And only Willard got attacked?"

"That's right."

"Did Jimbo and Billy fight them off?"

"Didn't have to."

"Strange. Did Willard get robbed?"

"I don't think so. Jimbo really didn't say," said Amanda. "Doesn't seem to want to talk about it."

"Did they call the cops?"

"No. They just brought Willard back to the ship"

"Has Willard seen the ship's doctor?"

"No. Willard said nothing's broken. He just hurts like hell. Said he doesn't want to talk about it. He just seems to want to forget the whole thing since we're not even in Colombia anymore."

"This doesn't make any sense."

Amanda shrugged, "You now know what I know. I was told to mind my own business."

"How's Zelma taking it?"

"You know, ... I guess she's just glad he's not hurt any worse than he is."

"Is there anything we can do?"

"Not to my knowledge."

"Tell them how sorry we are."

"I sure will."

After Will and Betsy left Amanda and Suzzie and felt like they could talk in private, Will said, "That whole story doesn't make a lick of sense."

"It might if Alfonse Sauterno is Adolfo Soltero. Al did say he had a meeting to attend after he left us, and we did see that whole group discussing something in the lounge."

"The Soltero syndrome again?"

"Highly likely."

# CHAPTER 12

"I think I'll go up on deck and read for a while," Will said. "Wanta join me?"

"Not right now," Betsy replied. "I'd planned to wash my hair. Maybe I'll come up after that."

"Well, you know where to find me. I'll be on deck fourteen by the Lido pool."

"That's the one on the open deck, isn't it? Not the one under the skylights?"

"Bingo."

"If I'm not there by say eleven thirty or so, come on back to the stateroom, and we'll see what we want to do about lunch."

"Sounds like a plan."

After putting on his hat, a tee-shirt, and his bathing suit, Will took the elevator up to the fourteenth deck and got out of it next to the Horizon Court, the ship's buffet eatery. He ducked in momentarily and grabbed a couple of chocolate chip cookies and a glass of tea before heading out onto the open deck. The bar on one end was open, and he could see the open-deck movie screen at the other end. Nothing was playing on it. A huge open swimming pool and two raised hot tubs dominated the middle of the deck.

*Good. No movie. Quiet. So, I can read in peace.*

He grabbed a beach towel from the rack, found a lounge chair near to one of the hot tubs, and situated himself so that the sun wouldn't be in his eyes. Soon he was engrossed in his book, occasionally nibbling on a cookie as he read. As he was beginning his second chapter, Will heard two familiar voices behind him. He turned and peered over his sunglasses.

*Dickie-do Dunne and Tom Hamilton getting in the hot tub.*

Each of them had some sort of rum drink in his hand. Will pulled his hat down a bit, hoping they wouldn't notice him.

"Damn. This hot water feels good," Dickie-do said. "Almost as good as some hot snatch. Tell me, Tom, what's it like to be a famous rock star? I bet you have to beat the women off with a stick."

"It definitely made picking up girls easier," Tom said. "It's exciting at first, but the new wears off over time as you get accustomed to it."

"I bet you partied every night all night long."

"At first, but you get to the point that after a show you just want to go back to your motel room, kick off your shoes, take a shower, and just wind down by yourself."

"I don't think the new ever would wear off with me – Slicky Tricky Dickie-do, the Dickman. Not with a different piece of ass throwing herself at me *every* night."

"Oh, you say that, but you'd be surprised."

"I remember what it was like with the girls when we all played football together. A regular pussy parade. And I'm sure that's not even close to what you went through. Every time I look at Suzzie, I remember what a prime piece of meat she was. And also ... oh yeah ... the divine Miss M ..."

"Miss M?"

"Don't tell me you've forgotten that. Sweet as an M & M."

He began to sing, "Nothing would be finer than to be in your vagina in the morning."

"As my man Hank junior would say, a family tradition. You got some in those days too. Don't pretend you didn't. Yes, our S and M period. And as Frankie Valli used to sing, "Oh, What A Night."

Will's ears perked up, and he began to pay closer attention to the conversation.

"I thought we all agreed that we'd let the past stay in the past."

"Hell, if we can't talk to each other who can we talk to. It all worked out didn't it. Knockin' around and having a ball, and nobody got knocked up. No shotgun weddings. You *do* remember how those gals were asking for it. If their husbands only knew how hot their wives used to be. I could tell them tales that would make a sailor blush, but I bet they couldn't compare to some of your backstage bimbo blasts."

"Dickie-do, let's let it drop."

"Why? One of them married a chicken shit and the other married a goober. We may be the highlight of their social life for all you know. We were studs. People like dumb-fuck Danny couldn't have gotten a hooker unless he paid her double her asking price. I always thought he might be queer. Admit it. Didn't you too?"

For the first time, Tom noticed Danny sitting in a chaise lounge within earshot.

Tom elbowed Dickie-do and said, "I've said enough, and you've said too much."

Will glanced in the same direction as Tom and saw a seething Danny Pearce in a deck chair with the remnants of an ice cream cone. He had crushed it with his grip. Danny said nothing as he got up to return to his stateroom. He glared at Tom and Dickie-do as he left.

Will was pretty sure he had gone unobserved by all three of his classmates. At least he hoped that was the case.

# CHAPTER 13

Will walked into the Crooner's Lounge and saw Dickie-do Dunne at the bar. Will could immediately tell Dickie-do was either already smashed or well on his way. He noticed Will and beckoned to him to come over. He clumsily stood up as Will approached.

"How's they hangin', my man?"

He grabbed and racked his crotch as he spoke.

"No complaints," Will replied. "And you?"

"Getting' better all the time," Dickie-do said as he toasted himself. He stumbled slightly as he tried to find the bar stool to sit back down. "Waitin' on Quackenbush."

Will ordered a draft beer.

"Be even better if I could find something soft and sweet to get next to."

"I take it you're traveling alone."

"Yeah. I'm currently in between numbers three and four. On the prowl for five."

Will chose to let that topic drop without any of his usual witticisms and sipped his beer. He glanced to his left and saw Suzzie, Amanda, and Lydia Vallence, three of the old GHS cheerleaders coming in and taking a table across the small room. Dickie-do noticed him looking in that direction and saw them as well. Dickie-do held up his glass and toasted them. The group politely acknowledged his gesture but made no attempt to come over and speak. Once the women were seated, they exchanged a few words by whispering in each other's ear. As their words went around the table, each glanced over at Will and Dickie-do. While Will didn't know the gist of their conversation, he was pretty sure it was not in a positive vein. Dickie-do ordered another drink.

"Gimme another double."

The women noted his order and whispered something else to each other.

"I know two of those three," Dickie-do said, "*very* well. And I'd sure like to know more about the third. I bet I could make that Lydia howl at the moon if I had half a chance. You know, she had a reputation for being pretty fast in high school."

Will remained silent, trying not to encourage Dickie-do. Dickie-do glanced back over in the ladies' direction.

"I think Lydia's giving me the eye. I think she wants some of Dickie-do, the amazing dick man. I always thought she did. ... The one I missed. Don't know how I let that happen. But it ain't too late."

He glanced back over and toasted the girls before taking another gulp.

"And if she does, I'll be glad to accommodate her. Quackenbush says she's not married, and at this moment, neither am I. You think I'm right? You wouldn't happen to know what stateroom Lydia's staying in, would you?"

"Dickie-do, why would I know that? I'm a happily married man with a daughter."

"Good old straight and narrow, Wilson Black. Hell, you never came out to play with us in the old days. Shit, man. You missed a lot of good times over the years. I know you're a prude, but you can't tell me you wouldn't want to sample a little of that. You probably haven't even paid any attention to that fine piece of ass, Michelle, Paul runs with. As I was telling my man Jerry, I wouldn't mind knocking some of that bush off as well if the opportunity arose."

About that time, Jerry Quackenbush came in and joined them at the bar.

After the two high-fived each other, Dickie-do sang, "I'm so glad you made it, so glad you made it, you gotta gimme some lovin', gimme some lovin'."

Jerry joined in, started playing his air guitar, and singing, "Every day. ... Duhna duh duhna ...duh."

"Jerry, I think Lydia over there wants some serious lovin', something I've got plenty of to pass out."

*'If you don't pass out first,"* Will thought.

They high-fived a second time before Jerry said, "You never change, do you. You old dick-master."

"I've got my MDA, don't I?"

"MDA?" Will asked, immediately regretting doing so.

"Master of Dicking Accomplishment."

Dickie-do and Jerry high-fived a third time.

"And I'm going for my PHD – Professor of Hard Dicking."

"With a major in stroking?" Jerry replied.

"Alright, Jerry! Ooh! Ooh! S ... and ... M! S ... and ... M!"

*'What's this S and M crap? He was yelling that in the hot tub yesterday. On top of everything else, is Dickie-do some kind of pervert? I've got to get out of here.'*

Will was beginning to get embarrassed. He was sure this last exchange was loud enough for the former cheerleaders to hear. He turned and walked away to another table. The other two didn't even notice.

Tom Hamilton and DV and Cee Cee Craig walked into the bar and were waved over.

"S ... and ... M! S ... and ... M!" Dickie-do continued to blurt.

Tom was not amused. DV and Cee Cee looked perplexed. Then Tom noticed Will for the first time and used that as an excuse to disentangle himself from Dickie-do to walk away.

"Dickie-do, as I tried to tell you yesterday, there's some things that it's best to bury and not talk about," he said as he turned and walked towards Will.

"Pull up a chair," Will offered

"Thanks. You remember my friends DV and Cee Cee?"

"Sure. DV and I met the first night. But I've haven't had the pleasure of meeting the lovely Mrs. Craig."

She blushed and said, "I understand you live in the Keys. I'm a native Floridian myself. Orlando."

"So, DV? Are you from Florida as well?"

"A transplant. Originally from the West Coast."

"I kind of figured that might be the case when you said you toured with the Beach Boys. And you didn't sound southern. How'd you guys meet?"

"At Disney World. I left the Beach Boys to become part of a Beach Boys/Jimmy Buffett tribute band called the Landsharks. They play exclusively at Disney."

"So y'all live in Orlando?"

"Not anymore. I've recently left the Landsharks. I guess you might say I've kind of retired. We're in the process of moving to Jamaica. Bought a home there."

"I can't believe this. I can't wait for you to meet my wife, Betsy. We've spent a lot of time in Jamaica. Lived there for a bit. Got lots of friends there to this day. Where'd you buy?"

"Oh, I'm sure you've never heard of it. A little town near Ochie called Discovery Bay."

"Heard of it? That's where we lived. Damn! I wish Betsy was here. What a small world! I've definitely got to introduce y'all to Betsy. I wish I could introduce you to some of the people we know who live there as well."

Tom was then almost forgotten about as Will and the Craigs began talking Jamaica. It seemed like in a matter of minutes that they had become immediate old friends. It seemed like the Craigs had a thousand questions which Will tried his best to answer.

"So, what villa did you buy?" Will asked.

"Ever heard of Mount Corbett."

"Heard of it? My God in Heaven!" Will said, raising his voice again in excitement. "Betsy and I have been in it many a time. It's right up the hill from Sundance, where we used to live. Sundance is on that big curve before you go on up the hill to get to Mount Corbett. It's walking distance. They even tried to sell it to us at one point, but since we're still working stiffs, we weren't in a position to do anything about it. But if we had been in a retirement mode, we definitely would have considered it. After all, how many people can say they own a house originally built by a member of the British royal family. We have got to introduce you to our friends Henry and Rose Davis. They live just above Mount Corbett on Primrose Lane."

"It'll be a while until we'll be able to relocate. We've got to get our affairs in order in Florida first and take care of some family business. We don't want to have to be running back and forth all the time. Also, the sellers rented it back from us on a month-to-month basis while find a suitable place to buy and move into. It worked out well for both parties."

"Well, let us know when you get all the i's dotted and the t's crossed, and we'll hook you up with the Davises."

"Will do. It'll all come together when the good Lord decides the time is right."

Will finally thought to look at his watch and remember that he had told Betsy he wouldn't be gone that long. After he and the Craigs exchanged cabin numbers, he excused himself.

"Tom, I am so glad you introduced us," Will said, shaking Tom's hand.

Tom just shook his head and repeated, "Small world. Who'd a thunk it."

"I hope you have an irie day," he said as he turned to leave.

Will looked over and Suzzie seemed to be squinting and eyeing him as if she was dying to find out what they had been talking about.

Will stared back and wondered, *Is it my imagination, or is Suzzie glaring at us with daggers in her eyes?*

# CHAPTER 14

Will opened the curtain separating their dark stateroom from their balcony. The bright morning sun streamed in, immediately illuminating the room. Instead of endless ocean extending to the horizon in every direction, he saw nothing but scrubby tropical vegetation seemingly only a few hundred yards from the ship.

"Land-ho," he called out to Betsy. "On deck ye scroungy tar, or I'll keel haul ye right where you lay."

He began to sing the lyrics to Darby O'Gill's "Jack Tar."

*A sailor was walkin one fine summers day*

*A squire and his lady were passin his way*

*And the sailor heard the squire say: Tonight with you love, I mean to lay*

*With me doomy-amma dingy-amma doomy-amma day*

"Please. Spare me," Betsy begged as she threw back the covers, "It's too early to listen to you sing off key."

Will responded by strutting back and forth in his underwear like a drum major da-daing to John Philip Sousa's "Jack Tar March."

"God forbid. That's even worse," Betsy said as she jumped up in self-defense and hurried over to where Will was standing.

"I guess this means we're approaching the canal," she said after Will hugged her and bussed her on the forehead. She peeked out onto their balcony.

"Uh, huh."

"Yep. Looks that way to me too," Betsy continued. "Some of your class members said they were meeting upstairs so they could watch the ship go through the locks as a group."

"Then let's get cleaned up and join them," Will said. "You take the bathroom first."

After they both showered and dressed, they took the elevator up to the fourteenth deck to the Horizon Court to get some breakfast. There was an air of excitement as the ship inched towards the Atlantic entrance of the Panama Canal. People rushed towards the top decks and the ship's bow hoping to be the first to see the iconic canal locks. A loudspeaker crackled overhead as Regency's Panama Canal expert narrated their upcoming experience over the ship's PA system.

"France began working on the canal in 1881 but stopped due to engineering problems and a high worker mortality rate. The U.S. stepped in 1904. The canal finally opened in 1914. It was considered to be one of the largest and most difficult engineering projects ever undertaken ..."

"This should be a helluva day," Will commented. "And look at that sky. Couldn't be more perfect."

The broadcast continued, "You're about to sail through a place that is unlike any on earth."

Will and Betsy walked in the Horizon Court and saw that some of their classmates had had the ship's staff pull several tables together for the group.

Some of his classmates were already there. Will saw Dick and Beth and walked over.

"Got room for two more?"

"Absolutely."

"We'll get some food and coffee and be right back."

The people already present were buzzing with excitement as they anticipated the day's adventure.

"Annual traffic has increased from a 1,000 ships in 1914 to 14,702 in 2008 ..."

By the time Will and Betsy had returned with their food, however, the mood had changed. A couple of the women were crying. The rest were engaged in a frantic conversation. Will looked to see what had changed. The only change was that Rusty Herring, the class's resident author had joined the group.

"How horrible."

"Does anyone know what happened?"

"I can't believe it. You've got to be wrong."

"How's his wife?"

"What's going on?" Will asked Dick.

"Willard may either be dead or dying according to Rusty," Dick answered.

"How's Rusty know that?"

"As you know, Rusty isn't just another passenger since he's working for the cruise line giving his literary seminars. He knows many of the crew members and has access to places on the ship that the rest of us don't. He said that one of his friends in the crew told him they have Willard either in the ship's infirmary or maybe even in the morgue. He's either sick or dead. Rusty's not sure which. It's not the kind of thing the ship wants the passengers to know about, you know. And risk causing a panic."

"What about Zelma?"

"Apparently she's sick as well."

"You've gotta be kidding ... After what Willard went through in Cartagena getting mugged?"

"I guess when it rains, it pours."

After the initial round of exclamations and denials, the table became silent as people listened to what Rusty had to say.

"I'm told they think they got some tainted food possibly from a food service basket left at their stateroom door," he said.

"Regency Crown food service? They seem to go so overboard on cleanliness and health. My God! They'll get their asses sued off."

"That's where things aren't so clear," Rusty said. "My contact in room service told me they haven't ordered room service even once on this trip."

"So, where'd the bad food come from?" someone asked.

"That's what the ship would like to know."

"Is that all you know?" asked another classmate.

"Right now, but as I learn more ... and I'm sure I will ... I'll let y'all know what's going on."

"And I thought this was going to be a great day as we got to see the Panama Canal for the first time. This certainly puts a damper on the whole thing," Tom Hamilton said.

"That's for damned sure," several people replied almost simultaneously.

# CHAPTER 15

"Do you want another cup of coffee?" Will asked Betsy.

"Nope. I'm about coffeed out."

"So, let's go out on deck and find some deck chairs so we can watch the ship go through the canal."

As they got up to leave the Horizon Court, Betsy noticed Billy and Suzzie Cobb sitting with Al Soltero a couple of tables down. They had certainly been close enough to have overheard the exchange his table had been having with Rusty Herring concerning Willard McFarland.

"Look," Betsy said and nodded.

"Interesting. Let's go over and say hello."

Will and Betsy walked over to Al and the Cobb's table. For once, Billy seemed sober.

"Good morning, Al. ... Billy ... Suzzie. I didn't know y'all knew each other," Will said.

"We don't really, but we know of each other through mutual acquaintances. Small world, isn't it?" Billy said. "And good morning to you, Miss Betsy. Couldn't pick a better day to go through the canal, could we?"

As Betsy was starting to answer, the speaker drowned out her voice.

"The U.S. continued to control the canal and the surrounding zone until the 1977 Torrijos-Carter Treaty provided for it to be handed over to Panama."

Betsy waited for a lull in the presentation before asking Al, "I guess you've been through this canal so many times the novelty's worn off."

"Ah, yes, but I still love to go through it. After all, it has been called the eighth wonder of the modern world."

"Did you hear about Willard McFarley?" Will asked.

"No. Something good I hope," Billy said. "He was overdue for his luck to change."

Suzzie said nothing but seemed to get a momentary look on her face that Will found hard to interpret.

Billy turned to Soltero and said, "Willard is one of our old classmates who's on this reunion."

"I'm not positive, but I think I may know who you're talking about," Al said.

Will gave Betsy a sideways glance that said '*BULLSHIT*' before he continued.

"Afraid Willard's luck hasn't changed since he got mugged in Cartagena. Apparently, he and Zelma have now picked up food poisoning."

"How awful?" Suzzie said. "Does anyone know how it happened?"

"Some of the crew members told Rusty about it, but his knowledge was pretty vague. I guess you know that Rusty's working part time for the cruise line giving literary seminars."

"Does Rusty know how bad it is?" Suzzie continued.

"No, but there's a rumor it could possibly be fatal."

"Oh, my gosh. I wonder if there's anything I can do. Maybe I should go to them," Suzzie said. "That's horrible."

"I think the cruise ship is trying to keep a lid on the whole affair while they try to find out exactly what happened so as not to upset the ship's other guests. Rusty said he'd keep us posted if he finds out anything more."

"I'll put them both in my prayers tonight," Suzzie said.

"That's kind of you to do that," Betsy said. "They're fortunate to have a caring friend like you. We're heading out on the deck to watch the ship go through the canal from a deck chair. See ya."

Will and Betsy began to walk away.

"My sincere condolences over your friend," Soltero said. "I'm sorry I never got to meet him."

"I am too," Betsy said. "I only met him myself on this cruise, but from what Will has told me about him, I'm sure you would have found that you had things in common."

"If you say so, I'm confident that it would be true. I have found that you are an excellent judge of people, Mrs. Black. I pray for the couple's speedy recovery."

Will cleared his throat and said, "My dear, we'd better get up on deck if we're going to find a vacant chair."

He turned to go.

"Caring friend? Liar, liar. Pants on fire," Will whispered to Betsy once they got out of the Horizon Court.

Will and Betsy found two unoccupied deck chairs on the front row by the starboard rail, got settled as the ship entered the first of the three locks they would encounter before it would be released into the man-made Gatun Lake, and listened to the loudspeaker.

"We will be going through the old canal today. You will note the unbelievably small amount of space on each side of the ship leaving very little room for error. But never fear, our experienced pilots are very adept in guiding our ship safely through this narrow space."

A few chairs down, Lydia Vallence seemed to be holding court with some of the other female members of Will's class. Some were drinking mimosas and some bloody Marys. They seemed to be paying more attention to Lydia than they were the canal lock. She seemed to have their full attention.

"I was sitting out by the pool reading my Kindle just minding my own business. I guess I must've dozed off, but then I felt something cold on my arm. It was Dickie-do Dunne holding two mai tais."

"Considerate of him," Amanda said.

"Well, he moved my bag down one chair and invited himself to sit down in the chair next to me. He seemed harmless at first but didn't seem to be able to shut up. Talked mostly about himself."

"Well, Dickie-do's favorite person was always Dickie-do. You know that," one of the other ladies commented.

The others agreed.

"Some things don't change. Well, the conversation gradually got more personal. He began to tell me that he'd had his eye on me for years and how I was the sexiest girl in the whole class."

"Is this going where I think it's going?"

"Sho' is. He told me that he had noticed that I'd always found him sexy as well."

"Did you?"

"Are you kidding? I always thought he was an egomaniacal goober who was full of himself. He'd have to be the last man on earth for me to even consider him."

"Me too. I can't imagine him trying to hit on me."

"I thought he might be queer."

"So, what happened next?"

"He put his hand on my leg."

"So, he had a boner to pick with you."

"And what'd you do?"

"Dumped my drink in his lap and left. And you won't believe what he said next. 'If you change your mind ..."

With that, all the women began to laugh, and Amanda said, "Speaking of legs, did I tell you the one about the couple who had a flat tire in the middle of a snowstorm?"

"Let's order another round before you begin."

"Great idea. After all, we're on vacation."

After the waitress brought fresh drinks, Amanda continued.

"The guy gets out to change the tire despite not having any gloves. Soon his hands begin to turn blue, and he gets back in the car. His girlfriend suggests he put them between her thighs so she can warm them up. He does, and soon they're warm again. He gets out to finish changing the tire, but his hands start to turn blue again. So, she warms them for him with her thighs a second time. Finally, he triumphantly gets the tire changed and gets back in the car so they can continue down the road. She looks at him and says, 'are you sure your ears aren't cold'?"

The group all laughed and toasted Amanda.

"Now I know what kind of jokes you girls tell when you're not in mixed company," Will said.

"Do you think men are the only ones who tell dirty jokes? You ought to hear the one about Little Red Riding Hood and the wolf."

"Tell me. Don't just leave me hanging limp."

"I'll give you the Reader's Digest abbreviated version. When the big bad wolf threatens to screw Little Red Riding Hood all night long, she holds a gun to his head and says, 'That's what you think. You're going to eat me just like the story says'."

"You're bad."

"By the way, Dickie-do's the one you overheard in the hot tub, isn't he?" Betsy asked Will.

"That's him. Dickie-do the self-proclaimed dick man. I guess you can say, being a dick man has its ups and downs."

"And can be dangerous too if he tries to dip his dipper in the wrong man's dipping."

# CHAPTER 16

"Rusty is doing one of his literary seminars this morning. Want to go?" Betsy asked Will.

"Where and when?"

"The Lotus Bar at ten."

"What's he talking about?"

"How to promote yourself at social functions like cocktail parties."

"Why not. Maybe we can pick up a fresh pointer or two about how to put our best foot forward at social gatherings even though I think we're both pretty good at it."

Will and Betsy climbed the stairs to the fourteenth deck and walked down to where the seminar was to be held. The room was empty except for the bartender and one waitress.

"Where is everyone?" Will asked the bartender.

"This morning's seminar has been rescheduled. Time to be announced."

"Did you have a lack of participants?"

"No. I think it had something to do with the instructor – a personal issue."

"Is he ill? We just saw him in the Horizon Court yesterday, and he seemed fine."

"Not sure. I'm telling you everything that I was told. I'm sure the Regency Rapper will announce his revised schedule."

Will turned to Betsy and said, "There's a presentation on our stop in Panama going on right now in the Regency Theater, but by the time we get there, it'll be half over. How about some ice cream instead, my dear? The ice cream joint's on this deck."

"Sounds good," Betsy agreed. "As my grandmama used to say. I scream. You scream. We all scream for ice cream."

"Try this one. Life is like an ice cream cone. You only have to lick it one day at a time."

"Forrest Gump?"

"Charlie Brown, actually."

Will and Betsy walked down to Swirls Ice Cream Bar. Rusty Herring was sitting there looking uncomfortable with his bandaged foot propped up on the chair in front of him. He had just completed a cup of chocolate ice cream. Some of it had spilled on this white shirt leaving a brown stain.

"Rusty," Will said. "You playing hooky from your own seminar?"

"Had a little accident," Rusty said and pointed to his bandaged foot.

He noticed Betsy looking at the chocolate stain on his shirt and as he dabbed at it with his napkin said, "Hard to bend over when you're foots propped up."

"So, what'd you do to your foot?" Will continued.

"Stepped on a razor blade. Had to get stitches."

"Ouch. How in the world did that happen?"

"It was standing up in my sneaker."

"Oh, come on now. How'd that happen?"

"I wish I knew. Somebody put it there. I don't even use razor blades. I've got an electric razor."

"Where'd it happen?"

"In my stateroom."

"So, you're saying someone came in your stateroom and put a razor blade in your shoe?"

"I know it sounds nuts. But, yes. I guess so. Ship's doctor said it could have hurt me much worse if it had cut my posterior tibial artery. I could've bled to death."

"Ye gads. That's scary. Did you hear any more about Willard?"

Rusty got a funny look on his face and said, "No, not really."

"Are he and Zelma going to be okay? We've sure had our share of accidents so far on this trip."

Rusty shrugged his shoulders and changed the subject.

"I'll reschedule my seminar. Give me a couple of days so I can get comfortable walking on this thing. I need to stay off it."

"You're doing right. Back to Willard ..."

Rusty looked impatient and barked, "There's nothing I can add. I'm not at liberty to talk about it."

Will glanced at Betsy. Her look said, '*Don't push.*'

"Sorry about your foot. Glad it's not any worse that what it is."

When they were out of earshot, Betsy commented, "It may be my imagination, but did Rusty seem scared to you?"

"I guess I'd be scared too if someone put a razor blade in my shoe. Gives me the creeps just thinking about it."

"Why is it that when I think of sadistically bad things I think of Al Soltero?"

"Now you're reaching. I don't think Rusty knows Soltero ... unless it's through Billy or Jimbo."

"Anything's possible. You didn't know Al knew Willard either. And now look at Willard. Surely, these 'accidents' can't all be accidental."

"You know, Shirley, you may have a point."

# CHAPTER 17

"I'm looking forward to seeing Panama City," Betsy commented to her husband.

"Same here. The former home of Manuel Noriega. I wonder how safe it is."

"I think when they got Noriega, they cleaned up a lot of the narcotics trade here. Did you know he was once an astronaut?"

"You're kidding."

"Got selected by NASA in the '90's, trained, and went on at least one mission."

The Blacks cleared ship security on deck four and were guided to their bus to begin their Regency sanctioned tour. Suzzie Cobb and Danny Pearce were in front of them in the line.

Will poked Betsy and said, "Danny and Suzzie. I hope we end up on the same bus."

"There's your musician classmate, Tom Hamilton, too. Who's he with?"

"That's the Craigs. The people form Orlando who are moving to Jamaica. The ones I told you that I was going to introduce you to. Let me do it right now."

Will introduced Betsy to DV and Cee Cee, but they were only able to talk briefly before they were called to board their bus.

As it turned out, Danny and Suzzie did end up on Will and Betsy's bus, but Tom did not. Will managed for them to get the seat across the aisle from them.

"Good morning," Will said. "I'm looking forward to this tour, especially Reprosa so we can watch them make jewelry. My brother, Bill, uses the lost wax casting method on his sculptures. Now I'll understand more about how he does it, even though his casting is done on a much larger scale. Where's Billy?"

"He decided to stay on the ship. Tours like this aren't his thing. We'd have to be visiting a rum distillery to get his interest. Now he can drink all day without me being there to nag him about it and take care of his buddy, Jimbo. I expect both of them to be shit-faced by the time we return."

"What do you mean take care of his buddy, Jimbo? Something wrong with him?"

"You didn't hear?"

"Hear what?"

"Jimbo took a tumble down the staircase on the ship. Got banged up pretty bad."

"How'd that happen?"

"No one knows. Apparently, no one else was there when it happened. He doesn't seem to want to discuss it. Probably alcohol related."

"When did it happen?"

"Yesterday morning."

"He was drinking in the morning? That doesn't sound right."

"He break anything?"

"We can always hope he broke his drinking arm or his pecker," Danny said.

Suzzie shrugged as if to say, "tell someone who gives a shit." Danny mumbled something about people get what they deserve and something vague about curiosity's been known to kill a cat.

"I was really surprised to see that Billy and Jimbo both knew Al Soltero. We originally met Al in Vero and then reconnected with him in the Keys. Small world, isn't it?" Will continued.

"Yeh. Too damned small sometimes."

About that time, their guide introduced herself to her charges for the day in perfect English.

"My name is Emily, and your driver is Pablo. This is bus number four. If you get confused, just ask any guide for either bus number four or for me."

Emily went on the explain how she had been the daughter of an American engineer who was stationed in the Canal Zone and how her mother had been a local. She went on the describe how she grew up in Panama but was then educated to be a nurse in Atlanta. She had remained in the Atlanta area for a number of years but had decided after being widowed to return to her roots in Panama.

"Our first stop will be the Old Panama Museum, where we will see exhibits on Panama's history and be entertained by a local folk dancing troupe."

Will and Betsy were surprised at the number of high-rise modern buildings as they drove along the wide, well-maintained, but traffic-packed streets. The American influence was very apparent. Soon the background changed when they were in stand-still traffic, and they saw soldiers with automatic weapons standing on the sidewalks. Cars were being loaded onto tow trucks and being hauled away. The drivers were being placed in handcuffs.

"Do you mind if I ask what's going on?" Will asked Emily.

"Not at all. In order to legally drive in Panama, you either must be a citizen or a tourist who has been in the country for less than 180 days. These tourists are permitted only to drive rental cars. These people are primarily either Venezuelans, Ecuadorians, or Nicaraguans who have come to Panama to work or are on their way to someplace else like maybe the U.S. We have a zero-tolerance policy when it comes compliance about such matters."

"So, what'll happen to them?"

"I really don't know, but we don't want unwelcome, undocumented aliens in Panama."

After touring the Old Panama Museum, the bus headed for Reprosa, Panama's renowned jewelry making facility and its handicraft boutique and showroom. The bus with Tom Hamilton arrived at the same time, and the guide took both groups into the building together.

"Tom," Will said. "I was hoping your bus would get here when ours did."

A guide explained the lost wax method of casting jewelry and how the molds for the jewelry were made. They watched from a catwalk as the precious metals were heated and then put in a centrifuge to fill the molds. When the tour was over, they were taken to a showroom and offered some rum punch as they shopped. Suzzie bought a gold pendant and a pair of earrings. Will and Betsy looked at some of the local handicrafts but didn't buy anything. Tom bought a rain stick and some maracas.

The relaxed atmosphere changed abruptly, however, when a security guard demanded to inspect Tom's bag. Tom readily complied and showed him the contents as well as his sales slip. The guard reached into the bag and felt under the maracas. When his hand came back out, he was holding a gold pendant. He held it up and inspected it. He checked to see if the pendant was on the sales slip. It was not.

"Señor, please come with us."

Tom seemed aghast. The Craigs looked confused.

"I've never seen that before," Tom protested.

"Then what's it doing in your bag?"

"I swear. I've never seen that before. And besides, how would I get it even if I did want to steal it? All your jewelry pieces are in glass cases, and only a salesclerk can get them out."

"Señor, please do not cause a disturbance. Please come with us. We will discuss this in the office."

He pointed at a door and gently shoved Tom in that direction.

Emily stepped up and said, "Bus four. We need to leave now if we're to stay on schedule and get you back to your ship on time. Our next stop will be the craft market. You will have forty-five minutes to shop there."

Tom's bus left right behind Will and Betsy's with Tom apparently left behind. The Craigs volunteered to remain with Tom, but the authorities insisted that they leave with the bus.

"Do you know what just happened?" Will asked after their bus was back on the road. "I wasn't paying much attention to Tom, but I did see him buy the maracas and the rain stick and pay for both. Did you see him take the pendant?"

Suzzie said nothing.

"I wonder what's going to happen to Tom," Will continued. "Is he going to end up in a third world jail? Will Regency help him out, or is he on his on? Billy's a lawyer. Do you think he could help Tom?"

"Tom should have thought about that before he tried to steal anything," Suzzie said. "I don't feel sorry for a thief, and I'm sure Billy'd say the same thing."

Betsy gave Will her let-it-drop look and whispered to him, "I'll talk to you at the craft market after we get off the bus."

When they arrived at the craft market and had disembarked, Betsy said, "Will, there's a concession stand. I'm thirsty. Let's go get a Coke."

After they had each gotten their drink and she was sure they were alone, Betsy said, "Will, that pendant Tom supposedly stole was identical to the one Suzzie bought."

"Oh, come on now ..."

"We women notice things like that."

"Honey, are you saying what I think you're saying? That Suzzie set Tom up? Why would she want to do that? Maybe Danny's the one who did it. After all, he's mad at the world. And he *was* holding Suzzie's bag while she walked around and looked. In fact, he held it for her when she went in the restroom. I don't know what Tom ever did to Suzzie. Plus, I don't think Suzzie's that kind of vicious person. Now, Billy. He's a drunken asshole, but Suzzie? And Danny? He's just plain weird."

"I'm just telling you what I saw. It was identical to the one Suzzie bought."

"I guess all we can do is keep our eyes open and see if we see her wearing her new purchase on the ship. My bet's still on Mr. Attitude -- Danny. He's the one who has a hard-on for the world."

"What do think the odds are of this many bad things happening to a group on a cruise? You've had Willard and Zelma ... and Rusty ... and now Tom? Is this ship cursed or hexed or voodooed or something?"

"You mean like cursed – like the Flying Dutchman? By the way, I bet you don't know why they call it the Flying Dutchman."

Betsy gave him Will her I-guess-I'm-about-to-find-out-whether-I-want-to-or-not-look.

"Because the Dutch are always high."

"Will, let's get serious. Something bad wrong is happening right under our noses while you're making tasteless jokes."

# CHAPTER 18

After Will and Betsy returned to the ship, they went back to their cabin to rest and clean up before venturing out again. They phoned DV and Cee Cee, but they could shed no light on what was going on.

"DV says they're as much in the dark as we are," Will said after he hung up. "I wonder what finally happened to Tom Hamilton. Gives me chill bumps to think he could be sitting in a Panama jail cell right now. Do you think we should tell anyone what happened? Or our suspicions?"

"Oh, I'm sure the ship already knows that he didn't make it back. And you don't want to be a part of the gossip-spreading group in your class."

"I guess you're right. I'm going to take a shower, and then I think I'll take a little nap," Will said. "Would you mind waking me up in an hour or so?"

"Actually, I was thinking about doing the same thing."

"Then, when we get up, we get up since we're not on a fixed seating plan for dinner. That's what vacation should be all about – no rigid schedules."

"Amen, my dear, but I'll set my travel alarm for five thirty anyway."

The brief nap accomplished its purpose, and both Will and Betsy felt refreshed when they left their cabin and went up to the open deck on the fourteenth level.

"Do you see what I see?" Betsy asked. "Tom Hamilton."

Tom was sitting at table alone drinking a cocktail. He seemed to have purposely chosen a table that was partially concealed by a post.

"I'll be damned. Obviously, he resolved the problem at Reprosa."

Tom noticed them and acknowledged their presence in a half-hearted manner. Betsy thought he seemed deflated and whipped as he stared vacantly at the glass he had cupped with his right hand. Will decided to approach him.

"Tom, thank God you're back on the ship. What a nightmare!"

Tom motioned them to a seat. A waitress walked up and took their drink order. Tom waited until she left but then immediately became defensive.

"I hope you don't think I stole that pendant, because I didn't. I don't know how the damned thing got in my bag when I bought those maracas. That's a woman's piece of jewelry. I had no use for anything like that."

"We didn't think you did."

"I don't know where the thing came from," Tom repeated. "I never saw it before in my life until that security man pulled it out of my bag."

"Something that small could have been in the bag all along. Maybe swept in there by accident when a clerk was cleaning the top of the glass case."

"Yeh. Damn right. But, believe me. I didn't put it there. If I'd have wanted it, I easily could have afforded to buy it. But I didn't even like the damned thing."

"What made them look in your bag?"

"A tip. They said someone saw me take it."

"Did they say who?"

"No. Wouldn't say."

"So, how'd you resolve it?"

"With money. Third world ugly American style. First, I offered to give it back to them and gave the security guard a hundred bucks if he'd forget the whole thing. Then, I paid for it but told them they could keep the damned thing and resell it to someone else. Shit. It was a no-lose deal for them. What were they going to get if they sent me to jail and the pendant got impounded by the cops as evidence? They'd have been stupid not take me up on my offer. Who was going to know? There was no one there in that office but the three of us. The clerk may have even pocketed the pendant rather than putting it back in the cabinet since it was paid for. I honestly didn't give a shit as long as I got the matter resolved."

"Hey. You do what you have to do. At least, you're back on the ship safe and sound, and the ship's sailed. You're out of there. No looking back."

"I guess you're right. Fuck 'em."

"Your bus left you. How'd you get back to the ship?'

"Caught a cab. When it got me back to the pier, I shagged ass straight back onto the boat. Couldn't get out of that God-forsaken place quick enough. I'll sure as hell never go back."

"I'd a done the same thing. Do you think it was an accident, or did somebody try to do you in?"

"I'd love to know. I tell you what. If I *do* find out that someone on this ship bagged me, they better watch out. Tom Hamilton has dealt with scumbags in the music business for years, and he is *not* a very forgiving person with a short memory. I do hold grudges, and I *will* get even. And if I can't do it, I know people who can and will do it for me."

"I hear you, but let's hope it was just a big mistake. Don't do anything rash that you'll regret. I don't know why anyone would purposely set you up unless they were jealous of your success as a musician. But, if we hear anything, we'll sure let you know. Glad to see you back, my friend."

# CHAPTER 19

"You ready to go yet?" Will asked Betsy.

"Almost. Gimme a couple of more minutes."

"We don't want to be late. I'll tell you a story while you finish putting yourself together. I'll call the parties involved Melissa and Claude. Claude made a date with Melissa. Melissa got ready and waited for two hours for Claude to show up. She finally decided she'd been stood up and decided she'd spend the evening watching an old movie. Well, she got her house robe on, took off her makeup, made some popcorn, and plopped down on the couch. About that time the doorbell rang. Of course, it was Claude. He took one look at her and gasped, "I'm two hours late, and you're still not ready."

Even though she was dressed, Betsy threw her robe over her sundress, tied the sash, and walked out.

"I'm sorry. What'd you say, Claude?"

"Touché. This should be fun tonight. The Dells are playing, and I understand they've invited Tom and DV to back them up. You remember them, don't you? You know, 'Oh, What A Night'."

"I wonder how many of them could possibly be left. Was that their only hit?"

"To answer your questions, none are left. All the originals died, but the grandson of their original baritone has reorganized the group. And yes, they had other hits. Actually, they hit the Top 40 eight times. Twice in the Top 10. 'Oh, What A Night' is the biggie they're remembered for but 'Stay In My Corner' also hit the Top 10."

"Aren't you a wealth of knowledge."

"Amazing what you can learn from Google. You ready? We better get going if we're going to get a table."

"Any time you are, Claude."

Will and Betsy took the elevator to the fourteenth deck. The concert was scheduled to be played out by the big swimming pool. Dick and Beth were holding a table for the four of them near the pool. Tom was comparing notes with The Dells as they prepared to get going while DV was checking his guitar tuning. Tom did the introduction. Cee Cee was sitting at a table by herself so Will asked her to join them.

"Welcome, my fellow classmates and passengers. I can't tell you how exciting it is for me to play with a group who's in the Rock 'n Roll Hall of Fame. I've listened to their music for most of my life, but I never dreamed I'd ever share the stage with them. Now, I present to you a legend – The Dells."

The Dells, dressed in pale blue tuxedoes with open-collared white guayabera shirts, stepped up to their mics and did a three-sixty spin before launching into their first number, a medley of "Always Together" and "Stay In My Corner."

Dick noticed Suzzie and Billy Cobb at another table with Danny Pearce and acknowledged them. Billy was already looking like he was headed for a night in the bag.

Dickie-do Dunne. Jerry Quackenbush, and Jerry's common-law wife had a table right next to the pool. It seemed obvious to Will that both Jerry and Dickie-do had had way too much to drink already. Both clapped and hooted as The Dells concluded their opening number.

Will commented to his tablemates, "Looks like those two have been drinking all afternoon."

"And are shit-faced already. Making asses of themselves as usual," Dick said. "Bet neither of them will remember this concert tomorrow."

When the Dells got to their signature song, "Oh, What A Night," Dickie-do stumbled up to the make-shift stage, dragging Jerry with him, and joined in with the band.

"Oh, what a night," the twosome warbled off key. "Oh, what and S and M night."

Then Dickie-do turned towards where Paul and Michelle were sitting and started sing "Michelle, my belle" as he humped the microphone stand. It was as if he expected Paul to be amused by his antics, but Paul didn't seem amused. Then he turned in the other direction and began to warble L-Y-D-I-A to the tune of "Gloria," the old Shadows of Knight frat-rock standard that had been popular when they were in school. Lydia Vallence looked both embarrassed and disgusted.

Tom's concert abruptly came to a halt. Tom stopped playing and led both of them away from the stage before Regency security could intervene.

The audience accidentally heard him say through his still live mic, "How many times do I have to tell you. Enough of this S and M crap, you piece-of-shit drunk. Let it go. Keep your goddamned trap shut, or I'm going to shut it for you – permanently."

Cee Cee whispered to Betsy, "Do you know what that's all about?"

"Your guess is as good as mine. Will says he's spouted that line on several occasions after drinking too much. We've have been asking ourselves what he means since the cruise began. Will says he doesn't have a clue, but it sure seems to mean something to Tom."

She glanced over at Suzzie's table. Suzzie was giving her husband a hateful look, but Billy was too far gone to notice. Danny reacted, however. He immediately rose, and after Tom had gotten the two drunks back to their table without saying another word, upended it, and sent both tumbling into the pool. Without looking back, Danny immediately stalked out through the automatic door to the elevators.

They overheard Suzzie telling her husband, "I've had enough. I'm leaving. You coming with me or not?"

"Give me a few minutes to have another drink," Billy replied. "Just one more."

"Then you can just have it by yourself."

Suzzie stomped out without saying another word.

"Wow," Will said. "Dickie-do and Jerry really rubbed both Danny and Suzzie the wrong way. Suzzie seemed disgusted, but Danny was like a time bomb. I wonder why this got under his skin so bad. He's seen Dickie-do make an ass of himself before."

"Because that guy's got a lot of stored up anger. I mean ... major issues," Beth commented. "He just totally went off the deep end."

"No," Betsy said. "Your boorish classmates are the ones who went off the deep end ... and into the pool."

# CHAPTER 20

Will and Betsy went through the breakfast buffet line the next morning and found a table. Will went back to get coffee for them both while Betsy watched their plates and returned just in time to overhear some of the class gossips reviewing the events that had happened at The Dells concert the night before.

"Your bigmouth, busybody classmates will have something to talk about all day today. That's a guaranteed for sure," Betsy commented to Will in a low voice.

"For many of us, baseball is the national pastime. For them, its gossip. By the way, do you know what a gossip is? Someone with a keen sense of rumor."

"I *always* heard that a gossip is someone who talks about others, while a bore is someone who talks about himself. And a brilliant conversationalist is someone who talks to you about yourself."

"Well, gossip *is* nature's telephone. I want you to notice Janie over there with them. She's got enough tongue for ten rows of teeth."

"I'll have to admit she doesn't drop names. She seems to throw them in a perpetual game of catch. Speaking of gossipees, here comes your buddy Jerry Quackenbush."

"He ain't my buddy. You know that age-old adage about how you can pick your friends but not your relatives. Well, the same thing goes for classmates."

Jerry found an empty table and sat down by himself. If he saw either Will and Betsy or the gossips, he didn't acknowledge any of them. Rusty Herring limped in and asked Jerry if he could join him.

"You used to be a helluva tackle, but I didn't know you were a championship diver as well until last night," Rusty said good-naturedly.

"Yeah, I guess there's a lot of things you don't know about me. I can swim too."

"Where's your buddy, Dickie-do?"

"Funny. I called his stateroom to see if he wanted to go to breakfast, but nobody answered. Then I went by and pounded on his door. Still no answer. He must still be in the bag from last night. I bet he's gonna really be hung sho' nuff when he finally wakes up. I'll try him again when we're finished here. Why don't you join me? Between the two of us, we oughta be able to get his attention."

"You think Dickie, the dick man, will ever grow up?"

"I doubt it. You know, Dickie-do's gonna be Dickie-do. Always has been and always will be to the day he dies. He's living proof that one thing you can't drink away is alcoholism."

Jerry and Rusty finished their meal and left the Horizon Court together. As they were leaving, Rusty noticed Will and Betsy and detoured by their table to say hello.

"We couldn't help but overhear your conversation concerning Dickie-do. Good luck straightening him out today – or any other day for that matter," Will commented.

Rusty rolled his eyes.

After Rusty and Jerry left, Will commented to Betsy, "Jerry's right about Dickie-do and alcohol. I guess you know alcohol is the perfect solvent. It's managed to dissolve Dickie-do's marriages as well as his family and his career."

An hour later, Will ran into Rusty again outside one of the shops in the ship's atrium.

"Well, did you get Dickie-do back on the straight and narrow?" Will asked.

"I'm afraid Dickie's straight and narrow days are over."

"What do you mean?"

"Dickie-do's dead. When the room steward went in Dickie-do's suite to clean up, he found Dickie-do dead in his Jacuzzi bathtub. Jerry and I got there right afterwards just as he was calling it in."

"Oh, come on now?"

"I'm serious as a heart attack. Deader than a doornail. Only thing I can figure is he was so shit-faced out of it that he drowned."

"You've got to be pretty plowed to die your bathtub. I didn't think he was that bad off. In fact, I would have thought his dip in the pool would've sobered him up."

"Yeah, normally that would've been the case, but there was a line of coke and a razor blade on the bathroom counter. Strange thing was that he still had on his clothes and his forehead was bleeding. Must've taken a drunken fall."

"Was the water running?"

"Strangely enough, no. Tub was full though."

"Was any of the furniture in disarray?"

"One chair was turned over."

"Where's Jerry? How'd he react?"

"It crushed him – just wiped him out. Dickie-do was his best friend in high school, and they've run together ever since. He said he's gonna get smashed today. Dickie-do would have wanted it that way."

"And I'm sure he's being true to his word."

# CHAPTER 21

The Petersons and the Blacks walked back into the Horizon Court expecting to have a leisurely lunch. The class gossips had already assembled and seemed to be in even more of a twitter than usual. It seemed that every other word was Dickie-do this and Dickie-do that.

"Didn't take long for the word on Dickie-do to spread," Will observed.

"Bad news travels fast," Beth replied.

"More like warp speed," Dick added.

"Evil news flies faster than good news. That's for sure," Betsy agreed.

Amanda, one of the gossips' leaders, saw them and waved them over.

"Let's pretend we haven't heard about him and just listen to what they have to say," Will suggested.

Betsy smiled and said, "this should be fun."

"Did you hear about Dickie-do?"

"No. He sure put on a show out by the pool last night though," Will said.

The women began to almost babble as each sought to be the first to put in her two cents worth.

"That didn't compare to the show that followed. He ..."

"Dickie-do's finally done ..."

"He was done years ago, and I don't mean well done ..."

"Oh, he was a rare one for sure. He rarely behaved himself."

"He wasn't a Dunne. He was just dumb."

"Yeah. He was about a sharp as a pound of wet liver."

"I guess you could say that the dickman'll never get it up again. As much as he drank, I'm surprised he ever got it up at all. Probably impotent, truth be known."

"Probably why his wives left him."

"I went out with him once. If his hands had been as fast on the football field as they were in the car, he'd be in the NFL Hall of Fame right now."

"You must've been really hard up for a date ..."

Beth looked at Betsy and both stifled an oncoming giggle.

Will interrupted at this point and said, "Why do you keep using the past tense? Did something happen to Dickie-do?"

The women all jumped to respond, each interrupting the other again in their haste to be the first to speak.

"You didn't hear? Dumb Dickie's dead. He ..."

"O. D. ed on drugs. Coke ..."

"I heard heroin ..."

"Crack was more his speed ..."

"I heard be was drunk and drowned in the whirlpool bath in his cabin."

"I heard they found a razor blade next to the spa."

"And someone was in the tub with him ..."

"Man or woman? I always thought he was kinky enough to swing both ways."

"I never really liked him anyway. I just felt like I had to pretend I did."

"You weren't alone. None of his wives liked him either."

Dick glanced at Will as if to say, *I think we've heard about enough.*

Will took the hint and said, "I'm truly sorry to hear about Dickie-do. I sometimes think he got a bad rap. I don't think he really was what he pretended to be. Be sure to keep us posted if you hear more. Good to see you, ladies. We need to get going now and get our lunch."

He turned around before anyone could comment further. When they were out of earshot, he commented, "Can you imagine living with anyone at that table?"

"What mouths! My guess is that the only time those girls are somewhat attractive to their husbands is when they're on their knees with those big mouths open."

"Even that's debatable."

"Dick! Will! Enough already."

"Sorry, but I almost became a babbling idiot in the five minutes we were standing there," Will added and began flicking his index finger up and down over his lips as he blabbered, "bu-bu-bu-bu-bu."

"Listening to them ought to make you glad we chose each other," Betsy said.

"My dear, I learned a long time ago not to laugh at your choices, since I'm one of them."

"Seriously though. These mishaps are beginning to add up."

"Way beyond coincidence. Let's walk out on the deck. I need some fresh air to get the bullshit scent out of my sinuses."

The foursome strolled out into the open air and saw Suzzie and Danny sitting at a table near the Lido Pool as they finished eating lunch with Al Soltero. They each had a now mostly empty plate of food that they had obviously gotten from the Horizon Court buffet line. Will waved at them, and Suzzie waved back. Danny just stared out into space like he didn't know them. As they approached the table, Soltero greeted them.

"Will and Betsy Black, two very dear people. So good to see you again. The sea air obviously agrees with both of you. If I were prone to jealousy, I'd certainly be envious of you two."

He then rose and politely excused himself. His bodyguard, who had been sitting at an adjacent table, followed him as he walked away.

"Al is always so pleasant," Will said. "He always acts like a perfect gentleman. He'd give Cesar Romero a run for his money."

"Don't forget. Sometimes people have multiple facets to their personalities," Dick said. "Like when Cesar Romero played the Joker in the Batman movie."

He seemed almost ready to elaborate, but a look from Beth shut him up.

"You've probably told me this before," Will said to Danny and Suzzie "but how did you guys get to know Al?"

"I never met him before this cruise," Danny said. "Suzzie knows him because of Billy. Actually, he asked us to join him for lunch when we go ashore in Costa Rica tomorrow."

Suzzie didn't elaborate further. An uncomfortable silence ensued until Will said, "I guess you've heard about Dickie-do."

"Yeah. I, for one, ain't gonna miss old Dickhead-phew," Danny mumbled.

"Agreed," Suzzie replied. "You *know* what I think about that show-off shithead. But what goes around comes around. All you have to do is wait long enough, and justice prevails."

"I'm sure everyone in our group either has or ...will ... hear about Dickie-do before the day is out," Danny added.

"We just came from the Horizon Court. It certainly was dominating some of our classmates' conversations."

"You mean the triple g's," Danny with venom in his voice.

"Triple g's?"

"Yeh. The girlie gossip gurus. We saw 'em, but neither Suzzie nor I wanted any part of that cat-scratch. Though, I'll admit, for once there is some justice in this old world. If you wait long enough, God will smite the wicked."

"I don't think this was the hand of God."

"From what I hear. More than likely the hand of the devil with a little help from OxyContin. ... Nope. Definitely not at the hands of God but maybe instead by a goddess ... or should I say godless," Suzzie spit out.

Danny rolled his eyes.

"Oh, yeah? What makes you say that? That sounds like something the gossip gurus might say."

"I'd rather not elaborate further."

"Come on, Suzzie. Give. Is this something you got from Billy?"

She glanced at Danny before responding.

"Well, my husband is a lawyer after all. Even though he is a drunken one half the time."

Danny reentered the conversation at this point and said, "What Suzzie doesn't want to say is that not only is Dickie-do's pusher is on this boat, but there's strong possibility that Dickie-do wasn't alone in his jacuzzi tub."

"Don't bait us, you two. C'mon. Spit it out."

"Well, you ... now ... out-of-state, out-of-towners wouldn't know this, but us locals know Dickie-do's not just a sot. He's been abusing narcotics for years – both the legal and the illegal kind. Why do you think he behaves so erratically?"

"I'll admit the only time I ever saw him was at reunions when he was always on stage," Will said. "Mind if we sit down? I want to hear the rest of this story – assuming *you* decide to tell me the rest."

Will and Dick each pulled out chairs for their wives and then looked around and found two more chairs they could drag over for themselves.

"Go ahead, Danny," Suzzie said. "You've opened up Dickie-do's can of worms for the whole world to see. Now you might as well tell them the rest."

"Several years ago, Dickhead-do tried to water ski on Lake Ferguson while he was drunk so he could show off for some bimbo. It wasn't good enough just to try to ski drunk, but the asshole tried to go over the ski jump and fucked up his shoulder when he crashed into it."

Dick and Will looked at each other as if to say, N*ot surprising*.

"He's been on pain pills ever since. When the prescriptions ran out, he got them any way he could."

"So, what's that have to do with his pusher being on this boat?"

"His OxyContin pusher was Paul Walcox's godless goddess and live-in squeeze, that junkie ex-cheerleader, Michelle. She got picked up for pushing other things as well. They said Paul ... you know he was a pilot, don't you ... was bringing stuff in from Colombia."

"Paul had a plane?"

"No. He flew Willard's plane."

"So, was Paul arrested too?"

"Nope. Never could prove anything against him, but he went down there all the time. And he always seemed to have money. You put two and two together. It don't take a genius."

Will and Dick looked at each other again but remained silent.

"Well, Michelle supposedly cleaned up her act after her last arrest, but she does have a record. Everyone in Greenville knows that."

"Well, not everyone," Suzzie said. "And don't believe everything you hear about her reformation. Don't forget that I have a source most people don't – my husband, big, bad Billy.

I guess you know he has clients who have been unjustly implicated in the narcotics business."

*Like Al Soltero,* Will thought.

Danny continued.

"As long as I've gone this far, let me finish. Last night as I was coming down the hall to go back to my stateroom, I saw Dickie-do unlocking his own door with two women. He seemed drunk ... as usual. I could only see the back of one of the women's heads, but that one sure looked like it could've been Michelle to me. Never saw the other one before. Not one of our group. Some barfly he picked up, I'm sure."

"Was Paul with them?"

"Not that I saw."

"So, you're saying Dickie-do may have died from an overdose of OxyContin?"

"On top of cocaine, I heard coke was found in his cabin as well," Suzzie said. "Ta da, and good riddance. Couldn't have happened to a nicer guy."

"You mean lousy, sorry cocksucker," Danny spit out. "I hope he burns in hell."

All Will could say was, "Wow."

"You didn't hear any of this from me," was Danny's closing remark.

"Don't you think you ought to report what you saw?" Betsy asked.

"Nope. Not getting involved. Wouldn't bring dickhead back anyway. And if you buttinskis do decide to report it, don't expect me to support your story. For the record, I didn't see nuttin'. I ain't heard nuttin'. A word of advice. Buttin' into other people's affairs ain't good for your health. And by the way, don't look for me at dickhead's funeral service – if they bother to have one. Suzzie and I will be too busy celebrating in the bar."

"For once, I'll have an excuse to drink with my husband," Suzzie added.

# CHAPTER 22

Dick and Beth went back to their cabin. They all decided to meet on the deck at noon and have pizza for lunch. After the Petersons had left and Will was sure he and Betsy were out of earshot of Danny and Suzzie, he said, "I think I'll go back to our cabin and get my Kindle. I think I'd like to read for a while on the deck."

"I'll join you."

"My sweet, as much as I'd love your company, let me go back up there alone. I'd like to catch Danny by himself and talk to him away from Suzzie. And I think it may work out better if it's just the two of us."

"Do you have a specific topic in mind?"

"I honestly don't know. But something's not right about a lot of things that have been happening lately. I just want to talk to him when there's no one else around. Maybe when he doesn't feel like he's got to bluster."

"Do you suspect that Danny might be involved?"

"I don't know what to think, but he sure seemed to have a lot of insider knowledge about the Dickie-do affair."

"You've got a point. And he sure seems full of venom. Okay. But fill me in later. Love you, dear."

Will grabbed his Kindle from their cabin and went back up on deck. Danny was reading alone in one of the deck chairs."

*Oh, good.*

The chair next to Danny was available, so Will came over and asked, "Mind if I take this chair."

"Don't own it."

Will began to read, and Danny continued the book he had been reading. Will did not open a conversation immediately but simply read in silence for a while. Danny said nothing as well.

After about half an hour, Will said, "I'm starting to get thirsty. Think I'll get a Diet Coke. May I get you one?"

"Sure."

He returned and gave Danny his drink. As Danny sipped on it, it seemed to Will that this might be an appropriate time begin to probe him. He still didn't know what he had in mind. He'd just play it by ear to see if he could get any useful information or understand Danny's mental state.

"Are you still working?"

"I don't know if you'd call it working, but I've got some rental property around Greenville. Keeps me busy."

"Your dad was a locksmith, wasn't he?"

"Yeah. Popa-Lock and Son. I was the son."

"So, you inherited the business?"

"Uh. Huh. Expanded it into a pawn shop as well."

"But you're not running it anymore?"

"Sold it. A locksmith chain bought it. They offered me what I thought was more than the business was worth, so I let them have it. Plus, the timing was good since I had my hands full dealing with Misty's health issues. That's where a lot of my rental property money came from."

"My condolences over Misty."

"Thanks. It's something I don't like to talk about."

"Did you guys have any children?"

"Misty couldn't have children."

Will decided to let that subject drop since Danny didn't seem to want to elaborate further. They sat in silence for a few more minutes before Will resumed the conversation.

"Let me ask you a question, Danny, since you're a lock expert. Hypothetical, of course. How safe are these ship staterooms? If someone wanted to get into one of 'em, are these digital locks that use plastic cards for keys easy to get into?"

"Not if you know what you're doing. Why do you ask?"

"Oh, just wondering. Kind of wondered if anyone could have gone into Dickie-do's cabin."

Danny suddenly looked wary and defensive.

"Why would anyone want to do that?"

"No particular reason."

"Are you planning to break into someone's cabin?"

"Of course not. Just wondering. I guess you might say I'm just nosy."

"Nosy people sometimes get hurt. If you're inferring that someone could have done Dickie-do in, let me just say this. Dickie-do was an accident waiting to happen. A naturally self-destructive person who was contagious. As I said earlier, the world ain't gonna miss that low-life, self-proclaimed cock-hound, pervert, and rapist. He finally got what was coming to him. Probably because of his own stupidity. Something that should have happened years ago. There's a lot of us who would be better off if he had never been a part of our lives. Now if you'll pardon me, I think I'll go back to my cabin. Thanks for the Diet Coke."

"Yeh. Good talking to you, Danny. I'll catch up with you later."

# CHAPTER 23

By the time Will and Betsy got to the Regency Pizzeria, Dick and Beth were already there waiting for them. They went up to the counter and ordered their slices of pizza and a got a soda before returning to the table.

Will held up a legal pad and said, "I want to pick your brains after we finish eating."

"Wow, a legal pad," Dick said. "You must be like the man who had an elephant on his brain. Do you know what I told him?"

"What's that?"

"Looks like you've got a lot on your brain."

"Please," Beth said. "I'm eating."

After everyone had finished, Will and Dick bussed the table. Will pulled out the legal pad again and began.

"There's eight members of our football team on this ship celebrating this reunion. For simplicity's sake, I've listed the first seven in the order they appeared in the cheerleader skit on our first night at sea. I'll read the names one by one. H – Jimbo Littleton, O – Tom Hamilton, R – Rusty Herring, N – Dickie-do Dunne, E – Paul Walcox, T – Jerry Quackenbush, and S – Willard McFarley. Number eight is Billy Cobb."

"That's a good portion of our first-string," Dick commented.

"Yep, and I'd say they were thick as thieves then and for the most part, still are today. We've been at sea now for eight days, and thus far, there've been four unfortunate occurrences. The common link in these so called 'accidents' is that every victim has been a part of this group. It started with Willard being mugged, then someone putting a razor blade in Rusty's shoe, then Tom got accused of shoplifting, and now finally Dickie-do's dead with the possibility that Paul's girlfriend, Michelle, could be implicated. Nothing has happened to anyone else in our class. Coincidence? Seems to me to be hard to believe."

"You forgot that Willard and Zelma got food poisoning from something possibly comped from room service."

"I forgot about that incident. Hope they're all right."

"Yeah. Will may have a point," Dick said. "Kinda like one eye said to the other eye. Something between us smells."

He crossed his eyes.

"Dick ... Be serious," Beth said in an exasperated tone.

"That leaves three football players who have had nothing out of the ordinary happen to them. ... Yet. Paul, Jerry and Billy."

"You forget Danny pushed Jerry into the pool," Betsy said.

"Yeah, You could say that Jerry just sort of went off of the deep end," Dick said.

Beth just shook her head and said, "I don't know this man."

"I wasn't sure whether that counted or not since it was sort of impromptu," Will said. "Do you think we should sort of ... advise the four remaining to be extra careful?"

"Duh. Hopefully, they're already aware of these coincidences. They may have been dumb jocks, but surely, they're not stupid. After all, some of them became accomplished, successful adults."

"But they could be repressing the whole issue."

"Yeh. Maybe we can get them thinking about the possibility that they have a common enemy."

"Like maybe Danny," Dick suggested. "Sometimes I don't think he may be all there."

"And he is a locksmith," Will replied.

"But what could his motive be? You've got to be full of hate to target a whole group. Especially after all these years."

"Or delusional."

"Maybe he was jealous of the football players' popularity. After all, we had a damned good team."

"Didn't he help out as equipment manager? Do you think they humiliated him somehow?"

"You're right. I'm thinking maybe he did do that for a short period. But come on. What's the worst that could have happened? He got a dirty jock strap hung from his face, or somebody popped him with a towel?"

"I think we may be reaching ... grasping at straws, folks," Beth observed.

"I'd rather reach and be wrong rather than regret doing nothing at all," Betsy said. "And you haven't mentioned one wild card – Al Soltero. Y'all don't know Al, but Will and I do all too well. He ... now. how should I put this? ... has a history of being around when violent occurrences that are not coincidental seem to occur."

"Well put, my dear. I'm not saying we should go on a campaign. After all, we're not law enforcement officers. But if an opportunity presents itself in a conversation, maybe we should broach the subject with different people and see what happens when we do."

"I disagree. We need to be more proactive. And maybe we'll create enough awareness to keep something else from happening."

"We could be saving someone's life."

"Assuming these events *are* related."

"As long as we're adopting a proactive stance," Betsy said, "let me say this. Our next stop is Costa Rica. A lot of these accidents seem to happen ashore. Let's keep our eyes open and see if we can learn anything that might harm those remaining football players."

"Can't hurt. Sounds like a plan to me."

"Our first opportunity may be right now," Betsy said. "Look who's coming."

They all turned and saw Willard and Zelma McFarley slowly walking across the deck towards them. It almost seemed like an effort for the twosome to maintain their balance. Danny and Suzzie walked beside them. They paused and leaned against the rail as if trying to catch their breath. Danny held Willard's arm while Suzzie helped Zelma. Both of the McFarleys looked pale and like they had lost weight since the cruise began. Willard's face showed several days of unshaven stubble, unusual for him since he had always been very fastidious about staying freshly shaven. Zelma was not wearing makeup. As they got closer, it became apparent why. Both he and Zelma had a scabby facial rash that was just beginning to heal. They also had bags under their eyes.

"Wow," Will said. "It looks like those two were shot at and missed and shit at and hit."

"A definite train wreck," Dick agreed.

They waved at each other, and then the McFarleys began to slowly walk towards them. Will and Dick rose to pull up chairs for everyone".

"We heard about your food poisoning," Will said. "The rumors were all over the map. I'm so glad to see you're up and around. There was even one rumor going around that it might have been fatal."

"Well, the jury was out for a while," Willard said. "I've never felt so bad in my entire life."

"Me either," Zelma agreed. "I'm still woozy and weak. And don't have much appetite."

"If you don't mind me asking, just what happened?" Dick asked. "We didn't know what to think. Rusty told everyone about it, but he was pretty vague about the details."

"You know I got mugged in Cartagena, don't you?"

"We heard."

"After we got back out to sea, we found a gift fruit basket along with a bottle of wine outside our cabin door. We thought it was the reunion committee sending it to us through Recency room service in sympathy for the Cartagena incident. I didn't recognize all the varieties of fruit, but after all, I'm not an expert on tropical fruits. One of the pieces of fruit was yellowish green and looked somewhat like an apple."

"Was there a card in the basket?"

"A get-well card."

"Signed?"

"No. Blank. Anyway, we took it out onto our veranda, and I opened the wine. Thought we'd just have a happy hour celebration since I wasn't hurt in Cartagena any worse than I was."

A waitress came over, and Willard ordered two Diet Cokes. She also offered to get them each a slice of pizza. Willard declined. Danny and Suzzie did so as well.

"Thanks. I don't think either of us could keep it down. But don't let us keep you from ordering."

"No problem. We just had some. But, okay. Go on. I want to hear this. What happened?"

"I cut the little apple-looking fruit in half and shared it with Zelma. Tasted pretty good. We now know it was a manchineel."

"Man – chi – neal? I never heard of that," Beth commented.

"Me either," Betsy agreed.

"We certainly hadn't. The ship's doctor told us what it was," Zelma said. "Most people call it a beach apple. It's one of the most poisonous tropical plants that there is. More often than not, it's fatal."

"New one on me," Will said, "and we live in Florida."

"It's found in both South Florida, the Caribbean, and Central and South America. You don't have to merely eat the fruit to get poisoned. It'll poison you if you touch the bark or the leaves or get any of the sap on you. ... Or even breathe the fumes."

"Boy, oh, boy. That sounds like one bad ass molly dodger," Dick said. "I'm glad we don't have those in Memphis."

The waitress returned with their drinks.

"Moments after we ate it, we noticed a strange peppery feeling in our mouths. This gradually progressed to a burning, eye-watering sensation, and our throats tightened up. We tried drinking the wine to alleviate the pain, but the wine just made it worse. We tried to eat a banana, but that didn't help either. Our lips began to blister, and a rash formed on our faces and fingers where we had handled it. Over the next couple of hours, the symptoms got worse and worse until we could barely swallow anything because of the excruciating pain and the huge lump that was obstructing our throats."

"So, what'd you do then?"

"Called our houseboy and told him to get hold of the ship's doctor. That it was an emergency."

"I thought for sure I was dying," Zelma said.

"The doc induced us to throw up and then took us to the ship infirmary. They gave us some milk. It seemed to help some. After about seven or eight hours our oral symptoms gradually subsided, and we thought we might make it. But our throats stayed extremely tender for several days afterwards."

"The doc said we were lucky it didn't kill us. Since then, we Googled the plant and found out that the Indians used to tip their arrows with the sap. That's how Ponce de Leon died," Zelma added.

"Did the fruit basket originate with room service?"

"No. Definitely not. Someone just made it look that way. The basket came from the straw market in Cartagena. The rest of the fruit seemed to come off the buffet in the Horizon Court."

"Who would want to do that to you? Do you have any enemies ... or made any enemies ... on the ship?"

"Not that I know of. I've always gotten along with some people in our class better than I have others, but who hasn't?"

Danny nodded his head as he agreed.

"And some of the rich, catty bitches in our class never got over the fact that Willard chose to marry me instead of one of them. Some of them snub me to this day, despite the fact that the McFarleys not only have an old family name in the Delta but could buy and sell some of rest of them as well."

"Well, thank God you survived. We were just talking about all the bad things that have happened so far on this cruise."

"I heard Dickie-do died. What else?"

"Somebody put a razor blade in Rusty's shoe. Cut his foot pretty bad."

"I didn't know about that."

"What about Tom's shoplifting charge?"

"I haven't heard about that either. Where'd that happen?"

"Panama City. He was lucky to able to work it out with the Panamanian authorities."

"I guess we're not on the inside track for gossip since some of the catty wives have chosen to ignore us," Zelma said. "Not that I'd have it any other way."

Will looked at Betsy as he thought back on the jewelry Zelma had bought hoping to impress this group she was now pretending to disdain. Betsy felt sorry for her.

"Do you know what the common denominator on all these people was?" Will asked. "They were all our ex-football players. Do you think this is coincidental?"

"How should I know? And maybe not," Willard acknowledged. "But I wasn't one of our football stars. If you'll remember, I got kicked off the team for violating training."

"Yes. Maybe so. But they were still your friends, and you ran around with them. Who'd want to do the whole group in?"

"Gosh. I don't know."

"Well, there's still three members of the team on this ship that haven't had a mishap. ... Paul, Jerry, and Billy. But we've still got a lot of cruise to go. I think all you football players ought to have a sit-down with each other and decide what you could have done and how you're going to protect yourselves as a group from the person you've offended. And then do whatever you have to do to right things with this person before someone else gets caught in the crosshairs."

"And maybe killed," Dick added. "Like Dickie-do did."

Danny and Suzzie continued to remain silent.

"I would definitely keep my eyes open going forward," Will said. "As I suspected, it seems apparent that y'all hadn't connected all the dots. And I'm not sure your teammates have either. We're going to make it a point to talk to each of them just like we just talked to you."

"It could save them a lot of grief," Dick added.

"I think you're overreacting to a bunch of coincidences," Danny said. "And sticking your nose in where it don't belong. People resent that. I know I do when it happens. You better just look out for yourself."

Suzzie was silent at first but then added, “I can’t believe there’s a plot going on. That’s really stretching it. Things like that only happen in the movies.”

“Zelma, we need to talk all of this over some more,” Willard said. “Do you think Will’s right?”

Zelma shrugged and said, “I’m feeling sick again. I think I need to go to the ladies’ room.”

“I think you’d be wise to be vigilant,” Will said. “We’ll definitely keep our eyes and ears open and let you know if we come up with any fresh ideas. And if we can help in any way ...”

“Thanks for the offer and the heads up.”

The Blacks and Petersons walked away. Will heard a familiar voice greeting Suzzie and looked over his shoulder. Al Soltero and his bodyguard were coming from the other direction.

Will paused and said softly, “Hold up. Let’s listen.”

“Let’s plan on disembarking at 8:30 tomorrow. Will Billy be joining us?” Al asked. “I’ll have one of my associates pick us up.”

“Don’t count on Billy. Too early for him. Do you mind if Danny takes his place?”

“I would be honored to spend the day with you both.”

Betsy gave Will that look that said, *Interesting. Very interesting. I wonder ...*

Will nodded his comprehension back, and they continued walking before Al noticed them.

# CHAPTER 24

On the following morning, the Regency Crown arrived in Puntarenas, Costa Rica, a historic port founded by Hernán Ponce de León in 1519. It's a small town that has about 15,000 permanent residents.

"Should be a good day to go ashore," Will commented. "Our room TV said it's about eighty-two degrees, and once again I don't see a cloud in sight."

They had signed up for a ship sanctioned tour called "The Best of Puntarenas." It had eight stops that included a river cruise, a visit to a coffee plantation, and a ride on an aerial tram over Costa Rica's lush rainforest. The Petersons had chosen a different tour.

Signs held up by tour guide employees on the dock guided them easily to their bus. They got a seat near the back. They saw that Jimbo and Amanda Littleton had chosen the same tour.

Will whispered to Betsy, "Jimbo – one of the last men standing. Or at least he's standing again. That fall on the stairs must not have been as bad as we heard. Maybe this'll give us an opportunity to warn him or to find out if anything is really going on."

Betsy nodded back.

About that time the Littletons were joined by Paul Walcox and his girlfriend, Michelle.

"Didn't I hear you say she was an ex-cheerleader?" Betsy whispered.

"And junkie as well ... but she's supposedly clean now."

Both Paul and Michelle seemed to be weaving a little bit as they got aboard, and Paul plopped clumsily into his seat.

"You sure about that?" Betsy asked.

The first stop was at the National Theater in San Jose where they saw a performance by a troupe of local folk dancers. Betsy bought some colorful maracas at the gift shop. They then reboarded the bus for their next stop, the jungle crocodile safari cruise on the Tárcoles River. They boarded a well-maintained, flat-bottom, open-air houseboat for their tour of the river. As soon as everyone was aboard and settled in the bench style seats, their guide greeted them over the boat's sound system.

"My name is Dr. Marie F. Orjuela. Bienvenido."

She began to explain what they were going to be seeing. By the time they got aboard, Will's classmates had already settled on a different aisle. Will waved at them, and they waved back.

Will and Betsy immediately noticed the richness of the avifauna and the river's large population of crocodiles.

"This river has the largest crocodile population on the American continent," the guide explained. "And surprisingly, it is still relatively unknown and unstudied by the scientific world. Unless we learn how to conserve and sustain nature's delicate balance that has taken millions of years to evolve, the results could be disastrous and irreversible. We hope that by exposing people like you through this tour to one of our natural treasures, we will be able to call national and international attention to our cause. We hope when you return home you will transmit this important message."

People began to lean over the side of the boat to get a closer view and to snap pictures of the wildlife. The guide continued to point out the birds and show them the plant life as they slowly toured the quiet, still river.

'And there you see a Roseate Spoonbill ... and that's a White Ibis ..."

"We may take a lot of these things for granted," Betsy said, "but what you wanta bet this is the first time most people on this boat have ever seen any of these things?"

"Except maybe in a zoo."

Paul was cutting up, reaching over the side of the boat to see if he could touch a croc. Jimbo playfully pushed him, and Paul almost lost his balance.

"Your idiot buddy Paul keeps that up, and he may join his teammates on the casualty list," Betsy commented.

"We all made mistakes when we were growing up, but some of us have kept making the same mistakes as we've grown older," Will observed.

"Growing up is hard, my love. Otherwise everyone would do it."

Her comments were almost drowned out by the guide telling them that the bridge they were approaching was called the Crocodile Bridge.

"The Tárcoles or what we natives call the Rio Grande Tárcoles is sixty-nine miles long and covers 524 acres," she continued.

The tour took about an hour.

The tour's next stop at a plantation was where they learned how important coffee production was to the Costa Rican economy. Paul bought a bottle of a local coffee liquor that he opened on the bus, and he and Michelle shared it on their way to their next stop, the rainforest aerial tram ride.

"I was wondering how he was going to get that back on the ship," Betsy commented.

"Won't be an issue."

When they arrived, Michelle missed the last step as she got off the bus. Paul caught her as she lost her balance, but then almost fell himself. Jimbo caught both of them just in time. Paul and Michelle giggled as Paul threw the empty liqueur bottle at a wire trash bin but missed it.

"What was that you said about ex and being clean?" Betsy asked.

"Darling, some people don't have X's. They have Y's as in Y the hell do they keep doing crap like that."

Betsy smiled and squeezed Will's arm.

"They remind me of a glug-glug joke," Will said.

"I've heard of knock-knock jokes, but what's a glug-glug joke?"

'With a knock-knock joke, you say knock-knock at the beginning. With a glug-glug joke, you say glug-glug at the end. Ready or not here I go. ... They may drink a bit, but at least they don't wine."

"Glug-glug."

"Very good, my dear. You're a fast study."

Their guide began to prepare them for their next stop.

"We are now going to the Veragua Rainforest, a nature preserve, adventure park, and research station. It covers 1300 hectacres and provides a buffer to La Armistad National Park, Central America's largest conservation area."

A half hour later, the bus arrived at Veragua Rainforest, the site of the aerial tram. They all got off the bus and waited for instructions from their guide.

"We'll take the tram ride," the guide explained, "and then we'll have a buffet lunch. After that, we'll take the walking trail, and I'll show you some of Costa Rica's indigenous plant and animal life. Those of you who signed up for the zip ride will wait to my left. You will go with Manuel here. The rest of you will stay with me. ¿Entiende?"

"I hope your loopy classmate didn't sign up for the zip ride," Betsy mumbled.

"Me too. He seems to be zipping already."

The group walked through the open-air tiki hut full of tables where they would have lunch and down a board walkway to get to the tram departure site. Paul and Jimbo stayed with Will and Betsy's group. Michelle detoured by the ladies' room and said she'd catch up with them. The steel gondola was rectangular and was tall enough for a person to stand. It had wire mesh side walls from about waist high down to the floor. Above that level, it was completely open. It was suspended from the cable that it moved silently along and had bench seats designed for about six people.

Will heard Jimbo's voice.

"Will. Why don't the six of us share a car."

"I guess ... uh ... Sure. Why not. Glad to see you're not hurt from your fall on the ship."

"I've got a few bruises, but it could have been much worse. I'm mainly sore."

Michelle caught up with them. She smiled at Paul and patted her canvas tote bag. When they were all settled in the car, it began to climb the steep cable that would soon have them above the canopy of trees. A knowledgeable guide pointed out the highlights along the way through their gondola's PA speaker.

When they began to level out over the treetops, Will and Betsy looked down at the virtually unblemished, lush tropical wilderness beneath them. In the sensory overload that was the rainforest, Betsy felt her limbs tingle and her brain race. Even after all the years she and Will had lived in Florida's subtropics, the reality still seemed somewhat alien. Back home, she knew the Keys so well that she didn't ever have to think about her surroundings. Here in the Veragua Rainforest where nothing was familiar, factoids kept popping into her mind about its mysteries and dangers. Despite the fact that she had never been the overly anxious type, each time the guide pointed out one of the toxic plants, one of the injurious animals, or poisonous reptiles, it just raised more questions for her to silently marvel at and analyze all over again.

The guide explained, "Costa Rica has over nine thousand species of flowering plants and over eight hundred species of ferns."

Will and Betsy almost forgot about their carmates as they pointed out to each other the varieties of gingers and bromeliads they recognized as well as the types heliconia, and wild orchids they had only seen in pictures. The guide brought a dazzling yellow-leafed Cortez tree to their attention as they passed over it.

Their attention returned to their companions when they heard Paul shout out, "What's that? It looks like a giant turd hanging in a tree."

Will looked at Betsy and laughed since he knew exactly what it was.

"Paul, what you see is a tropical termite nest."

"Holy shit. Look at that mutha. They ain't got dem in Mississippi."

Will couldn't help but add, "My friend, I bet you don't know what tropical termites eat for dinner."

Paul pulled out a bottle of Cacique guaro that had been sequestered in Michelle's tote bag, stood up, and took a swig. After wiping his mouth on his sleeve, he burped and asked, "Whut's that?"

"A table for two," Will said with a smile on his face.

"Paul looked puzzled for a second, but then his face broke out in a big smile as he said, "I git it."

He held out the bottle for Will to take a swig. Will declined, and Paul took another drink himself, leaning back as he did so. The gondola rocked, and he clumsily turned to face the forest, almost losing his balance before Jimbo caught him by the back of his belt to keep him from tumbling headfirst over the side.

"Paul, maybe you should sit back down and lay off the sauce for a little while," Will suggested.

"Nobody can say that Paul Walcox is a pussy who can't hold his liquor."

Will looked at Betsy. She sent a silent message back.

*Will, back off. Don't start a fuss with this drunken redneck creep. He ain't worth it.*

About that time the tension was broken by their guide coming back on the PA system.

"Look right below us, and you'll see something you don't see very often in the daytime. See that big bromeliad beneath us with the yellowish red cone shaped flower? See that snake wrapped around it? That's a Fer de Lance. They're primarily nocturnal so you don't see them often in the daytime. That snake is one of the most poisonous snakes in the world. Scientists say that one single bite has enough poison to kill over thirty people. Its venom contains an anticoagulant and causes hemorrhaging. And it works fast causing its victim's tissues to die. Unlike many snakes, it doesn't avoid its victims. It aggressively attacks. It's not something you want to mess with."

"I hate snakes," Betsy commented to Will.

The guide came back on, "But one good thing about them is they love to eat rats so if you have a Fer de Lance in your yard, you won't have a rodent problem."

"That's comforting," Will said.

Paul bared his fingers like fangs and hissed. Michelle seemed to find this highly amusing.

When the gondola had returned to its launch pad, Will and Betsy got out. Betsy pulled Will over to one side and said, "Will, let's get away from these people. OK?"

"Good idea. Folks, we're going to go to the head and then walk around the gift shop before we catch a bite so why don't y'all go on through the buffet line, and we'll catch up with you back on the bus."

He and Betsy walked way before anyone could object. When they deemed it to be safe, Will and Betsy found a table as far across the room as they could from Will's classmates.

Lunch consisted of a casido, a traditional Costa Rican plate lunch with beans and rice, cabbage, and sweet plantains. Will got pork for his meat course; Betsy chose chicken.

As they were eating, Will commented, "Well, that didn't turn out to be an opportune time to talk Jimbo or Paul about all the coincidental accidents that've been happening to their teammates."

"That's for sure. But I guess we can rule out Jimbo as a predator. If he had wanted to, he easily could have let Paul fall out of that car instead of pulling him back."

"Maybe he would have if we hadn't been there as witnesses. Shit! I don't know who not to suspect anymore – except you. But I don't know what motive he would have to harm Paul. They've always been buds even though both of them dated Michelle at different times way back when. She dated a lot of people. She even dated Dickie-do for a while. She dumped both Jimbo and Dickie-do and started going with Paul because he was our big-shot, glamorous quarterback and they were just on the team."

"Holding a grudge over that sure doesn't make any sense."

"Let's face it. Nothing about any of this makes any sense."

# CHAPTER 25

The bus returned Will and Betsy to Regency Crown later that afternoon well before their departure time, and they were quickly processed back onto the ship.

"I wish it was this easy to get scanned at an airport," Betsy said.

"I think most of what they care about here is keeping you from smuggling booze onto the ship. Good thing Paul and Michelle are carrying their hooch in their belly."

When they were taking the elevator back to their stateroom, Will commented to Betsy, "I don't know about you, but I'm worn out. Eight stops make a long day."

"Agreed. You wouldn't think that mostly just riding around would wear you out, but it did."

"I'm sure the sun and heat had something to do with it. Kind of like when you go to the beach."

"Our choice of companions might be part of it too. What you say that we just stay in our room for a while. We can watch the ship leave the port from our balcony."

"You can watch it if you want to. I think I'll take a shower and catch a nap."

"You're right. I'm bushed too. Then later why don't we go to the Wheelhouse Bar for happy hour, then have dinner in the main dining room, catch the after-dinner show, and call it an early evening. After all, we've got to get up early to go ashore in Nicaragua tomorrow."

Will turned on the shower.

"Ladies first."

"Don't you mean pearls before swine," Betsy said and winked at him.

After freshening up and taking a short nap, the Blacks took the elevator down to deck seven. As they walked into the Wheelhouse Bar, they saw that some of Will's classmates had pulled some tables together and already had a head start on them. He noticed Al Soltero and his bodyguard sitting alone not too far away silently enjoying a cocktail. Al didn't seem to notice them, so they didn't feel obligated to go over and speak.

Both Paul and Billy seemed well on their way to a long evening. Paul bellowed out their names and waved them over. Suzzie and Amanda looked like they were merely tolerating the heavy drinkers. Jimbo seemed to be in a one-way conversation with the perpetual petulant Danny. The waiter took their drink order. The obligatory glass clinking followed when their drinks had been delivered.

"So, how'd your day ashore go with Al Soltero?" Betsy asked Suzzie. "He really showed Will and me a good time in Colombia. Bet you and Billy got some good shopping in."

Will noticed what seemed to be a slight reaction from Al at the mention of his name.

"Oh, fine," Suzzie said evasively. "Billy didn't make it. Danny went instead. He took us to someplace called Guaitil. It was OK, I guess. Maybe I'll tell you about it later."

Betsy smiled and made eye contact with Will.

Betsy waited for Suzzie to elaborate further, but Suzzie seemed to notice Al for the first time. Will thought they possibly made eye contact. Just as it seemed like she was going to elaborate further, she suddenly became silent. Instead she seemed preoccupied, glaring at her half-drunk husband and then down at the empty glasses on the table in front of him as if she were keeping count.

After an uncomfortable silence, Betsy said, "I guess Jimbo or Paul told you that we all took the same tour today. Went on a river cruise and a sky tram ride as well."

"And we got to see some interesting plants and animals at both places," Will threw in, trying to stimulate the dying conversation. "We even got to see something our guide said very few tourists get to see, a normally nocturnal snake that he said is one of the most dangerous in the world."

"Can't we talk about something else," Suzzie said. "I hate snakes."

"I see I'm the only guy here who doesn't have a jacket on," Will said as he struggled to change the subject.

"Yeah. This is formal night," Amanda said.

"I totally forgot. Boy, formal night has sure changed since Betsy and I began cruising. I remember when it meant black suits or black tie. Now it just means a blue blazer and an open collar shirt, and you don't even have to wear socks."

About that time a piano player began his set with Frank Sinatra's "Love and Marriage."

"How old does this guy think we are?" Paul slurred. "That's the kind of shit my grandmama listens to. I bet if I slip him a buck or two, he'll play something from this century."

"Hell yes. Damn right," Billy yelled. 'Something like 'Born to be Wild'."

Danny and Suzzie looked at each other and both looked disgusted. Michelle giggled.

Danny said contemptuously, "And next, you two'll be singing 'Sweet Caroline' I bet."

"Maybe it's a good time for me to go to our stateroom and get my jacket," Will said. "I'll be back in a sec. You want me to order you another drink before I go, darling?"

"I'll go with you. My earrings are feeling too heavy."

Will gave her that look that said, *Now, that's an original excuse.*

Billy announced, "I'll talk to the piano-picker after I take a piss."

"Piano-picker? You're so funny," Michelle slurred.

"Yep. He's about as funny as a fart in an elevator. I'm outta here," Danny announced.

"Me too," Suzzie agreed and reached for her walking stick to help her get up. "I've had all the fun I can stand."

"My wife the party pooper. Even so, I'll walk you back to our cabin," Billy volunteered. "But then I'm going to come back down here for a bit."

"Well, my dear, I'm not surprised," Suzzie said. "As usual, you've managed to end this soiree on a up note."

"Why don't I walk you back instead," Danny volunteered.

"I want anudder drink," Michelle said.

"Sounds like a wonderful idea. I'll have one with you," Billy slurred. "Beats going back to the cabin with my sourpuss wife. I need to pee."

"And by God, then we shall all have that drink – soon's you get back from draining your lizard," Paul commented.

"Don't you mean siphon the python."

Suzzie gritted her teeth, and her hand squeezed on her walking stick until the veins protruded.

Billy staggered towards the elevator. Those leaving said their goodbyes. The party seemed to be over. Al nodded at his bodyguard who then silently left their table and walked in the same direction Billy had taken.

Will and Betsy rode the elevator up to their stateroom and got Will's blue blazer. As they reentered the lobby by the stairs, they heard a scream.

Billy was lying at the bottom of the staircase. His nose was bleeding and his arm seemed to be at an unnatural angle.

They rushed down to try to help. Will thought he saw a figure disappear in a hurry back into the hallway, but he couldn't be sure.

"Don't move him," Will said. "Just watch over him until I can find a porter and get back. I'll call from our room."

He went to try to find help. Billy mumbled incoherently something about tripping or being tripped. After Billy was taken to the ship infirmary, they rode the elevator back down.

Later, as they were having dinner, the Blacks talked about the incident.

"Another staircase accident – and someone on our short list. Do you really think it was another coincidence?"

"Well, there's something Agatha Christie used to say. Any coincidence is worth noting. You can always disregard it later if it's a coincidence."

"So ... bottom line ...do you think his accident may have involved someone else or was he just plain drunk?"

"He was pretty loaded," Betsy observed.

"But he said he was just going to the head. Why'd he go four decks up?"

"Who the hell knows what goes through a drunk's head. Maybe he wanted to get in the last word with Suzzie. Let's face it. He's probably been drinking all day."

"But what was this mumbling about being tripped. It may be irrelevant, but I swear I think I saw someone go back into the stateroom hallway."

"Man or woman?"

"Couldn't tell."

"Surely, Suzzie wouldn't ... Her own husband?"

"I don't think Suzzie would, but I wouldn't put anything past Danny."

"You're right. He's sure strange and getting stranger all the time."

"You'd think that if someone just happened along and saw Billy fall, they would have tried to help like we did, not just run away."

"You would think so, wouldn't you. Unless ..."

"Yeh, unless, my dear, unless his fall was not a coincidental accident."

"And maybe Jimbo's wasn't either."

# CHAPTER 26

Later that same evening, Will and Betsy returned to their stateroom. After dinner, they went to the Crown Theater on deck seven to see the production show. Tonight's show had been entitled "Way Down Yonder in New Orleans" and was a tribute to Louisiana music.

"Boy, most of those songs sure brought back memories," Will commented at the conclusion.

"That's for sure. That's the music we grew up with."

"And dated to. All in all, I think it was a pretty review."

"From Fats Domino and Ernie K-Doe up to Dr. John and Doug Kershaw."

"They did stretch it a couple of times – like with 'Lady Marmalade' and the 'House of the Rising Sun'. 'House of the Rising Sun' is an old Mississippi blues tune covered by The Animals who are British, and Patti LaBelle's a Philadelphia girl through and through. Though I remember both Eric Burdon and Patti did play one time at Jazz Fest. Remember. We were there. And, I also remember what you used to say about her. You said Patti screeches like she got her tits caught in a ringer."

"And I still maintain that. Well, both songs are about New Orleans – and both were big hits. I'm sure you were the only person in the audience who thought about those other nuances."

Will unlocked their cabin door and turned on the light. They began to undress and get ready for bed. As he was emptying his pockets, Will noticed a rather large covered piece of glazed pottery about fifteen inches high on their small credenza. It was shaped like a cookie jar and had a flat lid with a ceramic knob handle. It was royal blue and had contrasting abstract designs.

"Do you know where this came from?" Will asked. "Something you bought?"

"If I'd have bought it, you'd know about it. I haven't been anywhere without you. It is a gorgeous piece. I wonder where it came from."

"Look. There's a card next to it."

Will picked the card up. It had the Regency Crown name and logo on the top.

He read, "'Congratulations for having the winning bid at our Champagne Art Auction. We hope you will cherish this one-of-a-kind memento of your cruise.'

"Huh! Must be a mistake. We haven't been to any art auctions since we've been on board. And we weren't even here today."

"I certainly haven't attended one. Must've delivered it to the wrong cabin."

Then he noticed a second card. This one was handwritten in neat almost block-style printing. It said, "Raise and Call."

"What in the world does that mean?" Will asked.

"You got me. Call who? About what? Is there a phone extension number or room number on it?"

"Nope. Fuck it. I'm tired, and it's late. I'll straighten it out in the morning. However, it is pretty. I'm sure the real owner will be glad to get it back."

They continued to get ready for bed until they heard a rustling noise.

"You hear that?"

"Sounded like it came from the pot."

Will raised the lid slightly. A hissing snake head darted at him barely missing his arm. He yelled and slammed the top of the pot back down just in time.

"Holy shit! A snake! And the son-of-a-bitch almost bit me!"

He stood there trembling, holding the top down so the snake couldn't get out. The pot shook as the snake thrashed around inside it. Despite the cold room, Will broke out in a sweat.

"You sure he didn't get you?"

"Yes. But if I would have picked up the top all the way, he sure as hell would've bitten me for sure."

"What do we do?"

"Give me a moment to think. Christ! I almost pissed all over myself. Give me something heavy to put on this lid so I won't have to stand here and hold it while we figure this out."

"I brought a roll of packing tape. Think that'll do it?"

"Can't hurt. We'll tape the lid down until we can think of something better."

Betsy brought the tape over and began to tape the jar while Will still held the lid in place as the snake continued to try to get out. When she had used what seemed like half a roll of tape, Will took the pressure off the lid. It seemed to be holding for the moment.

"Get me that ice bucket. We'll turn it upside down on the pot and tape it down as a backup."

When this was done, Will told Betsy to open their balcony door and carefully took the pot out onto their small deck. After he set it down, he turned the table over to put additional weight on it. Then they closed the sliding door so it couldn't get back in the room.

"I almost had a heart attack when that fucking thing tried to bite me. That's got to be about as scared as I've ever been."

"I think I was as frightened as you were. So, what do we do now?"

"Gimme a moment to think and catch my breath – as soon as my heart stops racing. God! I hate snakes with a purple passion. Right now, flip the light on out there so we can watch and make sure that mean mutha doesn't get loose."

Will sat silently on the side of the bed until his blood pressure started feeling normal again.

"OK. I think I've got a plan. We've going to get that Regency Crown ship zipper bag you bought in the gift shop and the sharpest high-heel shoes you've got here with you. Then we're going to spray the inside of the bag with sunscreen or deodorant or mosquito spray or whatever we've got that might be harmful or distracting to the snake. I'm going to take the ice bucket off the top of the pot and you're going to loosen the tape while I hold the top down. Then I'm going to carefully flip the pot upside down and dump the snake into the zipper bag while you zip it closed. It's soft but it's pretty thick. When the snake is in the zipper bag, we'll beat it to death with the sharp heels on your shoes."

"Don't forget. We also have the knife that came with the fruit basket."

"Good idea."

"We'll kill the SOB with one or the other, and after we do, we'll throw the zipper bag as far as we can into the ocean."

"Sounds dangerous to me."

"You got a better plan?"

"No. But I had another thought. Why don't we put the tape dispenser in the bag and maybe the jagged edges will cut him as we beat the shit out of him?"

"Can't hurt. And let's put our jackets on to protect our arms."

After they had assembled the needed items, Betsy raised the table while Will made sure the top or the packing tape didn't come off. After the preparations had been completed, he eased the upside-down container into the zipper bag, and Betsy partially zipped it.

"I'm going to count to three. On three, I'm going to shake the hell out of the pot. The lid should fall into the bag and hopefully the snake will as well. I'll jerk the pot back, and you zip as fast as you can. I'll drop the pot to one side and grab the knife in case it tries to come after you. Then we'll beat the living crap out of the damned thing."

"Instead of trying to reach for the knife, just hit it with the pot if you have to. If it breaks, it breaks."

"Another good idea. Ready. One. Two. THREE."

Will shook the pot and immediately the zipper bag began to writhe as Betsy zipped. The zipper caught on something. It was the snake's tail. Will slammed the pot down onto it, and Betsy was able to zip the bag the rest of the way. They both began beating until the heels on both of Betsy's shoes fell off.

"Move over," Will said.

He got up and began to jump up and down on the bag with both feet.

"OK," Will gasped, out of breath. "Surely nothing could survive that."

He picked up the bag by its straps and shook it. Nothing wiggled. He shook it again. Nothing.

"I think it's dead."

Will opened the bag slightly, just enough to see inside of it. The snake did appear to be dead. Then a realization hit him.

"Betsy, look at this."

She nervously glanced down.

"Look familiar?'

"A poisonous fer de lance viper snake like we saw in Costa Rica! Get that thing out of here."

Will rezipped the bag and while holding the straps and threw it as far as he could off of their balcony.

"Now that that's done, I guess we ought to try to get some sleep since we're scheduled to go ashore in the morning," Will said.

"You might be able to sleep, but it's out of the question for me."

"You're right. Me too. Maybe a late-night cocktail will settle both of our nerves down."

"I really don't want to go back out to a bar."

"Tell you what. I'll go back up to one of the deck bars that's still open and bring something back to our stateroom."

"That sounds better. I'll take off my makeup and get comfy while you're gone ... and try to quit shaking."

"And maybe we can make some sense out of this before we go to bed. Cuba libre sound OK?"

"Double Cuba libre. ... With plenty of ice."

"Your wish is my command, my brave and fearless princess."

"Courage, my dear, is not the absence of fear but acting in the face of it. You did alright in that department tonight yourself."

Will was back within ten minutes with their drinks.

"To us."

They clinked their glasses.

"Got something to show you that I noticed while you were gone. Take a look."

Will glanced down at the upturned pot. Stamped on the bottom of it was "Chorotega Pottery – product of Costa Rica."

"Son-of-a-bitch. So that snake came back on board with a passenger today. That narrows things down a bit – to most likely one of my classmates."

"Maybe. Or it could have come back aboard with a crew-member. Don't forget that lots of them are Hispanic, and our 'pal' Adolfo Soltero has tentacles that reach deep into the Hispanic community. And we both know he's involved with something crooked on this ship ...

"And he was ashore with Suzzie and Danny today ..."

"Suzzie? Danny? That's a stretch. ... Billy maybe ... but they said he didn't go ashore ... and Billy's the one who fell down the stairs tonight ..."

"My dear. Don't underestimate Al. Remember his influence over the help at Club Tropic?"

"Boy do I ever. Good old Al wanted to muscle in on the Rum Reef Club Tropic in Islamorada. And it just so happened Uncle Adolfo had a nephew, Luis, working there, and he asked Luis as a favor to his mother ...

... who Al was supporting in Colombia ..."

"to disrupt Rum Reef's operations ..."

"Al's got to be the only person I know who could use an iguana and a homeless man on LSD to cause an undertaker's convention to disrupt a NAACP gathering."

"And come out of the affair lily white."

"I love your choice of words."

"All my words are crumbs that fall from the feast of my mind."

"Gimme a break while I go and puke."

"Seriously though. I think we ought to keep this whole situation to ourselves. And I mean don't even tell the Petersons. Just pretend it never happened and see what going to happen. Maybe someone will slip up. Somebody's got to be surprised that we're not dead. Let's just see what going to be the next shoe to drop."

"Sounds like a plan. Dang. I liked those high heels."

"A small price to pay. Sweetie, at this point, I'll admit that I don't have a plan. Sometimes it's best just to breathe easy, trust your instincts, shut your mouth, and see wait for a shoe to drop."

# Chapter 27

Will and Betsy were both up early the following morning despite not sleeping well the previous night. Sleeping-in wasn't an option since they were supposed to go another ship-sanctioned tour in Nicaragua.

"Why don't we catch some breakfast at the Horizon Court before we go ashore," Will suggested.

"Coffee! Coffee! My kingdom for a strong cup of coffee," came Betsy's answer.

"I didn't sleep worth a diddly-damn thinking about what happened last night."

"And with all your tossing and turning and up and down, you think I did?"

"Well, the time wasn't totally wasted. I've got a few things to bounce off of you as a result."

"Can it wait until I get my caffeine fix?"

"Oh sure. Why don't we take whatever bag we're going to carry ashore with us, so we don't have to come back to the room unless we want to."

"Works for me."

They took the elevator up to the fourteenth deck. After they sanitized their hands, a Regency employee with disposable gloves on handed them their plates.

"Do you want to take the caffeine intravenous line or go through regular channels?"

"Regular channels will be fine."

Will got his usual – two eggs over light, grits, a couple of link sausages, two slices of bacon, and whole wheat toast. Betsy chose the eggs benedict and some cut fruit. After they had gotten their breakfast, Will looked around the dining room. He was pleased to see no one that they knew.

"Good," he said. "No familiar faces. I was hoping we could talk alone. Let's get that two-person table across the room by the window just to be on the safe side. You hold it down while I get coffee for both of us.

When he returned to the table, Will cut up his bacon and sausage into bite size pieces and scooped them onto his grits. Then he poured the whole glop over his eggs and salted and peppered it all. He topped the mixture off with a pat of butter. With his knife and fork, he cut the eggs into small pieces letting the egg yellow coat the grits. Last, he put some strawberry jam on the toast he would use as a scoop and got out his spoon to dig in.

"Bon appetite."

"I've been watching you go through that morning ritual for how many years? And when you get through, it still looks like someone threw up in your plate."

"But it tastes so much better than if someone did."

"So, what did you want to discuss?"

"Things. Like Chorotega Pottery for one. I thought the name rang a bell, and at three o'clock this morning it hit me why. It's on one of the Costa Rican tours we didn't take. I thought I'd seen the name in the Regency Rapper. I pulled that day's letter out of the desk drawer, and I was right. And you'll never guess where it is – Guaitil."

"That's where Suzzie said Soltero took Danny and her yesterday."

"Your recall sometimes amazes me."

"That's because I'm a super-banker. So, either she or Danny ... or Al ... could have bought the pot and delivered it to our room ..."

"Mrs. super-banker, you have just earned yourself a 'coldbeer'."

"A little early for me."

"Chew on this comforting thought. Anyone on this ship who took that tour could have bought it."

"I don't think they sell ceramic pots with fer de lances in them as tourist souvenirs. I can hear it now. 'Sir, would you like your pot with or without a deadly snake? If it's a present, we can gladly giftwrap it for you. Will that be Mastercard or Visa?'"

"You're right. That probably rules out one of the tours. But it doesn't rule out a ship's employee under Al Soltero's control. As we were talking about yesterday, remember Rum Reef Club Tropic. Their employees who were in Al's sphere of influence totally disrupted their operations at his instruction with a series of coincidental accidents ..."

"And a druggie homeless person and a giant iguana. Not to mention the giant fish head they introduced into the buffet chowder. I'm beginning to see your point."

"And who else would know better how to bring contraband back onto the ship than an employee? And who would have a key to leave it in our stateroom? ... Or get a card saying it came from the Champagne Art Auction?"

"Good points. But don't forget. Danny *is* a locksmith. ... And Suzzie *is* a techie who probably knows how to hack things or get in electronic locks. And Billy is up to his neck with Al. But why us? Are we somehow a threat any one of them? Or all of them? Danny, I can see. He's weird and moody. But what have we done to Soltero lately? Or Suzzie? Ever? I only met her a few days ago, but she strikes me like a nice person with a rotten marriage to a shyster lawyer who now has also been an accident victim on this trip."

"Possibly not. Maybe he was just drunk. One thing we can do is to keep our ears to the ground and see if any of my classmates have attended an art auction since the cruise began. You know, they have them pretty much daily."

"Do you think one person is behind all of these accidents? Jimbo, Willard, and Billy are in bed with Soltero ... somehow. But Rusty wasn't. I don't think. Did he piss someone off by writing about them? Or Dickie-do ... He was just plain obnoxious. ... And a loser on top of that. ... Or Tom Hamilton ... he's a one- night stand, over-the-hill musician who probably hasn't had anything to do with this bunch for years outside of reunions. ... And you haven't associated with any of them for your whole adult life other than also seeing them at reunions ... Shoot, we live a thousand miles away. And don't forget, I don't even know these people since I just met them."

"With the exception of Soltero. Let's face it, my dear, we have interfered with his plans more than once."

"This is a lot to think about."

"Yeah, it is. But if we value our health, we damned well better give it some thought. Like it or not, apparently, somehow, we're right in the middle of what's going on. It would behoove us to find out why, as do it fast as we can."

"And tiptoe while we're doing it."

"Let's hope the last shoe has dropped on accidents."

"So do I, but I wouldn't bet the farm on it."

# CHAPTER 28

"Nicaragua here we come," Will sang as they left the Horizon Court.

"If you sing 'right back where we started from,' I think I'll lose my breakfast."

"Actually, I was going to sing, 'and I get to share it with my best chum'."

"Chum?" Is that what I am? Fish bait?"

"What would you rather be – a crumb or a bum?" After all I do have to do a rhyme in time."

"One more dumb poem is going to make me have a plumb numb spasm."

"Like orgasm?"

"No, more like a ho-hum spasm in my rectum."

"That's gruesome. So, I guess I better change the subject before we have a problem all over the floor. As I was about to say, my chum, I've always wanted to see Nicaragua since our old neighbors, Jack and Melissa, used to tell us so much about when they lived here. According to Jack, there's not a whole hell of a lot to San Juan del Sur Bay. Jack said it's only got about fifteen thousand permanent residents, most of whom are fishermen. And only a few one or two any-star hotels and some stores and restaurants. Other than fishing, cruise ships more or less keep the place alive."

"I guess that's why we're taking a tender in. It's not big enough to have a port deep enough to accommodate our ship."

Will and Betsy rode the elevator down to deck four to catch the tender that would take them ashore. After a very short wait, they boarded. The tender was a modernistic, hard-top, orange and white fiberglass vessel that almost seemed like it should be in a sci-fi movie. A passenger had the choice of sitting on a bench seat inside the vessel or on its open-air top. Will and Betsy chose to ride inside. Paul Walcox and Jerry Quackenbush along with their significant others, Michelle and Judy, were in line a few people in front of them.

Will heard Jerry's familiar voice as they climbed down the short steps, "Black, here. We saved you a seat."

Will gave Betsy that look that said silently, *I wonder if we're stuck with this bunch of rowdies for the whole day. Please God. Say no.*

He could tell by the look he got in return that she was thinking the same thing.

"Hey, mister," Jerry said impolitely to an older couple sitting across from them.

He shooed them with his hands.

"You mind moving down and giving our friends a place to set down?"

The couple obligingly slid down to make room.

When they were seated, Will said, "So what tour are you guys signed up for today? Betsy and I are going to the volcano. It should be very educational. Neither of us have ever seen a volcano before, and this one is supposed to be one of the premier volcanos in the whole world."

"You would. We didn't come here to get ed-icated. Don't you know what day this is?"

'Uh. Sunday last time I looked."

"It's Sunday Funday Pool Crawl Day."

Will and Betsy gave each other a puzzled look.

"You never heard of it? Where you been? Livin' under a rock? San Juan Del Sur every Sunday is where one of the biggest regular kick-ass parties in the whole world happens.... And since we're here on a Sunday, we're sure not going to let it happen without us getting our share of the booze. Certainly not going to waste this opportunity going to see some boring volcano. This is a once in a lifetime opportunity to p-a-r-t-y."

"Party! Party!" Paul chimed in.

"These folks drink all day and into the wee hours"

"Rum de rum rum. Rum de rum rum. Rum," Paul sang to the tune of Dragnet.

"But we're not going to be in port that long," Betsy said. "We've got to be back on the ship by four-thirty."

"So, we're going to do our own Sunday Funday Pool Crawl. See. We've got our bathing suits on under our clothes."

He pulled up his tank top to show them his bathing suit. The top had rolled over from his white, flabby belly.

Betsy shuddered slightly as she took in the whole scene from Jerry's hairy armpits to his scuffed, high-top work boots.

"I read up on it."

Will looked at Betsy as if to say, *I didn't know he could read.*

"It goes to four bars. What we're going to do is go to all four of those bars ourselves on *our* schedule and be back on the ship by the time it leaves."

"Just don't get so wasted that you miss the ship. You know they are not going to wait for you. They *will* sail without you and leave you stranded here."

"You worry about yourself. We'll be back, and tomorrow I gar-on-tee our stories are gonna be hotter than yours are."

"A bar story hotter than an active volcano?" Will commented to Betsy. "That's a hot one."

Betsy smiled and said, "I guess it depends on your perspective. Ole! Ole! Ole! Ole! Feeling hot, hot, hot."

"Do you know the bars that participate in this weekly debauchery?" Will asked.

"All I know is that the first one is some joint called Pacha Mama's. I'm sure they'll tell us where to go from there," Jerry said.

"I'm sure they'll be glad to tell you where to go," Will said and smiled.

"And something called The Naked Tiger. I may get me a t-shirt from that one. Describes me gurrr-rate," Paul added.

Within minutes, the tender arrived at the dock and began to quickly unload its passengers so it could return to the ship for its next load. Locals held up signs to help the new arrivals find their correct tour bus. Paul and Jerry rushed to try to get a cab to take them to Pacha Mama's.

When the Blacks boarded their bus, they saw Suzzie, Billy, and Danny and took the seat across the aisle from them. Billy's arm was in a sling, and he had a bruise on the right side of his face.

"I'm glad to see that nothing's broken from your fall last night," Will said. "I was afraid you'd really hurt yourself."

"Yeah. I guess I was lucky. I didn't break anything, but I did dislocate my shoulder and twist my ankle."

"You know what they say," Suzzie added with a frown. "God protects fools and drunks."

Will thought it best to change what was obviously a touchy subject, so he said, "We rode over on the tender with Paul and Jerry. They're planning on spending the day bar-hopping. Apparently, it's a Sunday tradition here in San Juan Del Sur called Sunday Funday."

"Wish I'd known. I might have joined them," Billy said.

Suzzie looked at Danny, and he rolled his eyes.

She added, "I should have let you go. Maybe I'd get lucky, and you'd break your neck this time."

The bus public address system came on and their guide for the day announced that they would now depart. Will and

Betsy welcomed this as an excuse to end the uncomfortable conversation.

"Welcome to Nicaragua, the land of lakes and volcanos. I am proud to be able to show you the geographic beauty of my native land. We are the home to a multitude of volcanos, making us an ideal location for those of you who enjoy viewing and photographing nature's wonders. After we visit the Masaya Volcano, our driver will take us on our return trip to the colonial city of Granada where we will have a buffet lunch. Now, sit back and enjoy the scenery. We have a pretty good ride in front of us."

Their first stop was the Catarina Viewpoint where they were allowed to photograph the Apoyo Crater and the towering Mombacho Volcano. The guide told them that these natural wonders dated back approximately twenty-three thousand years. They then continued on to their destination. The guide came on occasionally to briefly explain various things, but for the most part, Will and Betsy simply enjoyed looking at the Nicaraguan countryside.

When they neared the Masaya National Park, the guide began to explain things in more detail.

"Remember when you were a child and studied volcanos. I'm sure you all assumed that all the world's volcanos had big lakes of magma sitting around inside of them."

People nodded in agreement.

"Well, amigos, that's not how it works in the real world. In fact, this is true of only three very special volcanos worldwide, and you're about to see one of them. The other two are in Hawaii and the Congo.

"But before you get worried, let me give you some good news. Masaya has only had two lava flows since the sixteenth century. The most recent one was 1972. But ... we have had a few discrete explosive events in the last few years. In 2001, the crater exploded and formed a new vent in its bottom. This explosion blew rocks as large as sixty centimeters as much as five hundred meters from the crater.

"Before we get off the bus, let me warn you that Masaya does emit large amounts of sulfur gas. And let me warn you to be careful. A few years ago, we did have two people fall into the crater."

Someone asked, "Did they die?"

"Fortunately, no. But firemen had to rescue them using ropes and harnesses, and they were severely dehydrated when the firemen got them back out. We'll spend forty-five minutes here. Please be careful. I'll be wandering around and will gladly answer any questions that might arise."

The passengers began to file off the bus, and small groups headed in different directions. Will and Betsy immediately noticed massive groups of green parrots and bats flying around the volcano. The Blacks tried to distance themselves from their unpleasant travelling companions but kept them in sight.

Billy was limping halfway down a slope when they heard him yell as his head disappeared. Suzzie and Danny had been right behind him.

"Oh, shit," Will yelled and ran in Billy's direction. "I hope he didn't fall in the crater."

When he got over to Billy, he saw that Billy was merely lying face first and upside down on a pile of rubble. His arm had come out of the sling, and he had skinned his knee. He seemed dazed and trying to get back up, but he fell back down on his side. Suzzie and Danny were just looking at him as if they didn't know what to do.

Will gently turned Billy over so that he was lying on his back.

"Billy, are you OK?"

"I – I think so."

"Nothing broken?"

"No. ... But I hurt like hell. I think I wrenched my shoulder again."

"What happened?"

"I dunno. I think my ankle must have given way."

"C'mon. Let me get you up and help you back to the bus. Danny, you get on one side of him, and I'll get on the other."

Danny complied. Will got Billy up, and they supported him as Billy limped back to the bus. All this time, Suzzie had said nothing and did not volunteer to stay on the bus with him.

Later, as they were having lunch in Granada, Will commented to Betsy, "I thought for a moment there that another mysterious accident had occurred."

"Thought crossed my mind as well."

"Danny and Suzzie were with him when he went down."

"But Billy would have known if one of them had tripped him. You heard him say that his ankle turned on a rock."

"Well, he does have a bad ankle from the fall he took last night."

"We may be trying to read too much into this incident. Legitimate accidents *do* happen."

"Yes, they do. Let's hope that was the case today."

# CHAPTER 29

Will and Betsy found a row near the back of the bus on the trip back hoping to distance themselves from the Cobbs and Danny. It seemed to work. The threesome sat silently farther forward staring out into space and not even looking at each other for the whole trip back.

"Great. Maybe we've shaken them. I can only take so big a dose that bunch on a single day."

"Actually, I almost feel sorry for them," Betsy said. "They seem so miserable most of the time."

"Sorry? Remember what Henry Davis used to say in Jamaica. Sorry for maga dog, maga dog turn round and bite yu."

Betsy smiled as a mental vision of Henry came into her head.

"Do you think Paul and Jerry stayed sober enough to make it back to the ship?"

"We can only hope. They say that God looks after children, drunks, and fools."

"They're certainly at least two out of the three, and ...hmm ... Paul and Jerry *are* childlike."

The bus arrived back at the waterfront at the scheduled time and unloaded them at the dock. The Carnival ship that had been using the dock that morning had sailed, but the Regency Crown remained anchored offshore. Tenders were waiting to transfer their passengers back out to the ship. Higglers abounded to take one last shot at selling local crafts and souvenirs to the returning passengers. Betsy took a moment to walk around before they boarded the tender. She bought a Toña beer baseball cap to take to Wilson Soltero, their Nicaraguan pool man in the Keys.

"Wilson'll like this," Will commented. "Plus, it also gave us one more opportunity to shake the Cobbs and Danny once and for all. I'd prefer to spend my happy hour with only you and you alone."

"Hope springs eternal. Only you and you alone can thrill me like you do."

"Very good. That's a song you should be too young to remember."

"Flattery will get you everywhere. I'll have to admit, my dear, you were a hard nut to crack, but the sweet kernel in your center made it worthwhile."

Will squeezed Betsy's hand.

After they had rested and then cleaned up, Will suggested that they have their evening cocktail in the Pirate's Lounge on deck five instead of their usual haunt, the Wheelhouse Lounge.

"After spending all day with dysfunctional classmates, I prefer just to have a little down time with you this evening," he reasoned. "And this bar is a little more out of the way."

The Pirate's Lounge was a nautically themed bar dedicated to the pirates from piracy's golden age. The walls were lined with paintings of famous buccaneers of old. Some like Blackbeard and Francis Drake were very familiar to most passengers. Some like William Reed were more obscure. They chose a table by the wall. Above their table was the portrait of Bartholomew Roberts.

Will pointed at the picture and said, "You remember who this guy was, don't you?"

"Of course. The infamous Black Bart. Looking around, it seems like the decorator purposely chose pirates from various nations, not just England."

"Smart. This cruise line caters to guests from all over the world."

A laminated drink menu had a wide variety of pirate themed drinks. Things like a Wrecked Pirate, Pirate Punch, and a Pirate's Last Call.

Their pirate-damsel waitress came over and welcomed them.

"Today's special is an Angry Pirate."

"What's that?" Will asked.

"Coconut rum, peach schnapps, melon liquor, pineapple juice and 7-Up. They're yummy."

"Yarrr, me favorite wench! Feel like an Angry Pirate?" Will asked his wife, "or would you rather get your usual grog?"

"Shiver me timbers if you must, but I think I'll pass on both. It's the end of the day, and I'm too tired to be angry this late in the afternoon. A gin and tonic sounds nice and refreshing."

"So be it. Settled. Make it two."

He turned to the waitress and said, "Fair maiden, hie thou rapidly to yon barkeep and deliver our libations without fail, or I'll be forced to run you through."

Betsy looked at the waitress, shrugged, and said, "I don't know him. He just insisted on sitting here."

As they were waiting for their drinks to be served, Will heard familiar voices behind them.

"So much for choosing an out of the way bar and unwinding. Maybe they won't see us."

The voices were becoming increasingly animated. They could hear Paul's over the rest.

"Those wet-back, cocksucker, mother fuckers ... I'll ..."

Then they heard Jimbo say, "Paul, you won't and can't do anything. Let me handle this."

He turned and saw Paul, Michelle, and Jimbo but no Jerry or Judy.

"Jerry's probably passed out in his stateroom," Will whispered to Betsy. "Could be Judy's up there trying to nurse him back to health."

"Or up there passed out with him."

Before Will could reply, they overheard Michelle say, "I can't believe it. We would've known."

About this time, Al Soltero came through the doorway from the opposite direction from Will and Betsy and joined the group. His massive bodyguard sat at a different table. Jimbo began to explain something to him in a voice so low that Will and Betsy couldn't hear what he was saying. A waitress came over to get Al's drink order. Al's bodyguard rose and waved her away.

"Not, now, miss. Please leave them alone for the moment. I'll come get you if he needs you."

Jimbo continued to speak. When he finished, Al sat upright in his chair as if he were digesting and sorting out the information Jimbo had just imparted.

Then in an even and controlled voice he said, "I have connections in Nicaragua. Let me handle this situation."

Then Al looked at Jimbo and said, "Do not take any action without consulting me first."

He looked at the rest of the table and then said, "And the rest of you. Do not discuss this affair with anyone. Do you understand? No one."

"But our classmates are bound to notice," Michelle said.

'And they're bound to ask."

Al said nothing, but his eyes spoke for him.

Jimbo said, "Señor Soltero's right. Silence. If anyone asks, he's sick in his cabin."

Al looked at Jimbo and said, "I'll add this favor to your tab."

Jimbo nodded his understanding.

Al rose and nodded to his bodyguard. They left through the same door he had used before. The remaining people stayed huddled at the table listening to Jimbo say something.

"What in the hell is going on ... ?" Will whispered.

"Why don't we slip out before we're noticed. I feel a sudden urge to finish this drink out on the deck," Betsy whispered back.

"So now Al's now got his claws into Jimbo as well as Billy and Willard."

"Sounds to me like they've been there quite some time."

# CHAPTER 30

The following morning Will and Betsy went out on the deck after they had finished breakfast at the Horizon Court. They leaned against the rail, enjoying the forenoon sea breeze and the accompanying solitude. The sky seemed to be full of both billowy and wispy clouds that were gently bathed in light from the sunlight shining above them.

"You think God could cram anymore clouds into this picture," Will commented.

"I don't think so though behind each cloud there seems to be another cloud."

"If you use your imagination, you can see lots of things in cloud formations. For instance, to my left I see a castle."

"Unusual architecture though."

"There are no structural rules to cloud architecture."

"I guess that rule book is in heaven. Not to spoil your reverie, but company's coming."

Paul and Michelle approached them. Will waved.

"So, how'd Sunday Funday go yesterday? Did you leave anything for the locals to drink for the rest of the week? You don't look any worse for wear. Was it everything you expected?"

"Oh, fine. I guess," Paul replied.

"Just fine. I thought this was supposed to be a frat party that would rival the one in 'Animal House'."

"Oh, like I said, it was fine," Paul said, not elaborating further.

"So, did you make all four bars?"

"Actually, no, we didn't."

"Where's Jerry, your partner in crime, this morning?"

"I dunno. In his cabin I guess. Good to see y'all."

"Well, stay out of trouble."

"You too."

Paul and Michelle kept on walking.

When they were out of earshot, Betsy said, "Well, that was the biggest bust of a conversation I've heard in a while."

"Sure as hell isn't the braggadocios Paul I expected. I thought he'd say that he and Jerry drank the whole town under the table ... at each and every bar. Shit. He acts like they went to a funeral yesterday instead of the party of the century. Whatever happened, Soltero and Jimbo must've really taken them down a notch in the Pirate's Lounge last night."

"I'd sure love to have heard what they were talking about."

"Since Al's involved, we may not want to know."

"Look. Here comes Jerry's girlfriend Judy. Let's see if she's as down in the dumps as Paul and Michelle were."

Judy was alone. She seemed kind of wobbly, but when she looked up and saw them coming, she ducked into a doorway before they could get close enough to call out a greeting.

"So much for that. Do you think she was trying to avoid us like Paul and Michelle seemed to want to?"

"One way to find out. Let's follow her through that same door."

Will opened the door and said, "After you, my pet."

"Pet? Makes me sound like your dog, my snookum."

"Snookum? Haven't heard that word in a long time."

"OK, my bebé. That's colloquial Spanish. After all, we are in Central America."

They entered a lobby area and looked around. Judy was nowhere to be seen.

"Damn! She's quick for someone who's supposed to be hung over."

"Must have been one hell of a head banger since no one seems to want to talk about it."

"Yeah. A real partizzle.

"A ...partizzle?"

"Yeah, I'm cool. That's hippity-hop, hop-along, hip English talk for Fizzled party."

"Sigh. Mama warned me about you, but she didn't think to tell me to check and see if I might be marrying a cowboy hippie rabbit."

"Maybe you just weren't listening."

# CHAPTER 31

Will drew back the drapes in their stateroom and winced slightly as the bright early-morning, eastern sun streamed in over their deck that suddenly bathed their room in light.

"Another gorgeous day and another exotic port," he commented.

"And another third-world country and another all-day excursion," Betsy said. "Boy, a new road trip every day. I never thought I'd just want to see a sea day. These stops are beginning to all run together in my mind."

"Are you trying to say that too much of a good thing is a bad thing?"

"I wouldn't go that far. Let's just say that good is not as gooder as it seemed a few days ago. I guess you could say that some of the novelty has worn off. What's the name of today's town?"

"H-U-A-T-U-L-C-O. It's pronounced wah-tool-coh. According to the Regency Rapper, we're about 500 kilometers below Acapulco. It's primarily known for having a shit-pot-load of some of Mexico's most unspoiled beaches and is named after it's nine bays. Was supposedly mostly developed in the eighties. I guess kind of like Cancun."

"Beaches – i.e.tourist traps. What you wanta bet? I guess we're scheduled to see them all."

"I suppose. But we're also scheduled to go to their arts and crafts museum and see hand-made rugs being made. Anyway, snap to. We better start getting dressed if we want to have time for breakfast before the bus leaves."

"Yasir, Massa Will. Don't beat me. I'se doing my best."

"I wish we had more time. I'd like to do something else to you instead."

"Hold that thought for when we get back."

After departing from deck four, Will and Betsy were guided across the pier to an air-conditioned bus. Will glanced around the bus and didn't see any of his classmates. Just before the bus left, Judy, Jerry Quackenbush's common-law wife, boarded. Will and Betsy waited to see if Jerry would be joining her, but it never happened. The driver shut the door, and their guide gave them her usual preliminary welcoming speech, giving the passengers an overview of the day's tour.

"I guess Jerry's not going to be joining us," Will observed. "Surely he's not still hung over from Sunday Funday."

"Maybe he had more fun than his body could withstand," Betsy answered.

"What were we saying earlier about too much of a good thing? Remember the old Frogman Henry song, 'I ain't got nobody'? Well, it looks like today Judy ain't got nobody."

"Because Jerry ain't got noo - body left to abuse. As long as I've known him, he's always been one of these people who don't think too good because he don't think too much or too often."

Over the course of the morning, the tour took them to see not only Huatulco's nine bays but the ancient Copalita ruins as well. The guide told them they would be having lunch in Santa Cruz at a restaurant named La Doña and would then get to shop and to see rug-making that afternoon.

La Doña was not what Will and Betsy expected. Instead of a rustic, adobe-type restaurant, it seemed more like a strip shopping center diner in the States. It was air-conditioned, had standard commercial glass-paneled doors and a solid wall of floor-to-ceiling plate-glass windows on the front side. The interior was one big room with a stained acoustical tile ceiling. The walls were mostly white, but one wall did have wide-striped black and white wallpaper. The counters and floor were plain, cold-looking, off-white glazed tiles. Each square, black Formica table would each sit four people and had clunky armless black wooden chairs. A flatscreen TV hung from one wall. The other wall had a few neutrally themed, framed prints.

Will commented to his wife, “they must be making it on their food. It’s certainly not on their atmosphere.”

“Got about as much personality as a doctor’s waiting room. At least it looks clean.”

“I’m still not going to drink the water.”

They noticed Judy had sat alone at a table in one corner.

“Let’s go grab those chairs at Judy’s table before someone else does. I’d love to know where Jerry is today.”

“You mean so you can snoop.”

“Any detective or reporter will tell you the first step to information is snooping. Might as well get my info from the horse’s mouth instead of from the gossip circuit.”

He made a beeline for Judy’s table. Betsy followed.

“Mind if we join you?”

‘Whatever.”

The waitress brought them a special limited menu that La Doña had designed for cruise ship tours along with some taco dip and chips and asked them what they wanted to drink. They each ordered a Corona.

“Soup or salad? Today’s soup is a tortilla chicken soup,” the waitress asked.

To be on the safe side since they weren’t sure whether to trust the lettuce, they each ordered the soup.

“A burrito bowl, fajitas or tamales?”

The ladies each chose the fajitas while Will went with the tamales.

As soon as the waitress left, Will asked, “So where’s Jerry today. Hope he’s still not recovering from our last stop.”

There was an uncomfortable silence. Judy began to tear up. She wiped her eyes with her napkin.

"Is there something wrong? If so, maybe we can help."

Another silence followed as if Judy was trying to think of what to say next. She looked around to see if anyone were listening before she spoke in a low voice.

"I -- I guess I might as well tell you. I'm sure you're going to find out anyway. Jerry won't be finishing the cruise."

"Did he get sick?"

"No. I dunno. Maybe he is sick."

"Is he in the sick bay?"

"He's not on the ship. He's in jail. Jerry got arrested. They're holding him in Nicaragua. ... I know this doesn't look good, ... you know. Me being here ... but after what happened, I had to get off that ship today anyway so I wouldn't have to face y'all's classmates. ... I don't know why I'm telling you this. I hardly know you. But I need to tell somebody."

"Is this something connected with Sunday Funday? A fight? Is he hurt?"

"No. Worse than that. They're trying to say that he tried to arrange to pick up a child prostitute."

"Jerry! Oh, come on now!"

"A twelve-year-old boy. Every time I think about it, I want to puke."

"I can't believe that. Jerry's about the most, how can I put this, non-gay person I know. If anything, he's a rough and tumble man's man. How'd this happen?"

"They're saying he reserved a Nicaraguan boy from the ship using his computer."

She stopped there and looked like she was about to hyperventilate. Will gave Betsy that *Holy Shit!* look but said nothing. Betsy broke the silence.

"How'd the authorities come to that conclusion?"

"They arrested him at Pacha Mama's, and when they did, they told the rest of us to butt out unless we wanted to get charged with something as well. They wouldn't tell us then what they were charging him with. "

"So, how'd you find out what was going on?"

"We came back to the ship and found Jimbo. Fortunately, he hadn't gone on any ground tours that day, or I don't know what I would've done. We told him what had happened. ... He's a lawyer, you know ... and he said he'd try to get to the bottom of it."

"Did he?"

"Yes. He was able to find out what Jerry's being accused of. ... I'm so ashamed. ... I'm not sure I can bear to talk about it. And I'm not so sure I understand it all."

"Judy," Betsy broke in. "Let me assure you, one lady to another, that we're not here to be judgmental."

"Or gossipy," Will added.

"They said something about he went on a website or program or something named 'Tinder.' If I understand it right, it advertises itself as a dating service, but it's actually a prostitution site. They said he accessed it through the ship wi-fi. I didn't even know he knew how to use it. I don't.

"They called him a deviant. Said he even gave the scum a picture of himself and chose a specific child. ... This is so horrible ... and ... and ... and the trafficker was supposed to bring this child to Pacha Mama's to meet up with him. The ship's key-word filter picked up on it and notified the local cops who were waiting for us at Pacha Mama's. I understand at the same time they also got the child's pervert handler."

"I find all this hard to believe."

"You do? I'm the one who's been living with Jerry. And left him alone with my kids when I went to work at the restaurant. No telling what he could have done with them. It makes me sick every time I think about it. I was living with a pervert and didn't know it!"

"I don't know what to say. Somehow, it doesn't make sense. Where did he expect to take this person? Y'all would be together all day. And Paul and Michelle were there."

"Maybe Paul's a sick pervert too. I just don't know what to think. And if Jerry's in jail, what's going to happen to our house. We're not married, and my name isn't on it. And I can't afford the payments by myself. ... I don't have any savings. I just live paycheck to paycheck. Where are me and my kids going to live? I'm not an educated person with a lot of options. Being a waitress is all I know how to do. I – I don't have any family to turn to. Jerry and my children are all I have. ... and now I don't even have him. I can't afford an expensive lawyer. I – I – just ..."

Judy choked up and began to cry.

"I'm sure Jimbo will advise you what to do. He and Jerry go way back. And keep in mind, you're convicting him before he's even been tried. All this may be a mistake for all we know."

"I've been wondering ever since. And thinking about – you know, signs that he was sick. I do remember he told me once when he was drunk that he'd been part of a gang bang way back when. He seemed very ashamed of it, but he said it did happen."

"If he was part of something like that, I don't know anything about it. I know some of the crowd he ran with got a little rowdy every once in a while, but far as I know, they just drank too much. Did he give you any details about this supposed past incident?"

"No. He was shit-faced at the time, and I was too. The next day when we both sobered up, I asked him what he was talking about, and he denied the whole thing. ... I – I should have known something was wrong with him then, but I just put it out of my mind. Now I think, how stupid could I have been?"

"Judy, something about all this just doesn't ring right. I'll be very honest with you. We've all always known Jerry had a lot of rough edges. But I'd classify him as homophobic if anything – somebody who might beat up this kind of person. I've heard him say a lot of crude things about women. But I also attributed that to insecure male blustering. I hope you don't take this the wrong way, but Jerry was never exactly a ladies man. If anything, he's overweight, crude, and spits Skoal. And he's certainly not rich. Hell, he works construction. Jerry's just – you know, Jerry. I'd have a lot easier time believing he might secretly lust after an underage girl – and that's a stretch – but a twelve-year-old boy? That goes against everything I know about him. It just doesn't compute."

"It's easy for you to say. You don't live with him – or leave your children with him. I swear if he had ever touched one of them, I'd kill him. I swear to God I would."

"We think that Jimbo might have gotten a Señor Al Soltero involved. We've known Al for a long time. Let's see what he comes up with before we condemn Jerry."

"I don't want to get back on that ship. ... And even if he gets out, I'm not so sure I want to be on it with him anymore. And I don't think I can face those people in y'all's class."

"I don't know what to tell you. Just do the best you can for the time being, and see where this thing goes."

# CHAPTER 32

Will and Betsy decided to wait until they returned to the ship to recap their shocking lunchtime discussion with Judy so they could do so in privacy. They offered to keep her company for the afternoon portion of their tour, but she begged off and told them that now that she'd gotten the story off her chest she just wanted to be left alone to think about what was in store for her when the cruise was over. They reemphasized that she would definitely need competent legal advice and suggested that Jimbo was a logical candidate to provide it.

"Wow," commented Betsy when they were alone once more, "What a mess?"

"That's for sure. I think we both can agree that Jerry Quackenbush is a beer-guzzling, fat slob of a redneck with no couth and disgusting personal habits, but I never dreamed he'dempty seat be a pervert. He's always been the type of person who was liable to call an effeminate man a queer in a bar and then maybe push him around or beat him up just to show how macho he was around his drinking buddies."

"That was my assessment of him. I still remember him from that first time I met him on deck the day the cruise started when he was gorging himself on pizza and spitting tobacco."

"That's the Jerry I know – a blue-collar cretin who may possibly have gone somewhere in football, but instead became a school dropout and a manual laborer. Can you imagine if this got out with his white-trash buddies or the workers on a construction site? Dumb bastard'd never live it down. Those people are not known for their broadminded, enlightened, forgiving attitudes."

"Oh, he'd be blackballed as a redneck. That's for sure. But I feel sorry for Judy. She seems to be a nice person, but let's face it. She doesn't have a whole lot going for her. She isn't especially good looking. Doesn't appear to be especially smart. Not educated – has a menial, dead-end job."

"And has the baggage of being a single mother on top of that. You're right. Truth of the matter is she probably doesn't think she can do any better than Jerry and was lucky to find him."

"I hate to say it my dear, but maybe she can't."

"So now that we know what's going on, what do we do about it? She doesn't deserve to be dragged down with Jerry."

"First of all, don't forget. We promised her we'd be discrete. Can you imagine what a field day your class gossips would have at her expense?"

"Or his football buddies, for that matter? No sympathy from any of that bunch, that's for sure. Her life would be a living hell for the rest of this cruise. She may have a long enough row to hoe when she gets back without starting to hoe it before she has to."

"Maybe we ought to share this conversation with the Petersons and get their feedback. I know that they'll keep the matter to themselves. They may have some ideas."

"OK. I'll agree with that. ... But let's still keep our little snake incident to ourselves for the time being. We don't have to tell anybody everything."

"And whatever we do, it needs to stay low key. Somebody already thinks we're we're sticking our nose where it doesn't belong."

About that time there was a knock on their stateroom door. Will went to see who was there. He opened to the door, and Dick and Beth were standing there.

"Come on in. Your ears must be burning. We were just talking about you."

"You know what they say about great minds running in the same channel. Or in our case is it the same rut? What've we done wrong now?"

"It's not what you've done wrong, but someone else we know may have."

When the Petersons had gotten in the room, Will said, "What I'm about to tell you is for your ears only."

"Cross my heart and hope to die. Stick a needle in my eye."

Will then explained what had happened to Jerry Quackenbush and their subsequent conversation with his common-law wife, Judy. Dick and Beth were as surprised as Will and Betsy had been.

"*I'm* not going to say anything, but you can bet your booties that this will get around sooner rather than later no matter what the four of us say. Bad news travels faster than shit through a goose. I wouldn't doubt that it's not already being talked about. Now, before we analyze that situation, let me tell you an even later news release. This one is about Jerry's asshole buddy Paul."

"Now what?"

"Word is Paul's been arrested too."

Will stood up and walked over to the window.

"In Nicaragua?"

"Oh, no. This supposedly happened here in Mexico."

"What for? I didn't know they had laws against being a boorish redneck in Mexico. Drugs, maybe? You know what they say about his girlfriend. Who got him?"

"Try being a threat to homeland security. Word going around is that Homeland Security's holding him."

"Wha ...? Gimme a break. He's not that smart. What was he supposed to have done? Insult the Democrats? We both know he's a right-wing nut case, but come on now? He's mostly just tasteless."

"Do you call trying to get into a terrorist training camp tasteless? If this is true, what he's being accused of isn't supposedly Grand Wizard KKK Dixie flag-waving shit but trying to join a real terrorist training camp."

Will began to pace as he thought. He stopped and shook his head.

"That goes against everything I know about that boy. ... And I've known him since kindergarten. He's ... it's ... I don't know what to say."

"Out of character?" Betsy said. "Need I remind you that we just said that Jerry's problem was out of character too?"

"Something's rotten in Denmark. Both of these guys are stupid. ... But I ... uh ... Does anyone here disagree? And I'm not even sure either one of them is intelligent enough to do the things they're being accused of using a computer. They are what they are – dumb fucking bullying lowlifes who never amounted to a hill of shit who are still living their football glory days ... which are long the hell gone."

"Until now. Maybe they're finally making their mark."

"I can't get over one of them doing some stupid out-of-character crap, but both of them. That's too much of a coincidence. There's got to be more to this story."

"One more accident, or should I say misfortune?" Betsy said. "They're sure starting to mount up."

"And all ex-football players! Are there any left unscathed?"

"I don't think so," Dick said. "Glad I was in the band. Maybe it wasn't as cool, but it certainly seems to be safer in the long run. Hold these thoughts. You know it is five o'clock somewhere, and my internal clock tells me that the somewhere is now. Let's adjourn this meeting to the Wheelhouse Lounge."

# CHAPTER 33

The Petersons and the Blacks took the elevator down to the deck seven. The Wheelhouse Lounge wasn't that crowded, and they easily found a table. The waitress told them that the drink of the day was Long Island iced tea.

"That'll grow hair on your chest," Dick said. "Correct me if I'm wrong, but don't those bad boys have four different kinds of booze?"

"Five, I think. If you count the Triple Sec," Will corrected him.

"I don't need any hair on my chest," Beth said. "But maybe it'll put some back on your head."

After a little more cajoling, all four ordered the drink special. The waitress left to fill their orders. A short time later, she returned with their drinks.

"Remember when we took geography?" Will said, raising his glass. "All I remember from it was that Long Island had the best iced tea. A toast, my friends."

"Hear, hear. Over the lips. Through the gums. Look out tummy. Here it comes."

"We're getting to that age where it's 'Over the lips. Through the gums. Look out dentures. Here it comes'."

"Speak for yourself, old man."

"Who are you calling ...?"

"Enough! Both of you," Betsy and Beth said simultaneously.

"On a more serious note," Betsy added, "Isn't that Paul and Jerry's squeezes over there talking to Jimbo? Alone?"

"Sho' is. I wish I was a lemon twist on one of those glasses. It looks like a very serious discussion. Damn. I wouldn't trade places with any one of them."

About that time Danny walked in. He glanced their way and turned to leave.

"I'll be right back," Will said and pushed back his chair to get up. He caught up with Danny in the hallway and returned with the reluctant Danny in tow.

"Danny's going to join us for happy hour," he announced as the two of them approached the table. He pulled out a chair from the adjacent table before Danny could object. As he sat down, Danny noticed Michelle, Judy, Jimbo for the first time. He seemed to glare at them. The waitress returned, and Danny ordered a draft beer.

"Did you know that both Jerry and Paul have been arrested?" Danny asked.

Will looked at Betsy. She could read his mind.

*So much about secrets.*

"No," Dick said.

And I wasn't surprised," Danny continued. "I can't say I feel sorry for either one of them. What goes around, comes around. They've gotten away with murder for years."

"Oh, yeah? Do tell."

"Hell, everybody knows that when we were in school, they were allowed to run wild. Just because they were foooot-ball players. And they always treated me like I was dirt under their fingernails."

"How's that?"

"I'm sure you don't remember, but I was equipment manager ... for a while. One of the biggest mistakes of my life. Everyone was involved in some activity, and I wasn't an athlete. And I couldn't play an instrument like you could, Dick. And I wasn't good enough to be on the yearbook or newspaper staff. So, I became the team's equipment manager. Big mistake. The players treated me like I was their slave. Did everything they could do to make my life miserable. I wish I could have gotten even, but in Coach Beech's eyes, they could do no wrong. He even thought they were funny."

"Man, that's too bad," Dick said, picturing a dirty jockey strap on Danny's face or him getting popped with a wet towel.

"Finally, they got me in trouble – with both the school and my dad."

"How on earth?"

"Part of my job was doing the team's dirty laundry. One day someone went behind me and put a whole bottle of Rit dye in the washer while the team's things were still in it. I got blamed for it. They told my dad, and he had to cough up the money to replace the ruined items. I had to work off the money at Dad's locksmith shop until he was paid back."

"Did you ever find out who did it?"

"Nope, but I caught hell from the whole team for months afterwards, just for the pure old meanness of it. They thought it was funny as hell. ... But I damned well didn't. ... Mother fucking animals!"

"Man, that's awful. I don't blame you for holding a grudge. Kids can be so mean."

"Mean kids become mean adults."

"May I ask you one more thing? You probably know this since you spent so much time around the players. What was that 'S and M' stuff Dickie-do kept yelling about? It seemed like some inside joke that the football players had."

Danny said nothing. He simply stared at his half-drained beer glass as if he was thinking.

Finally, he said as he pushed back his chair, "Don't know. I was only a lowly equipment manager. Not one of them. I guess I need to go now. Good to see y'all."

He glared at the table where Jimbo was sitting and without another word walked out, leaving his undrunk beer on the table.

As soon as Danny was gone, Dick said, "Boy, he ended that conversation in a hurry when you brought up the 'S and M' business."

"That's for sure," Beth agreed.

"I think Danny probably knows more about what that phrase means than he was willing to let on," Betsy said. "Did you see the way he stared at that beer glass? It was almost like he was in a trance."

"And look at that crumpled napkin. Something really upset him. I swear I think he was gritting his teeth too."

"Could've just been reliving the Rit incident. You'll have to admit. That's a pretty shitty thing to do to someone."

"I disagree. It wasn't that. He wadded the napkin up *after* you asked him about 'S and M', not after he told us about the dye fiasco."

"You're right. You know what comes to mind – sadism and masochism."

"The team ... or certain members of it ... must've really treated Danny like sadistic shit."

"Yep. Big shot bullies. Just because they could get away with it."

"Too bad it had to happen to Danny. He certainly seems to be one psychologically fragile individual."

"And definitely an unhappy one."

# CHAPTER 34

On the following morning, the Regency Crown arrived in Puerto Vallarta. Will and Betsy once again had a leisurely breakfast in the Horizon Court before going ashore.

"I'm glad we didn't sign up for another tour today," Will said. "I'm looking forward to just visiting some of Puerto Vallarta on our own and see how much it's changed since I came here before we were married for a company conference. I'll sure never forget that meeting. Everything that could go wrong did go wrong."

"You've told that story so many times that I feel like I was there."

"Just be glad you weren't."

"It'll be fun to stroll around the downtown Malecón area and see if it's everything we've heard it is."

"I truly don't know what to expect."

"Me neither. I guess since we have no expectations, we won't be disappointed. I try to limit my inflated expectations to matters related to you."

"Don't forget. I'm not here to live up to your expectations, and you're not here to live up to mine."

"You haven't fallen off your pedestal yet."

"Nor have you, darling. Maybe we can find Richard Burton and Elizbeth Taylor's old house."

"They sure made this place. This town wasn't shit until they made it famous by filming "Night of the Iguana" here. Funny how one film shoot can make a town."

"Not just any film shoot, my dear. An academy award winning movie written by one of the most important modern play writes of all time and staring some of the most famous actors in the world – not only Burton but Ava Gardner and Deborah Kerr. It doesn't get much bigger than that."

"I guess you're right."

"Aren't I always?"

"I won't go there. Let's just say that you're never wrong. There's just different levels of right."

"Yes, my dearest, but just remember being right isn't as important as knowing when to shut up."

"Touché."

Will and Betsy got processed off the ship and then took a cab into town to the Malecón.

"So, this is the Malecón Boardwalk. So, where are the boards? This is more like a waterfront esplanade."

Indeed, there wasn't a board in sight at the Malecón. Instead, they found themselves on a wide, winding, modern cobblestone walkway clearly defined on both sides by continuous chair-height, backless concrete walls. It was spotlessly clean and well landscaped with well-maintained tropical plants. Every ten to fifteen feet they saw recently trimmed coconut palms with lower trunks that had been painted white. On one side of this barrier was a beach. On the other side, you could take wide, winding sidewalks to every kind of retail business imaginable – outdoor cafés, gift shops, restaurants, arts and crafts stores, and of course, t-shirt shops. Behind it all, they could see hills rising in the distance. Some people leisurely strolled around. Others sat on the walls in small groups chatting or just simply looking out over the pristine Pacific Ocean and the contrasting relaxing blue sky. Everything around them seemed to be taking place in a lethargic. easy-going manner.

"So, are you disappointed?" Will asked.

"If anything, the brochures don't do it justice."

"You know what they say about a picture being worth a thousand words. Which way do you want to walk?"

"You pick it. I understand this whole thing is about a mile long, so I don't guess it makes a whole lot of difference."

The morning breeze coming in off of Banderas Bay felt refreshing as they walked along. About every fifty to one hundred feet outdoor sculptures dotted the walkway. There were no "do not touch" signs. These sculptures were obviously meant to be felt, sat on, or in some cases climbed. Some were classical; others were whimsical. Some were just plain odd. There was a preponderance of four to five-foot-high heart shaped sculptures, each unique in its own way. They passed a tall, vertical, tower-like bronze with a giant hourglass in its middle. Another bronze featured a mermaid and merman. There was a ladder to nowhere. with bronze figures hanging off of it. Tourists were climbing it as well so they could hang off of it and have their pictures taken.

"I don't think I've ever seen as much of an art-driven city as this appears to be," Betsy commented as they listened to some street musicians.

They poked their head into one of the shops featuring ladies clothing. Betsy saw a colorful cotton blouse she liked and looked at its price tag.

"Four hundred and fifty dollars?" she gasped.

"No, my dear. That's pesos and considering the fact that the peso trades about sixteen or seventeen to one American dollar, that's really more like thirty-five or forty dollars."

"Shoot. It's a bargain then."

"See if it fits and if it does, it's yours."

They ended up buying the blouse.

As they approached an amphitheater with four grand arches, Betsy said, "I see a place to sit. Why don't we take a break and people-watch for a few minutes?"

As they sat and looked around them, they heard a voice.

"Will Black."

Will turned and saw Lydia Vallence.

"Isn't this place something else?"

"That's for sure. Will you join us?"

"Don't mind if I do. I don't guess I've had a chance to visit with you since this cruise began."

Will introduced Betsy to Lydia.

"Lydia was one of our cheerleaders. She was on the same squad with Suzzie Cobb."

"Well, not quite. I was an alternate, but Suzzie's the reason I ended up a regular."

"I didn't remember that. How'd that happen? I thought you were there the whole time."

"Just our senior year. Suzzie and Misty quit after at the end of football season our junior year. It was sudden and dramatic. Nobody expected it, and they'd never talk about it. I always thought maybe it had something to do with grades. And I'm pretty sure some of the players had the hots for some of the cheerleaders. Who knows. Maybe their parents made them quit. Only thing Suzzie would say was that it was something she had been thinking about for a while and that she wanted to have more time for senior activities during the upcoming senior year. I dunno, but it gave me a chance. And Pat Karls too."

"How come Pat?"

"Because Misty dropped out at the same time as well. She transferred back to Riverside School for the second semester. You know, that's where she went to school before she came to GHS."

"No. I didn't know that. But Misty graduated with us."

"Yeah, she came back for our senior year. I never understood it all. Like I said, the rumor was that it was grades related. But I guess she missed Suzzie and wanted to graduate with her."

"I knew they always seemed to be best friends.

"I think Suzzie may have had something to do with Misty starting to date Danny."

"You know how that happened, don't you? Danny and Suzzie are second cousins – on her mama's side, I think."

"I never knew that. That certainly turned into a tragic situation. She and Danny must have really been in love because her death certainly seems to have messed him up for good. I've been told her mental problems may have come from the fact that she and Danny couldn't have children and that led to her depression issues."

"I don't think that was it. Her depression issues seem to have started when she came back from Riverside to GHS for her senior year. She was very moody even then. It was like Suzzie became increasingly her only friend until Danny came into the picture later on. Suzzie and Misty became even closer than they were before. None of us understood what was going on. Misty kind of distanced herself from all the rest of us and became very dependent on Suzzie. So, we started just sort of staying away from her. You know how teenagers are. It was all pretty mysterious. But I guess whatever it was, it wasn't any of my business."

"Now it seems that Danny is the one dependent on Suzzie."

# CHAPTER 35

When they got back to the ship, the Blacks rested for awhile before going up to the fourteenth deck to watch the ship depart.

"I'm glad we ran into Lydia today. You think you know people, but I certainly learned some things I never knew about Danny and Suzzie."

"I'm sure my former class at Murphy has its secrets too."

"It whet my appetite to know more. Something about Danny has been bothering me since this trip began."

"Something? Pretty much everything about this trip bothers me. I haven't gotten over that snake incident yet. I get the shivers every time I think about what could have happened. And I sure think of him. You know, being a locksmith, he would probably know how to break into our cabin."

"And he's just unbalanced enough to do something like that. But why? Unlike some other people, I've never been anything but decent to Danny no matter how unsociable he acts. And how would he have gotten the damned thing back onboard? Don't ask me why, but I'd really like to know more his married life to Misty. She might not have been the only nutcase in that relationship. Why don't I try to catch that little-old-wine-drinker Billy alone and see what he has to say about things in general."

"And maybe Beth and I can catch Suzzie by herself and get her take on things as well. You know, a girl to girl talk. I'll clue Beth in ahead of time, but I'll plan on taking the lead."

"Works for me. But I still think I'll try to talk to Billy by myself. I've got a feeling if anyone else is there, he'll feel ganged up on."

"And I've got another idea. Why don't we just mention in passing to each of them that we think we've got a quandary of sorts on our hands. . Don't make a big deal out of it. Just kind of mention it off-handedly. Definitely don't say anything about the snake. Just say that our room steward found something in the cabin when he was cleaning up and gave it to us thinking it was ours. But that it was nothing either of us had ever seen before, and we've been wondering how it got there ever since."

"Sounds like an interesting idea. But let's put more teeth in the matter. Instead of being so passive about it, say we're pissed since that's breaking and entering. And that if we could find out who it was, we'd prosecute the offender unless that person had a good excuse. Then say maybe that the item we found is unusual enough that it shouldn't be hard to trace it back to its owner. And after that we wait and see what kind of reaction we get, if any."

"Why not? Can't hurt."

"Might try that on some other people as well. Who know what snake-in-the-grass we might turn up if we turn over a few rocks," Will agreed.

"Don't even mention snakes. I'm not sure I ever want to see one again."

"Keep in mind we're looking for a human snake. But they can be poisonous too."

"Agreed. Old rockhound husband of mine. You know, you're pretty smart for a white boy. And I thought you just had rocks in your head. Maybe I'll just keep you around."

"Come on over to the bed, and I'll show you rocks."

"Not now, big boy. But hold that thought for maybe later."

"Well, don't forget that's not all I'm good for. I also bring home the Rocky Road every so often. I guess you might say I'm one kind of rockhound or the other."

"I guess once a rockhound always a rockhound. By the way, what if someone asks what we found?"

"Just be evasive. Say something like it was a personal item or something like that. I dunno. I think we're better served if we keep our adversary wondering. You know, make them worry a little bit."

********************

The following morning Will got the opportunity he was looking for to talk to Billy Cobb when he ran into him on the fourteenth deck by the Lido pool. Billy's arm was still in a sling.

"Morning, Billy. Another gorgeous day. Where's you lovely wife? She letting you out alone nowadays?"

"Suzzie went to that art auction at the Wheelhouse Lounge. I'm not sure why. Those things bore the shit out of me. All they're doing is selling overpriced crap. Where's your wife?"

"I think I agree with you on the art. Betsy and Peterson's wife are going to a cooking demonstration in the Regency Theater this morning. I wasn't particularly interested in it. Told her I'd meet her when it was over. In the meantime, why don't you let me buy you a beer?"

They strolled over to the Lido bar, and Will ordered two draft beers. They found a table.

"I'm glad to see you didn't really hurt yourself when you took that fall the other night."

"I'm sore, but nothing seems to have gotten busted. My shoulder's just sprained."

"If you don't mind me asking, exactly what caused you to fall? Did you just trip?"

"I guess. I take blood pressure medicine that sometimes gives me an equilibrium problem."

*Especially when you're blitzed.*

"I've heard of that happening with some medications. Some especially don't mix well with alcohol, and we had all had a few drinks. Were you alone on the stairs?"

"I dunno. I wasn't paying close attention. There was a big guy coming up the stairs next to me. Maybe I tripped over his foot."

*Hmmm. I did notice Al's bodyguard leave the room about the same time Billy did. You don't think ... But why?*

Will looked at his watch and said, "Billy, you mind if I call my wife before she leaves our stateroom. There's something I forgot to tell her earlier. I'll be right back."

He immediately found a house phone and called Betsy.

"Hon, Will. Guess who I ran into moments ago? Billy Cobb. We're about to have a beer together up by the Lido pool. He told me that Suzzie has gone to that art auction in the Wheelhouse Lounge. This might be a perfect opportunity for you to catch her alone."

"You're right. I'll let Beth go to the cooking seminar, and I'll head up to the art auction."

Will hung up and headed back out on the deck so Billy wouldn't think he'd been abandoned.

"Caught her just in time. Thanks for waiting. Now, where were we? ... Oh, yeah. ... Had an interesting turn of events in Puerto Vallarta yesterday. We ran into Lydia Vallence down on the Malecón. First time I've had a chance to talk to her since the cruise began. I'd forgotten that she didn't make first string on the cheerleader squad until our senior year. Said she and Pat Karls got lucky after the football season was over the year before when Suzzie and Misty both decided not reup as seniors. Boy, our junior year was a helluva year, wasn't it? Who ever dreamed we'd end up state football champions? I guess there weren't any more hills to climb for a lot of people after being a part of that."

"I remember. We had seven people off that team that ended up with college scholarships. Too bad a lot of them like Jerry and Paul never graduated."

"Funny how things work out. In some cases, though, like with Tom and his music, it didn't make any difference."

"But everybody's not a lucky as Tom was. Just because you're a football prima donna doesn't make you smart. Or a scholar. I reckon in too many cases once a meathead always a meathead."

"I guess for some of them it was the top of their mountain. And for a brief period, they could get away with more than most people. Aren't you glad we didn't peak that early in life?"

"Uh, huh. And they took advantage of things too. Both Coach Beech and Coach Ward let the ass-wipes get away with pretty much anything – with the principal's blessing. If they'd been anyone else, they'd gone to jail as juvenile delinquents for some of the crap they pulled. Hell, instead, they got away with murder."

"Murder? Aren't you being a little tough on them?"

"I'm being sarcastic and euphemistic, Will. And I wasn't just jealous of them because I didn't get a scholarship. I secretly looked down on and despised some of those self-absorbed lowlifes then and still do. I just had to hide my feelings."

"I also didn't remember that after that, Misty transferred to Riverside School for second semester. Lydia said they were all shocked because it seemed happen so suddenly right after the season was over. Best I remember, she and Suzzie were so close they were like sisters. Bet they really missed each other. Did she ever tell Suzzie why she left? Do you think it had anything to do with the team?"

"Who knows. Suzzie never told me."

"Must have made a big mistake though because Misty was back for our senior year. I'm surprised they both didn't try out again for cheerleader."

"I guess they had other priorities rather than being around those jockey-strap delinquents again."

"Something else I didn't know until Lydia told me yesterday is that Danny and Suzzie are second cousins. Who'd a thunk it?"

"Yep. Small world."

"And Danny and Misty must have really had a good marriage."

"It had its ups and downs because of her depression."

"I wonder what brought that on. She always seemed to have everything going for her before she transferred out. Was she always like that?"

"I think it started coming on when she was a senior."

"Strange. You'd have thought that would've been one of the happiest periods of any girl's life. When you're a senior, you're the top of the heap."

"It can have its pressures ... and challenges."

"I guess it can. By the way, changing the subject, I heard Dickie-do using the expression here on the ship "S and M" several times with both Jerry and Tom. Also, with Rusty, now that I think about it. You may have overheard it too. It's like some kind of football player insider's joke. The only thing that comes to mind with me is sadism and masochism. Surely, that's not what he was referring to."

"No. the pervert meant Suzzie and Misty."

"Why them?"

"Oh, he and some of the other players all had crushes on them, but Suzzie and Misty wouldn't give them the time of day. Hurt their egos since as football heroes they thought their shit didn't stink. Suzzie still looks down on them today."

"But you, Jimbo and Willard are still friends."

"I wouldn't call it friends as much as we have some business interests in common."

"But back to Dickie-do. Sounds like what we'd call sexual harassment today. Is that why Suzzie and Misty quit the cheerleader squad? Because he was becoming a pest? Do you think Misty was trying to get away from them when she transferred back to Riverside?"

"It went deeper than just harrassment. They were jocks with damaged, inflated egos being crappy and mean who could be downright dangerous because they couldn't get what they wanted. But that's ancient history. I really don't want to rehash it after all these years. Those days are over and gone now, and what's done is done."

"On a different subject again, have you had any problem with strangers coming in your cabin?"

"No. Why do you ask?"

"Our room steward gave us something he picked up in our cabin, but it didn't belong to either one of us. Had to be left there by someone else. It didn't exactly give either one of us warm and fuzzies that someone else's key might fit our lock. And that they might come back. And on top of that, I think it may give me some insight into all these freaky calamities that have happened since this cruise started."

"No shit! What'd he find?"

"Oh, just a personal item. Rather not say right now. But I'm sure whoever lost it will be desperate to get it back when finds it missing. It was unique enough that I think I'm going to eventually trace it back to its owner. And when I do ... the mutha fucker better watch out because you can bet your booty, I'm going to turn it over to the cops so they can singe his sorry ass."

There was an uncomfortable silence. Billy looked at his watch.

"I think I'll go see if Suzzie's art auction is over. Thanks for the beer."

"Since we're both in Florida, let me swap business cards with you. You never know when one of us might be in the other person's back yard. Let's try to keep up better instead of just seeing each other at reunions."

"Sure thing. I'd like that."

Billy stood up and got a card out of his wallet. Will did the same. Then Billy turned and left without another word.

"See ya," Will called after him, but if Billy heard him, he didn't acknowledge it.

*Well, I didn't learn much from that. I guess one beer wasn't enough to loosen Billy boy up. Only that Billy and Suzzie don't much care for some of our old classmates any more than Danny does. And at least now I know for sure what 'S and M' stands for. I guess Betsy and I need to noodle over that one.*

Then he glanced down at Billy's card.

Carlos, Valdes and Perillo PLLC

Attorneys at Law

*Holy shit! Every one of those names are surnames of Colombians who have been in bed with Al Soltero in the past. Granted they're all fairly common Hispanic names, but surely that's not a complete coincidence since I've seen him talking to Al on the ship so many times. ... And Al spent the day with Suzzie and Danny in Nicaragua. I sure wish I could have worked Al into the conversation I just had with Billy. ... And I'd still like to know how Willard fits into the picture. Or Jimbo, for that matters. But maybe it's best I didn't let Billy know how well I know the slick-as-owl-shit Señor Soltero. It might've gotten back to Al.*

*I can't wait to show this card to Betsy.*

# CHAPTER 36

Betsy tried to call Beth, but no one answered. She left word that something had come up.

*Probably gone to breakfast. I guess I'm doing this interview with Suzzie by myself. Probably better anyway.*

She then immediately caught the elevator up to the Wheelhouse Lounge and looked around for Suzzie Cobb.

*Oh, good. She's alone ... and, lucky me, there's an empty seat next to her.*

She went in the doorway that Suzzie was facing and feigned surprise when she saw Suzzie and waved as she headed over to Suzzie's table.

"Good morning. Anybody sitting here? I'm glad I'm not the only art aficionado on this ship. Will doesn't especially care for these things. Good to see a familiar face. Mind if I join you?"

"Not at all. Good to see you too."

"What are you drinking?"

"A mimosa."

"Sounds good. I think I'll have one as well."

A waitress arrived, and Betsy ordered her drink.

"How long until this thing starts?

"Oh, about fifteen minutes or so, I think."

"Great. That's give us a few minutes to visit before the auction begins. You'll never guess who Will and I ran into in Puerto Vallarta yesterday – his classmate, Lydia Vallance. I gathered that you two were cheerleaders together."

"Well, yes. More or less."

"Lydia said the same thing. Said she was an alternate until y'all's senior year and only got to be a first stringer after both you and Misty decided not be on the squad anymore."

"Yeah. I suppose that's true. We had our reasons."

"Will has told me that the football team won the state championship y'all's junior year. That must have been a really exciting time. And I bet they had a great team coming back for their senior year too. I'm surprised you two could walk away from that limelight. Did they win it again the next year?"

"No. I guess the stars all aligned that junior year since our team was a dark horse. Unfortunately, it did, however, bring out the worst in some people. Other teams were gunning for them the next year. You know, on everybody's radar screen. But a bunch of them did get college scholarships anyway. Most of them went to Mississippi State."

"Must be what Alabama feels like every season. You become everyone's big game. She said that team is a local legend until this day. I guess now I can now appreciate that cute HORNETS skit the ex-players put on our first night at sea."

"There was more to that horny part of Hornets than most people know. That bunch always thought they were funny, but some of their antics weren't always as funny as they thought they were. In fact, some of them could be downright mean, sadistic, and illegal. But because they were who they were, they went unpunished."

"To use a trite expression, I guess boys will be boys."

"Which is bullshit. Why don't people use the excuse 'girls will be girls'?"

"I couldn't agree with you more. Why don't we just say that teenagers don't always exercise the world's best judgement? And some adults don't either."

"That's for sure."

"So not to be nosy, but why'd y'all walk away? If I'd been lucky enough to be part of a dynasty, I don't think I could have given it up. I'm sure some of their popularity had to rub off on you."

"If some of those jocks had had it their way, more than that would have rubbed off on us. Like I said, prima donnas can be pretty insufferable at times."

"Oh, yeah? How's that? Like trying to put the mash on you?"

"I'd rather not go into specifics. I wouldn't want it to get back to their spouses what louts some of them were. Let's just say I've just tried to repress those days rather than celebrate them. You know ... put that timeframe behind me."

Suzzie sighed and took a sip of her mimosa.

*I guess that's about as far as this line of conversation is going. I'd better change the subject while I still can.*

"Lydia said you and Danny were kin to each other. Will said he was surprised to hear that. Said he never would have suspected."

"Well, not close kin. We're second cousins on my mama's side."

"I think that's great. And from what Will and I have seen maybe you're not close blood kin, but it does appear that you are still very close friends. I wish some of my cousins and I had that kind of relationship. And from what I've heard said, you and Misty were best friends back then as well. So, I guess you played Cupid with Danny and Misty. I think that's cool."

"I may have had a little to do with it, but I'm sure they'd have found each other anyway."

"They must have really been meant for each other. He seems to be still lost and unable to move on with his life."

"Oh, they both had their issues."

"Don't we all. What kind of issues?"

'Danny didn't tell you?"

"Not really. I never met him until this cruise."

"If he doesn't want to talk about them, I guess I shouldn't either.

*Well, scratch that as well. ...Ahh! Let's make one more last-ditch effort.*

"Will and I have a mystery we're trying to solve. We think someone may have gotten in our stateroom by accident."

"What makes you think that?"

"Our houseboy gave us something he found while cleaning up that he thought belonged to us, but neither one of us had ever seen it before. It sheds a lot of light on what's been going on with some of our classmates. Someone must have left it when they came in our cabin. I thought you were pretty safe on a cruise ship, but now I'm beginning to wonder."

"I'm sure there's a logical explanation. What'd he find?"

"An ... unusual item. Rather not say right now. I've got it safely hidden in my nightstand drawer. We're waiting to see if whoever will miss it and return to get it at some point. And I haven't seen Will so pissed in a long while. He takes the invasion of his privacy really seriously. He said he thinks that it's distinctive enough for him to find out who owned it. And he said when he does, that person better have a really good excuse not only about this but about a lot of other things as well. He's on a tear about this and really thinks he's on to something. You've only seen his nice side, but when he gets like this, he's like a pit bull. A few years back, Will had a lawyer mess over him. He got like he is now and stayed on that guy's back for three years. I tried to tell him to forget about it ... told him it wasn't worth it, ... but he was determined. It took him three years, but he finally got the bar association to suspend the guy's license. He can really be tunnel-visioned when he decides to be."

Suzzie wadded up her napkin as she mulled the matter over but had no response except to point out to Betsy that the auctioneer had picked up his microphone and tapped it to see if it was working. Betsy silently wondered if Will's interview with Billy Cobb had been as big a bust as hers had been with Billy's wife.

# CHAPTER 37

Will got back to their stateroom before Betsy did. He flipped on their TV, and "Mama Mia" was playing on one of the movie channels.

*Oh. What the hell. I'll watch a little of it and use it to kill time until Betsy gets here. I still can't believe someone had the imagination to take all those old ABBA songs and wrap a cohesive story around them.*

It was just getting to "Super Trouper" when Betsy walked in. He turned down the volume on the TV somewhat as she entered.

"Ah, my super trouper returns," Will said. "So, how'd it go? Were you able to talk to her?"

"Oh, yeah. As much good as it did. She clammed up when I pressed her for info. She wasn't a wealth of hard information, but she made it clear that she didn't idolize y'all's football team – even if they were champions."

"Funny you should say that. I got the same vibes from her husband, and he was one of them. Some of those guys must have been real jerks off the field. I did learn what 'S and M' stands for, however."

"Strong-willed and masculine?"

"Not hardly. And not stout and musclebound either. Get this -- Suzzie and Misty. Seems like some of the boys wanted to date them, but they wouldn't give them the time of day. Think about that for a second."

"Do you think that some of the players spread nasty rumors about the two of them since they wouldn't got out with them? And that's why Suzzie dislikes them to this day?"

"And if Suzzie dislikes them, I'm sure it rubbed off on her husband as well. If someone was saying crappy things about you, I'd sure be pissed."

"As I would about you. And maybe that's why Danny seems to dislike them as well. I'm sure he got a dose of venom from both his wife and her cousin."

"Well, he did have his own reasons to have a hard-on against them. Remember he was the team water boy or whatever you want to call it, and the players used to pick on him."

"And what you want to bet, that's why S and M quit the cheerleader squad right when the program should have been on top of the world?"

"And maybe used parental pressure and grades as an excuse? Could be. But for Misty to transfer schools? That seems a little overboard."

"Depends on how bad it was. But if rumors were going around all over school, surely some of your classmates would remember the whole affair. I remember the shoddy treatment some people in my class got to this very day – and thank God I wasn't in their shoes. Teenagers are pretty vulnerable and tender and can often blow things out of proportion. I think they take things harder than grownups do."

"Do you think that whatever happened had something to do with Misty's depression problems?"

"Wouldn't doubt it. Teenagers can be awfully damned mean. Aren't teenage suicide rates higher than those of the population as a whole?"

"I think so. I brought the depression business up with Billy and he did say that he thinks Misty's senior year may possibly have been when her depression began."

"Mmm, huh. Whatever it was, it must have *really* been bad. Do you think the boys spread the word that Suzzie and

Misty were the class sluts? Girls take that kind of thing very seriously even today. Despite the fact that mores have become considerably more liberal than when we were in school. In those days, an accusation like that would have devastated a girl. Especially if it was a lie."

"Wouldn't have made some girl's future spouse feel really good either. Could that be part of Danny's problem?"

"How'd you like it if the whole town was calling your beloved a whore or a round heels? That's as devastating to a girl as calling a boy a fag."

"Good point. Did you bring up our cabin 'visitor' with Suzzie?"

"Yep. And told her what we've found had far reaching implications. But I couldn't get a solid read on her reaction. She looked a little uncomfortable at first but then more or less poo-pooed it and acted like there must be a logical explanation. I will say this. When I told her something got left behind, she was curious enough to ask what it was."

"What'd you tell her?"

"Just said it was an unusual item. Something that we should be able to trace back to its source. Told her you were super pissed and determined to find out who our intruder was. Thank goodness, she didn't keep on pushing me for specifics. But she did look uncomfortable."

"That's good. I told Billy more or less the same thing. He didn't even ask that much. Just looked uncomfortable, chugged the rest of his beer, and said he needed to go."

"Interesting. I'm glad we haven't backed ourselves into a corner regarding what it is in case we want to use it as a playing card later. And we need to spread the word about our visitor with your other classmates so we can judge their reactions."

"Uh, huh. Can't hurt. I'd like to see Al Soltero's reaction as well. We may have made him start to feel threatened. Maybe his bodyguard was dispatched on a black-hearted mission. That variety of poisonous snake bite seems like something he would not only know about but a dirty trick that would be right down his alley.

"But changing the subject ... while not changing the subject, I've got something here I want you to look at."

Will handed Betsy Billy's business card.

"Any of those names ring a bell?"

"This is a pop test, right? Is this one of those I get three tries, and the first two don't count quizzes? Or maybe I should ask you. Does a one-legged duck swim in a circle? You ask if these names look familiar? Of course, they do. Looks like Al Soltero's steering committee."

"An A plus and a blue ribbon for the most beautiful lady in the room. If anyone says your mama raised a dumb daughter, just tell them to come to me, and I'll set them straight."

Betsy stood up and curtsied.

"I think I'll talk to Jimbo next. I'd like to get his take on the 'S and M' situation. Maybe we can find out what might have been being said way back then. Chances are he ought to remember. After all, he was a first-string linebacker on that team, and part of the core group. And I find myself wanting to talk to him anyway and see if I can learn how Al Soltero fits into this whole cruise picture. I still don't buy that Al's presence here is purely a coincidence. There's something going on between Billy, Jimbo and Willard that I'd sure like to know more about."

"How do you propose to do that?"

"I think I overheard that Jimbo works out at the ship's fitness center most mornings. Instead of walking the deck, I think I'm overdue to work out myself."

"My husband, a jock of all trades. A private investigator *and* an athlete."

"But you forgot. ... It's a bird. It's a plane. It's a SUPER-STUD."

"A stud for all seasons? We won't go there. At least not right now. But later ... who knows. You may get lucky, big boy."

ABBA's "The Winner Takes All" began playing on the TV in the background.

# CHAPTER 38

When Will walked into the fitness center, Jimbo Littleton was already running on the treadmill. Will went through some stretching exercises while he waited for another passenger to finish running on the treadmill next to Jimbo, and when it opened up, he grabbed it. He greeted Jimbo and made a few small-talk, preliminary comments about the weather and how he really needed this workout since there was such an abundance of tempting food on the ship rather than immediately broaching the topics he was really interested in. He looked for an opening to change the subject, and within a few minutes it came.

"Well, I guess Puerto Villarta was our last port of call for this cruise," Jimbo said.

"It was the only one I had ever visited before, and I went there for a company meeting before Betsy and I were married. Betsy and I decided not to do an organized tour but just went and hung out on the Malecón instead. Lydia Vallence ended up with us. I learned things from her that I had never known before – or maybe things that I'd just forgotten. I didn't realize that she and Pat Karls only made first-string cheerleader our senior year after Suzzie and Misty quit the squad. Or that Suzzie and Danny are kin to each other."

"Yeah. I guess a lot of things changed after our junior year – some good, some not so good."

"Only state championship team Greenville ever produced. The town was really proud of y'all's team – and they still are."

"It got a lot of us in college. That's for sure."

"And some people like you ended up with a law degree. Didn't you and Billy practice together for a while?"

"Yep. As a matter of fact, we did."

"As big a buddies as you two always were. I'm surprised y'all still aren't partners today."

"Well, truth of the matter was, it *was* a pretty mediocre practice. We were making a living, but it never really took off like we hoped. I think some people around town never got over just seeing us as ex-athletes."

"That's certainly a problem. In some people's eyes, some of us never grow up. They always see us a wet-behind-the-ears teenagers. So, how'd Billy get to Tampa?"

"His mother's family ... she was a Valdes ... I guess you know that Billy's dad did a stint in the air force. He was stationed for awhile at MacDill in Tampa. That's where he met Billy's mom. Plus, Billy went back to Florida to go to law school after he couldn't get in at Ole Miss. Ended up getting his law degree at Nova."

*Definitely know the Valdes name. Betsy and I had our run-in with that boy. Small world, ain't it.*

"Even though Billy's parents had moved to Greenville, she still had some connections there so it just kind of worked out. They never made me an offer, so I just stayed put after he left. It was an amicable parting. Of course, we're still friends. The Tampa people just didn't want both of us."

"Billy gave me his card the other day. Looks like all the firm's partners are Cuban or something."

"Let's just say Hispanic.

*Yeah! Colombian Hispanic!*

Will wiped his brow with his towel as he continued to run.

"Possibly maybe Colombian? That must have been how Billy got to know Adolfo Soltero."

"Do you know Señor Soltero?"

"Betsy and I have known Al for years in both Vero Beach and the Keys. Mysterious guy with tentacles in a lot of things. But he's made a lot of money. I know quite a bit about him, but I'm always finding out there's a lot I don't know. He's been a client of both mine and Betsy's. In fact, he's even been our neighbor. So, should I assume that you and Willard met Al through Billy?"

Jimbo gave Will a look that Will interpreted as being defensive. It was like he was debating with himself how evasive he ought to be. Finally, he just said, "Small world, isn't it?"

"I can understand how Al could possibly do you and Billy some good, but Willard? A farmer way over in Mississippi? That's an enigma."

"Not as much as you might think. Remember when Willard had his major falling out with his parents because they didn't approve of Zelma? Did you ever know he tried to break away from them and start a flying service?"

"Vaguely. Refresh my memory."

"He wanted his independence, but he didn't have any money. He got what he needed to buy two planes as a loan from Soltero. Got a new Grumman Ag Cat and a 172 Cessna. They don't give those babies away. You're talking total of a million plus for both planes. Billy was the go-between who introduced them."

"Well, I'll be dog. But then Willard made up with his parents and ended up with the farm, didn't he? So, he was able to let the flying service go? Did his folks give him the money to pay off the airplane loan?"

"No, but Al let Willard work off the debt. And because of Billy, they stayed in touch."

"I see. I've seen you, Billy, and Willard talking to Al here on the ship. Do they still do business with each other? Like maybe Al carrying paper on Willard's plantation?"

"I shouldn't comment. It would be inappropriate."

"But Billy continues to represent Al?"

"Al continues to be a client of Billy's firm."

"But he's not a client of yours. But I guess *you* still deal with Willard."

"I have handled some matters for Willard over the years."

"Interesting. Very interesting."

They both finished their treadmill runs. The free-weights were being used by another passenger, so they took a water break.

"Noticed when you were running that you seem to be a hundred percent. Didn't you take a fall early in this cruise?" Will asked.

"Yep. Matter of fact I did. Fell down the main staircase."

"How'd that happen? Just miss a step?"

"To tell you the truth, I still don't know. It wasn't like I was drunk or anything like Billy was when he took his fall. I was ... going down. The stairs were packed with people. And then all of sudden I tripped over somebody's tote bag that had been dropped on the step in front of me just as someone else nudged me. Darndest thing that ever happened to me. One second, I was walking down, and the next second I was plummeting down headfirst. And you know, nobody ever did come back to claim the bag. Just left it there. Only thing I can figure was that they'd rather forfeit what was in it rather than get into a negligence dispute."

"Hmmm. Are passengers liable if they cause another passenger to have an accident?"

"I'm not sure. There's probably a precedent somewhere or other. I was sore for a few days, but at least I didn't break anything."

"Well, thank God you weren't hurt any worse. On a different subject, something else I've just learned. ... I can't tell you how many times I heard Dickie-do – and Paul or Jerry, as well for that matter -- holler 'S and M.' And I also heard him say 'oh, what a night.' In fact, now that I think about it, it seemed to be kind of a sore subject with both Tom and Rusty. They both told him to shut up. Then I finally learned what 'S and M' means – Suzzie and Misty. Strange. ... How'd all that get started?"

"I probably shouldn't say. Let's just say it was teenage meanness and bad judgement and kid crap."

"Could that be why Suzzie and Misty quit being cheerleaders? Or maybe why Misty transferred out to Riverside for a bit? Or part of her ongoing depression problems?"

"Will, I hope you don't think I'm being rude, but if Suzzie or Danny don't want to dredge up ancient history, I'm not sure I should. Hell, that was forty years ago. There's been a lot of water under the bridge since then. It'd be best to just let it drop."

"OK, if you say so. By the way, have you had anyone get in your stateroom?"

"Not that I know of. Why do you ask?"

"Our cabin boy found something in ours that didn't belong to either me or Betsy. Don't know how it got there unless someone got in the room while we weren't there and accidentally left it."

"I guess someone could go in by accident while the maid was cleaning. Are you missing anything?"

"Don't seem to be."

"Then I wouldn't worry about it. I'm sure there's an innocent explanation."

"You're probably right. But if I find out who it was, I'm going to make his life very uncomfortable. I've got the evidence hidden in my nightstand. Oh, I was about to forget. Did you find out what was going on with Paul and Jerry? I saw you meeting with their lady friends."

"Both of them claim they were set up. They're both still in custody. The ship couldn't wait for them. Both of them could be in major trouble. They're going to need a lawyer. That's for sure."

"Not you?"

"I haven't been hired to represent either one of them. They need a specialist. I know it sounds far-fetched and please don't repeat the charges since we don't know how true they are. But they're calling Jerry a pervert who was soliciting, and they say Paul is a Homeland Security threat."

"I find both charges hard to believe."

"So do I. But ... Looks like ... Who knows? ... Oh, good. Looks like the free-weights are available. Do you use them?"

"No. You go ahead. I'm going to use the machines instead."

"I wouldn't worry about someone getting in your cabin again."

"You're probably right. But when and if they do, I'm going to nail the bastard. They don't know it, but they did leave a clue  not only to their identity but also to a lot of the other shit that been happening on this ship as well."

"Just be careful. It's not worth getting hurt over. You've been asking me some questions. You mind if I ask you one?"

"Fire away."

"Have you been going in the casino?"

"I think Betsy and I maybe walked through it once. Why do you ask?"

"Because there's a rumor going around that you have a gambling problem and that you lost a shit-pot load of money in the casino."

"What? That really pisses me off. Who's saying that? It's a complete and total lie. I don't even like to gamble. I think it's stupid to engage in any activity where the odds are stacked against you like they are there. Random is random, and it always will be. Who's saying that shit?"

"No particular source. I can tell you this though. There's a lot of people talking behind your back."

"Next time you hear it, please straighten them out. And if I hear it, I'll lay out the son-of-a-bitch who's spreading that poison. Hell, I don't even buy lottery tickets."

"Will do. Just thought you ought to know."

"Buddy, thanks for the heads up."

At that point, they parted ways.

*Wait until I tell Betsy the gambling rumor. If they think I'm pissed, they ain't seen pissed until they see Betsy.*

*Other than that, did I strike out again? No. Not completely. I guess I'm gradually piecing some facts together, but I sure wish I knew what they meant. ... Or how they tie together. ... Or even if they're relevant to anything. But we must be rattling somebody's cage.*

*Whatever happened with Suzzie and Misty was, and I guess still is, pretty hush-hush. Was it something bad or, like he said, just kid crap?*

*Jimbo didn't seem have much of a reaction to our cabin break-in either. Interesting that he's the first person who didn't ask what the cabin boy found. Especially since he's a lawyer. I always thought they were nitpickers for detail.*

*Cock-sucking-mother-fucking hell! So now Betsy and I are on the gossip list after also almost being on the accident list? Who considers us a threat? And why? Apparently, we've sure created a scared enemy. God, I'd love to know who it is. Now I'm convinced more than ever that all these accidents aren't what they appear to be on the surface.*

*Are we going away? Not only no, but hell no. We'll just keep on digging. Sooner or later surely, we'll find out whose nerve we hit. That snake didn't walk onto that ship and into our room by itself. And that gambling bullshit rumor didn't start itself.*

# CHAPTER 39

The following morning Will and Betsy saw Al Soltero on the deck. He seemed to be in a spirited conversation with one of the crew. They were animatedly talking in Spanish. Al's back was to them.

Will put his arm on Betsy's and motioned for her to stop walking. They tried to listen to the conversation, but it was unintelligible to them. They wondered about the topic being discussed. It seemed to be more than just Al ordering a drink or some other mundane activity. The way Al put his hand on the man's shoulder seemed to convey familiarity.

"Is it my imagination, but do those two seem to know each other? And does that steward seem especially deferential to Al?"

"I think you're right on both counts. I'm always amazed at how many people Al seems to know."

"Or how many know him."

"Sometimes it's almost like he's their Colombian godfather."

"Like if Al made this guy an offer, he couldn't refuse it?"

"Uh. Huh. Which reminds me of another quote. It goes something like 'The world is so hard that a man must have two fathers to look after him. That's why there are godfathers.'

"I'm sure I paraphrased the reference, but you get my drift."

"Oh, yeah. And as we have seen in the past, Señor Soltero has been known to fill that role *very* well. You've got to wonder just how many workers on this ship's crew are under his thumb."

"And could bring contraband reptiles aboard a ship? Or leave poisonous goodies for some unsuspecting slob to eat? ... Or do other favors up and above usual expectations?"

"My dearest, I think we've landed on the same page. You know what they say. Great minds ..."

"Run in the same gutters?"

"Something like that, but you'd accuse me of being foolish if I disagreed with you."

"Would I do that to you? After all, it's a free country. I can't force you to agree with me and always be right."

"Shh. Heads up. Al's heading our way."

A big smile broke out on Soltero's face when he saw the Blacks. He approached them with his arms extended. His bodyguard lurked silently a few steps behind him. Will noticed an old scar below one of the bodyguard's eyes for the first time.

"Mr. and Mrs. Black! A fine good morning to you. Seeing you two has made a perfect day at sea just get even better. After all, you are poster children for the ideal cruising passengers."

Al bussed Betsy on the cheek and then vigorously shook Will's hand. Betsy smelled the subtle scent of Al's mandarin orange cologne. As usual, Al was nattily dressed in a buttoned up double-breasted linen coat with a paisley silk handkerchief in the breast pocket. His freshly pressed shirt was open collared, and a matching silk ascot adorned his neck.

"Al, you missed your calling. You should have been a diplomat. What are your plans for the morning?"

"Oh, something that probably seems dull to you. One of the ship's best held secrets is that on the days it is at sea, they serve a complimentary breakfast in the Bordeaux dining room. I've been meaning to try it since it's not a buffet like the Horizon Court but a refined breakfast off of a menu. A more elegant breakfast served on china with crystal glasses and cloth napkins. It would truly be a shame if I had to eat alone. It would be an honor if I could persuade you to join me."

"Sounds delightful. Something special to do on my birthday."

"That's even a better reason for you to honor me with your presence. It's not every day I get to share someone's milestone."

When they arrived at the elevator, Al's burly bodyguard silently punched the down-button with a meaty but manicured finger and watched for a car to arrive while Al and the Blacks stood back and waited. When the door opened, he held it for them to join him and then hit the button to take them to the fifth deck. He accompanied them into the restaurant. When they were admitted, he walked back out again towards the atrium to wait for them.

The waiter led them to a table. Al pulled back Betsy's chair and held it for her to sit down, and then the waiter handed them each a menu.

"Welcome, Señor Soltero. A pleasure to see you."

Will couldn't resist glancing over at Betsy. Her eyes told him she understood perfectly well what he was thinking.

*Been meaning to try this breakfast? Hmmm! Is there nobody in the Latin world Al doesn't know? Or who is not in his sphere of influence?*

The waiter then turned to Will and Betsy and said, "My name in Nico. Welcome to the Bordeaux dining room. I will be your server today. Would you like a beverage before I take your breakfast orders? On the back of the menu are the selections we have available."

"You know. A salty dog might just hit the spot," Betsy said. "Do you have fresh grapefruit juice?"

Before the waiter could reply, Al looked down the list and asked, "Betsy, have you ever had a sangria melon cooler? I think you'd like it."

"Never even heard of it," she replied. "What's in it?"

"I couldn't tell you all the ingredients, but in Colombia they are a very refreshing addition to a morning brunch."

"Sounds delish. Cancel my salty dog and make it a ... what'd you call it?"

"A sangria melon chiller," Will said. "Make it three of 'em."

Will and Betsy each ordered eggs benedict and coffee. Al chose to have huevos pericos and an expresso to be served later.

"What's that dish you ordered?" Will asked.

"Nothing fancy, I'm afraid. It's just scrambled eggs with tomato and onion added," Al replied. "I'm just a simple man with simple tastes."

"I don't see it on the menu. Or the melon cooler, for that matter."

"Rico is familiar with both and is kind enough to convey my wishes to the staff. They're nothing out of the ordinary, I assure you."

Will gave Betsy that look again.

*Sure!*

The waiter returned with their drinks.

Al raised his glass and said, "A birthday toast to you, my amigos."

Betsy tasted her drink and exclaimed, "Al, as usual, you're right. This *is* refreshing. Not all what I expected. OJ and wine?"

"Actually, if they make it like my tia does, sauvignon blanc and orange juice with some Triple Sec."

"With wedges of cantaloupe and watermelon," Will added. "Al, you're consistently on target. Speaking of on target, is this cruise living up to your expectations? And before I forget, thank you again for introducing us to your delightful aunt in Cartagena."

"She enjoyed your company as well. But back to the cruise. Absolutely. Regency is a wonderful cruise line. Almost hate for the trip to end. I've managed to get in a little business and a little pleasure. As you Americans say, 'all work and no play makes Johnny a dull, dull lad'. ... And how about you?"

"Ours has been a bit more stressful, I'm afraid. As you know, we're here on a high school reunion. It seems that an inordinate number of my old classmates have been involved in either accidents or incidents."

"That's unfortunate. May I ask the nature of these occurrences?"

"They've varied greatly. They range from death, to injury, to even arrests. In fact, one incident occurred while we were with you in Cartagena. One of my classmates who I think you may know – a guy named Willard McFarley was involved in a street mugging."

"Unfortunately, we are not immune to such incidents especially with vulnerable tourists who are perceived to be wealthy. After all, Colombia is a poor nation. Was he killed?"

"No. Just banged up pretty bad. If you'll recall, I think you were introduced to Willard by my classmate Billy Cobb."

"Yes. I do recall him now. You meet so many people on a ship this size. If memory serves me right, he was a pretty pleasant fellow. I don't recall his line of work."

*BULLSHIT. Try farmer and pilot. And possibly more than that ... like maybe one of your drug runners ... if I'm most likely correctly reading between the lines on what Jimbo Littleton didn't want to admit. But what you want to bet that that's probably all Foxy Al will ever admit to with-*

*out a subpoena. Let's take a different tack and see what he says.*

He glanced over again at Betsy. Her look said *move on.*

"But you know Billy Cobb pretty well, don't you? He gave me his card. I didn't know that all the partners in his Tampa law firm, Carlos, Valdes and Perillo were Hispanic. Do you work with them?"

"Yes, I work with many law firms. Carlos Valdes has handled some matters for me from time to time. And I think Mr. Cobb was occasionally assigned some of my work by one of the senior partners."

"Like possibly Valdes. Someone told me Billy's mother's maiden name was Valdes."

"Could possibly have been. We never discussed it. ... Oh, our food's here."

The waiter brought their breakfast and for a few moments everyone was silent as they ate their meal. When he came over to refill their coffee cups Al told him to pass his compliments on to the chef. After the waiter left, Will reopened the conversation.

"Billy Cobb's wife, Suzzie, told us that she and her friend Danny had a delightful day with you in Puntarenas. Where'd you guys go?"

Before Al answered, he tried to find out what either Suzzie or Danny had already told the Blacks.

"Did they say what part of the day was most meaningful to them?"

"She said something about having lunch in Gu-ya ... something or other."

"Guaitil. I remember now. Any place else?"

"That was the primary place she mentioned."

Al smiled. He now had some parameters and was confident he was he was on safe ground. This should enable him to use a reasonable amount of literary license to recreate the rest of his day with Suzzie and Danny. He then related other events for that day.

When he finished, Will said, "Oh, I almost forgot. She did mention going to a pottery factory ... uh ...Chorotega Pottery. Even brought us a pot from there. I guess you forgot mention them."

Al seemed to pause but recovered quickly and merely said, "I guess I did."

Will waited for Al to elaborate further, but it didn't happen. So, he plowed on.

"We think we had an intruder in our cabin."

"Oh, what makes you think that?"

"Something our cabin boy found that didn't belong to us. He seems to think he can trace it back to its original owner."

Once again Al was silent. Both Will and Betsy were surprised at his lack of curiosity. It seemed uncharacteristic of Al.

Finally, he said, "Do you still have the item?"

"As a matter of fact, we do."

"If you'll allow me to borrow it, I might be able to use some of my connections to shed light on the mystery. Not to be braggadocios but I can possibly get someone to put in more of an effort to find the object's owner than you can."

"We wouldn't want to put you to the trouble. We already have someone working on it."

"Did you turn the item over to them?"

"No. It's still safe in our cabin, tucked away in our end table where no one would ever think to look. If this item tells me what I think it's going to, I think some shit's going to hit the fan. I'm going to be able to shed a lot of light on some of the recent unexplained occurrences both on and off this ship."

Al did not comment further. Their talk then turned to other matters. When the meal was concluded, Al said he had some matters to attend to and thanked them graciously for joining him at breakfast. As they emerged from the Bordeaux dining room, his bodyguard silently appeared and followed him as he walked back to the elevator.

Later that day, a thirty-two-ounce Tortuga rum cake was delivered to their room. It had a handwritten note on it written in neat almost block-style lettering that said, "Can't think of anyone else who is more deserving of an incredibly happy day. Happy birthday. Your friend, Al."

# CHAPTER 40

When they were alone again, Betsy commented, "Well, another strikeout."

"Maybe or maybe not. We'll just have to wait and see. Did you expect any of these people to just jump and say they had been in our stateroom?"

"What you want to bet if Al had gotten his hands on our made-up mystery item, that would have been the last of it?"

"We've talked to how many people now?"

"I've lost count. Probably at least a dozen."

"And we're right where we started. I think it's time for plan B."

"And what would that be?"

"We need to encourage another break-in. But before we do that, we need to make sure each person we've already talked to knows where in the cabin to look, even if they don't know what they're looking for."

"Like the nightstand you mentioned to Al?"

"Sounds like as good a place as any. And we'll hide out on our balcony and see if we can catch them in action."

"What do you plan to put in the end table. A mousetrap? Or a poisonous snake?" Betsy said. "I'll say again for the five-hundredth time. That thing scared the living crap out of me."

"A snake would serve them right. But how about nothing? Why does there have to be anything in it? If we catch some-one ransacking our bedroom table, we'll have our culprit."

"And then what do we do?"

"I dunno. I guess it depends on who it is. I'm not about to confront Al's bodyguard if that's who was involved. Someone else? ... We'll see. ... We'll just play it by ear."

"And what do you propose we do? Hide on the balcony for the rest of the cruise?"

"Of course not. On the last night, my class is supposed to have an informal get-together in the ship disco. There'll be plenty of confusion, so it'll be easy for us to go unnoticed. We'll RSVP for the thing but stay in our cabin. But we'll make sure we tell everyone we're going to be there."

"I've got an idea. If Dick and Beth are going, we'll use them as cover. We'll say we're going with them, but if anyone asks where we are at any point in time, they can say we're on the dancefloor, or in the head, or getting a drink. Maybe I can even go up briefly and walk around the room and be seen while you wait here for me to get back."

"Now you're getting the idea. Nothing may happen, or then something might. Who knows? Nothing ventured; nothing gained. And if it doesn't work out, we'll spend the next twenty years wondering who put a snake in our room and why. But then again – shit – it's just crazy enough that it might work. I know this much. If we don't solve this mystery while we're on this ship, it ain't never gonna be solved. ... And time's running out fast."

"I've got another idea. Why don't we put some tape or something on all the drawers in the room so if someone goes through them while we're not there any other time we'll know about it. I know it won't catch them, but at least we'll know someone is continuing go come in our cabin.

"What the hell. Works for me. Should we take a vote on plan B?"

"I think we just did, but all in favor, say aye."

Will began to sing, "Aye, Aye, Aye, Aye. Conta y no llores, Porque cantado ..."

Betsy jumped up and pretended to pull at her hair.

"Enough! Enough! I surrender. I'll confess to anything if you'll just stop singing."

# CHAPTER 41

"Betsy, there's another person I want to talk to alone."

"Who dat, daddy rat?"

"The rat I had in mind is Willard McFarley. I wonder if I can find out more about his association with Soltero than Jimbo was willing to disclose. If his dealings with Al are ancient history like Jimbo said, I can't understand why we keep seeing him in Soltero related conferences. Al's not the kind of person who gets together with people just to relive the good old days."

"How do you plan to do that? We're running out of cruise time."

"Call him and say just that. We're running short on cruise time, Willard, and I feel bad that we haven't had a chance to visit much this whole trip."

"Sometimes the straightforward method is the way to go, my devious dear. Are you planning on grilling him with Zelma present?"

"That's where you come in. Since she's a shopaholic, I thought maybe I'd suggest that you two look for some earrings or something to take back for our daughter. And how you'd like for Zelma to join you since she seems to have such exquisite taste. I think she'll jump at the chance if we stroke her ego since she's been snubbed by so many of other women in my class."

"And do I have your authorization to actually spend money?"

"If you see something Lexie would really, really like, go ahead. After all, she does have a birthday coming up. But don't feel like you have to buy something just to be buying something. After all, money doesn't buy happiness."

"My dear, whoever said *that* just doesn't know where to go shopping."

Will called and set up a meeting. Willard said Zelma would be thrilled to provide her input into picking out a present for Lexie. Will set a time for the two of them to meet Willard and Zelma in the Crooners Lounge after lunch. Willard and Zelma arrived on schedule, and the couples made some small talk before the ladies departed on their shopping excursion.

"What you drinking?" Will asked Willard.

Willard said a beer would be fine.

"I can still see some bruises from your Cartagena episode. Otherwise, are you OK?"

"I'm still somewhat sore, but otherwise, I guess I'm fine."

"I'm surprised you're the only one who got mugged. I would have thought that if the local thugs were after the Yankee dollar, they would've attacked all three of you."

"I haven't told anyone this, but I seem to have been singled out. One of the muggers grabbed my wallet and looked at my driver's license. He then said something to the others in Spanish that sounded to me like éste. That's when I got pummeled while the others held Billy and Jimbo back."

"Wow! That's strange."

*I wonder why neither Billy or Jimbo mentioned that tidbit. This whole thing is getting a Soltero aroma about it, and the smell ain't good.*

"I heard you were coming from a business meeting when it happened. Hope the meeting went better than its aftermath. Not to be nosy, but were you doing business with Adolfo Soltero?"

"Uh. Uh. ...You know him?"

"Betsy and I've known Al for years. We even done some business with him ourselves from time to time."

"No shit! Small world. Though, I don't know whether that's good or bad. I've had some dealings with him in the past myself. Billy introduced us back when I had my flying service."

"You're not cranking that back up, are you?"

"Oh, no. Actually, Al wants to buy my plantation. I told him it wasn't on the market, but Billy insisted that I meet with him and his bankers anyway and just to hear their offer and terms."

*I know all about Al's interpretation of the word terms. And they're often not negotiable. ... But he has a way to make them clear. ... And he can be emphatic.*

"Al's a wheeler-dealer investor alright. And I would certainly think he could afford your property on a cash basis. And he can be quite persuasive. ... And insistent. So, were his terms attractive?"

"Oh, yeah, but that land's been in my family for generations. You don't just give up your legacy and your heritage on a whim without getting some expert advice. That's a big decision to ask a guy to make. Like, for example, I don't know what the tax ramifications would be. And what about our children? I'd planned to leave it to them. That's just one of several questions. Besides that, I don't think I'm ready to retire yet. But you're right. Soltero can be very insistent."

"As well as persistent. So, did you leave the door open or just flat turn him down?"

"I guess you could say I turned him down. But I didn't close the door completely. He didn't like that one little bit. In fact, he kind of scared me after he didn't get what he wanted. He acted almost like he's two persons. You know a kind of a Jekyll and Hyde."

*Boy, do I ever know. Wouldn't want to be in Willard's shoes. Slick Al doesn't take rejection well. I wonder if he sent his henchmen to put the fear of God into Willard when the meeting didn't go according to Hoyle. I also wonder just why he wants Willard's place. I can't see Al as a Delta farmer, but I can see him using a farm as a front for appearing to be a legitimate U.S. businessman and to have an ideal money laundering mechanism. There's also some special provisions in the tax codes to benefit farmers. I wonder if Al files a U.S. tax return.*

"Do you still have a landing strip on your place?"

"Oh, yeah. Just because I gave up commercial flying didn't mean I gave up flying completely for fun. Actually, for years, I did my own crop dusting."

*Yep. Bingo! The strip must be of the attractions to Al for his smuggling operations.*

"Best I remember, your place is kind of in the middle of nowhere."

"Yeah, it is. Thirty thousand acres not close to much of anything except Greenville. Ain't much else there but farmland until you get down to Vicksburg."

*Remote. Definitely attractive for illegal activities. Kind of like Mena Arkansas was for drug smugglers back when Slick Willie was governor of Arkansas. Yep. Slick Willie and Slick Al. Two peas in a pod.*

Will thought he saw Willard suddenly shudder and look down at his beer. He glanced to his left to see what Willard had seen. It was Al Soltero's bodyguard standing over near the door giving Willard a stern look.

Willard suddenly seemed like he wanted to change the subject.

"Oh well. Enough about that. I guess I was always destined just to be a poor hick farmer living in the sticks. So, tell me, Mr. Florida sophisticate, what life's like in the Keys. Always wanted to visit there. Also, before I forget. You seemed to do OK for yourself in the wife department, my man. Zelma and I have both been impressed with Betsy. Both good looking and smart."

"I guess I got lucky. You know what they say. A good-looking woman is a good-looking woman but combine that with a brain and you've got a sho' nuff lethal combination."

For the next few minutes, Will gave Willard his standard speech about Florida and the Keys while he looked for an opportunity change the subject back to topics that he was more interested in without making it look like an interrogation.

When there was a pause again, Will said, "Did you ever figure out how that poisonous beach apple got in your fruit basket?"

"Never did. God, neither one of us can remember ever being so sick. But the ship's doctor said we got off lucky. He said people die from eating those things."

"Are you going to hold the ship responsible?"

"I don't know how we can. I wasn't one of their gift baskets. It had to be some kind of gigantic mistake."

*Riiight! If you believe that, I've got the bridge over Lake Pontachartrain I'd like to sell you.*

"Willard, there's been entirely too many mistakes on this cruise for them to have all been just mistakes. Look at Tom, and Rusty, and Jerry, and Paul, and Jimbo. And of course, Dickie-do. Even Billy's had an accident."

*Not to mention Betsy and me in our poisonous snake encounter, but I won't go into that right now. But maybe it is a good time mention our break-in and watch his reaction.*

Will repeated what had become his standard spiel about the intrusion and only got a blank look back from Willard.

Will concluded saying, "But whoever it was, he was dumb enough to leave a clue to his identity behind, and I'm going to use it to nail the asshole. He doesn't know it, but he's given me a clue to a lot of these unexplained things. Got it hidden under some stuff in my nightstand."

*Still no reaction. Not surprised. I didn't really think Willard was who I'm looking for. Let's go to 'S and M' matter and see what Willard can tell me about it.*

"I can't tell you how many times I heard Dickie-do shout 'S and M' around some of the other football players. And 'oh, what a night.' But every time he brought it up no one seemed to want to talk about whatever it was. Willard, you were part of that football clique. What the hell is that BS all about? If you know, please tell me before I die of curiosity."

"It's kind of embarrassing, but I guess it can't hurt to talk about it now. It happened our junior year after the Corinth game. If you'll remember, that was the game that nailed the championship down for us. I'd been kicked off the team for doing some stupid stuff by that time, but I took daddy's station wagon to the game anyway. After all, these *were* my friends, and Greenville had never won a championship before."

"Those were sure heady days alright. Too bad you didn't get to share the glory with the rest of them. They walked on water around town for a while after that season."

"It is too bad, but I was stupid. My own fault. Nobody to blame but myself. If I hadn't been such a dumbass and kept breaking training, I might have even gotten to play some college ball like a bunch of them end up doing."

"Hey, buddy. We all have regrets. ... Go on. I've been wanting to hear *this* story."

"Well, they were giving the ACT exam the next day. So, some of them wanted to get back to Greenville earlier than the bus would get them home. So, I volunteered to let them ride back with me. Shit. I had plenty of room in daddy's big old station wagon. And Suzzie and Misty joined us as well because they wanted to get on back. Anyway, we were all about to piss all over ourselves we were so excited about winning the big final game, so I thought we'd get some beer for the ride home. I guess you remember that Corinth was dry as a bone in those days, but it's only a few miles away from the legendary Selmer honkytonks."

"In the wrong direction. That was Bufford 'Walking Tall' Pusser country. But go on. I didn't mean to interrupt."

"Anyway, since I was driving instead of going back to Greenville, I just ... sort of took it on myself ... across the state line on 45 to get some libations. I don't think the girls realized I was detouring until I pulled into some place ... I think the name of it was ... Junior's.

"When Suzzie and Misty realized what I'd done, they weren't real happy, but my deception tickled the shit out of the players. Hell, they were in the mood to celebrate our championship whether Suzzie and Misty liked it or not. Bottom line is Suzzie and Misty didn't have a whole lot of say-so in what was going on."

*Bet that's got to be the understatement of the year. I can see them now having a hissy fit.*

"Anyway, we went in. There was a country band going. Paul and Jerry insisted that Suzzie and Misty dance with them. That's when things started to go bad. Some drunk redneck wanted to dance with Misty and big, bad Jerry hit him with a cheap shot. Knocked the shit out of the boy. He came up with a knife. Just so happened high-sheriff Bufford ... I didn't know who he was at the time ... was right there. He ordered the redneck to drop the knife, but the redneck slashed out at him instead. Bad Mistake. The sheriff started wrestling with the drunk over the knife and turned the knife back on him. ... Anyway, the bottom line is the redneck lost and ended up taking the knife in the gut. Bufford ripped him stem to stern."

"You gotta be kidding?"

"Oh, no. If I'm lying, I'm dying. It was a bad scene. Shit! The girls were screaming because they got some blood on them. After I settled them down, I decided we needed to get the hell out of Dodge during the confusion. Otherwise we were gonna be there all night. We were pretty shook up, however. I needed gas for the drive home. While we were at the gas station, I bought a case of Bud for the drive. I guess that's all of the story. We got back to Greenville in one piece."

Will drained his beer and ordered another one.

"So, that's it? All this is about a bar fight? Is that why both Misty and Suzzie quit the cheerleader squad? Over a damned bar fight? And is that why Misty transferred out? It doesn't make any sense if that's all that happened."

*What you want to bet I just heard the sanitized Reader's Digest version of the whole affair.*

"All I know about. They were so upset, they never confided in me. All I know is that they were doubly pissed. And it did scare the crap out of them. Guess they weren't used to low-life dives like I was. And I guess they'd never seen anyone get killed before. Plus, I think I heard them say that they didn't do as well on the ACT as they wanted to and blamed me for it."

Willard glanced back over his shoulder. Al's bodyguard was still standing there, but now he was using his cell phone. Willard once again looked uncomfortable and told Will he better go and find his wife before she spent him dry. Before Will could offer to accompany him, Willard pushed back his chair and got up. As he exited, Al's bodyguard left walking in the same direction as well.

*That's all that happened on 'oh, what a night'? Oh, come on now! Surely, that can't be the whole story. And Dickie-do was still rehashing it forty years later?*

*Questions. Questions. Why do I keep having questions?*

*Why did Al's bodyguard's presence seem to upset Willard so much? Did Al have Willard mugged to try to scare him into a deal on his plantation?*

*And did this shit start Misty's long-term depression problems? Boy, that seems to be an overreaction unless she had problems anyway. But I guess that could have been.*

*And Dickie-do, knowing what a sensitive topic it was, rubbing it in after all these years in front of God and the whole class? If that's the case, he was one sadistic, sick bastard. No wonder none of his marriages worked out. I never liked him or thought he was as funny as he thought he was anyway. And now since he's dead, apparently, I'm not the only one who wasn't entertained by his shenanigans and showing his ass. I wouldn't have minded popping a knot on his head myself. Fucking insensitive asshole!*

# CHAPTER 42

“I guess you could say it’s now or never. I feel like I must’ve repeated our break-in story to half the ship so far. Now if we don’t get a second break-in, I guess we can call it a day on getting to the bottom of our snake-in. You know. LSMFT.”

“Huh.”

Yeah. Lotsa snakes mean freaky times.”

‘Will, that acronym is a new low even for you.”

“They can’t all be wieners.”

“That’s a fact. My hot diggity dogger. And if you sing ‘do what you do to me,’ I going to bop your ears.”

“So, now we’re getting erotic. My wiener’s into that. And so are his friends, Harry and Sack.”

“Later, gator. We’ve got more important things to do right now. We’ve got a big evening ahead of us.”

“I’m glad you’re the one making an appearance in the disco with the Petersons while I stay here since we don’t know who may be coming. I’d hate to think you were trapped here alone with a big brute like Al’s bodyguard.”

“If that’s who it is ... assuming we have a visitor at all ... But I hate to pop your bubble, my darling, ... but, honeychild, if that’s who it is, you’re out of your league as well. And that piece of cardboard you printed ‘surprise’ on, would probably just provoke him into a lethal orbit.”

“Still, if that’s going to be the case, I’d rather his tirade be against me rather  than you. Have I told you lately that I love you?”

“Not recently.”

“Then remind me, and I’ll tell you sometime.”

Betsy smiled and gave him a kiss.

After Betsy left with Dick and Beth, Will positioned himself on their patio with his Smartphone. He tested the curtains to make sure they were open just enough for him to see yet closed enough to hide his presence. He left the sliding door ajar with the TV running to test how well he would be able to hear through it and took a couple of test pictures of the room with the lighting dimmed. He took the SURPRISE message he had Magic Markered on a piece of shirt cardboard and put it faceup under some magazines in his bedside table.

*Surprise! Surprise! Surprise! Might as well let them find something so I can watch their reaction.*

When he was satisfied, he pulled up a deck chair up behind the slider and waited.

About a half hour later, the stateroom door opened. A head peeked in and looked around.

*Suzzie Cobb. Well, I'll be damned.*

Suzzie carefully closed the door, leaving it slightly ajar. Will began to snap pictures with his Smartphone. Suzzie looked around and then silently padded over to the bedside table on Betsy's side. She leaned her walking stick against the bed, and began to rifle through the drawer, finding nothing of interest. She then retrieved her cane, hobbled around the foot of the bed, and began to search the bedside table nearest to Will until she got to Will's piece of shirt cardboard. Will kept snapping pictures. Suzzie held it up and momentarily stared at it quizzically. Then it seemed to hit her that the Blacks had expected a visitor. As she tried to shove the cardboard back into the nightstand, Will almost spoke, but then he saw a shadow move behind Suzzie.

Suzzie couldn't see behind her, but Betsy had returned and was silently letting herself back into the room through the door Suzzie had mistakenly left ajar. Betsy held her vertical index finger up to her mouth. Will waited until Betsy was in the room before he spoke.

"Finding anything interesting?"

Suzzie looked to see where the voice was coming from as Will opened the slider and walked in. He was purposely holding the Smartphone out in front of him so Suzzie could see it. Suzzie tried to snatch it out of Will's hand, but he jerked it back out of her reach. Suzzie picked up her walking stick to go after Will with a roundhouse swing, but the swing stopped in midair. Betsy caught the stick from behind and snatched it out of her hands while simultaneously pushing Suzzie onto the bed face first mashing her face into the bedspread. Betsy threw the stick for Will to catch.

"Oh, no you don't, bitch. I'm the only one entitled to hit my husband."

Suzzie looked up, and it registered for the first time that she and Will were not alone in the room. A shocked expression spread across her face as she realized she had been trapped.

"Let me go," Suzzie gasped.

"Only after we've had a talk. I don't know who I expected tonight, but I'll have to say you weren't at the top of my list," Will replied.

"What do you want?"

"Uh, uh. I'm going to be asking the questions and you're going to be answering them. And if I don't like what I hear, you're going to have major problems."

"Fuck you."

"Sorry, only my wife gets that privilege. And let's get one thing straight from the get-go. I don't want to hear any abbreviated lies. And before you start, let me tell you right now that we know about happenings after the Corinth game and also about Billy's association with Adolfo Soltero."

"Who told you about the rape?"

Will and Betsy looked at each other with shocked looks.

*Rape? Holy shit! So Jimbo didn't tell me the whole story! My gut was right!*

"I'd rather not say, but suffice it to say, we do know all about it. And before we let you leave this room, we're going to hear it again from your perspective. And don't leave anything out. I'll be recording what you say. And don't think I won't know if you're not being forthright," Will bluffed even though he didn't have a recorder.

Suzzie started shaking.

"Betsy, get Suzzie a chair."

"Will, please tell me. How'd you find out?"

"As I just stated, I'd rather not say. But go on. We want to hear the entire story from the beginning."

"Oh, OK. If ... I have to."

"You have to."

"After the boys won the championship in Corinth, Coach Beech was going to reward the team by letting them spend the night instead of having to make that long drive back. Some of the team's backers had agreed to pay for the motel rooms and meals. Some of us though needed to get back, however for the ACT exam the next day – there were also some people who had weekend jobs -- and since Willard had his daddy's Buick station wagon up there, we decided to hitch back with him."

'Define we."

"Oh, Willard, Paul, Jerry, Dickie-do, Rusty, Jimbo, Tom, and Misty and me."

"That agrees with what we've already been told. Go on. I'll let you know if I think you're not being truthful."

"Well, Willard was driving. But instead of heading back to Greenville, he detoured in the wrong direction and we ended up in some Selmer Tennessee honkytonk."

"I know. Called Junior's," Will said to make Suzzie believe that he'd heard the story before. The disclosure had its desired effect.

"They insisted we go in and dance with them while they drank a few beers. A bar fight broke out on the dancefloor and a drunk got killed so we left. They bought some more beer at a gas station. Dickie-do and Paul tried to make out with us in the back of the car. When Dickie-do refused to leave us alone, I elbowed him in the balls as hard as I could. Misty scratched Paul's face with her fingernails. This didn't help things. It just pissed them off and made matters worse.

"They accused us of thinking we were too good for them and said they'd show us. We were really starting to get scared. Dickie-do ordered Willard to pull down this dirt road and stop. By that time, he was completely out of control."

"You poor things," Betsy commented.

"Paul and Dickie-do dragged us out of the car and told the others to hold us down while he and Paul showed us 'what happens to snotty bitches.' They held us down and ripped off our panties and raped us. Then they told the others that they weren't men but fags if they didn't each take a turn with us as well."

"So, you got gang-raped?" Betsy gasped. "Did they all do it to you?"

"Not everybody. Tom and Jimbo didn't screw us, but the bastards didn't help us either. They just let it happen."

"So, why'd you let them get away with it? You could have sent them all to prison."

"Because they said if we ever told anyone they'd spread the word that we were the class sluts and that the whole thing was consensual as our way to reward them for winning the championship. And since my dad worked for one of Willard's father's businesses, that he'd get daddy fired. Jerry said that since his dad was chief of police and that all their dads were Masons that he'd see that our families were run out of town. I guess you do remember that Willard's dad and Jerry's dad teamed up to get him out of a drunk driving charge where the other person got hurt real bad."

Will got up and began to pace the room as he ran his fingers through his hair.

"A date-rape gang-bang? So that's why you two quit the cheerleader squad."

"That was only part of the reason."

"There's more?" Will said, momentarily forgetting that he was supposed to be already familiar with Suzzie's story. She had become so worked up and close to hyperventilating by then that she didn't notice his faux pax.

"By Christmas, we strongly suspected that Misty was pregnant, and of course, we had no idea which one of our rapists impregnated her. One thing for certain was that she had no desire to try to find out and then force him to him marry her."

"How horrible. I'm not sure they had the technology in those days to nail down the culprit anyway," Betsy added. "Plus, the social stigma for girls in those days was awful."

"Misty was determined keep the whole thing from her parents," Suzzie continued, "but I confronted Willard since he had more money than any of the rest. We decided that the best way to keep it quiet was for her to insist that her parents allow her to transfer back to Riverside School for second semester."

"So, what about the baby?" Will asked.

"There was a colored woman who lived on Willard's daddy's plantation. She acted kind of like a nurse or pseudo doctor to the coloreds who couldn't afford to go to a real doctor. She aborted the child."

"And so, that's why she was able then to come back to GHS for her senior year."

"But there was still another problem. Misty ended up sterile after the abortion. That's when her depression issue began. I've blamed myself for years. If I hadn't gone to Willard and helped arrange the abortion, none of this might not have happened to Misty."

"Suzzie, let me say this one woman to another. You can't blame yourself. You did what you thought was right. And that eventually led to her suicide? I assume Danny knows all this," Betsy asked.

Suzzie nodded but otherwise said nothing.

"Is your bad leg the result of the rape?"

She nodded again and finally said, "that's another reason cheerleading was out. My hip was permanently damaged."

"What horrible stories. Those sorts of things shouldn't happen to anyone. Now I can understand why you and Danny are bitter to this day, and I understand your common bond. But now I'm going to ask you a delicate question, and your truthfulness will determine what I do with what I've learned so far. Did you or Danny have anything to do with Dickie-do's death?"

Suzzie looked down, wrung her hands, but didn't respond.

"Well?"

"As bad as I hated Dickie-do and the rest of those players, I couldn't kill anyone. I'm just not like that. I can't speak for Danny, but I don't think he could do it either."

"Look me in the eye and repeat that. What about some of the other things on this ship that have been happening?"

"I ... uh ... OK ... I ... I'll admit ... I was involved in the dirty tricks on Paul ... and Jerry ..."

"And Rusty?'

She shook her head.

"Willard?"

She shook her head again.

"What about Tom?"

Suzzie nodded and finally said, "They deserved it. As you know, I'm a network engineer. I was able to hack into Paul and Jerry's computers and frame them. ... And I did drop that gold pendant in Tom's bag and then report him for stealing. I'm not sorry one little bit. I hope both of them get convicted and sentenced at last for the part they played in what happened to Misty and me. It should have happened a long time ago. Please don't turn me in. Does it matter what they get punished for as long as justice is finally served? You can't tell me they deserve to get off scot-free for what they did. ... Especially to Misty. They might as well have put a gun to her head."

"I've got to give this matter some thought," Will said and glanced over at Betsy. He thought he could see in her eyes sympathy for Suzzie's vigilante actions.

'Suzzie, you've clarified Paul, Jerry, and Tom, but the other situations still bother me, especially Dickie-do. After all, he's dead. Does Billy know what you just told us?"

"He knows about the past, but he doesn't know all the names. I never told him that Jimbo was there because they were such good friends and have mutual clients to this day. Also, Jimbo wasn't a rapist. He just helped hold us down while the others mauled us. And to answer your question, Billy also doesn't know about my recent attempts at retribution."

"Have you been in this cabin before today?"

She shook her head.

"Then I don't understand why you broke into it tonight. Why'd you do that?"

"Because I thought Billy had possibly been here and left something behind that would get him in trouble. You know, he already has trouble with the bar association, and if he got involved in a breaking and entering charge, he would lose his license to practice once and for all. And if he did, the scandal would be too much for him to take. Can't you see? That would finish him off. He'd drink himself to death for sure then. Will, he's my husband. The father of my children. I couldn't risk that happening.'

"How'd you get in our room?"

"Danny's a locksmith. I got him to teach me what I needed to know, but I didn't tell him what I planned to do with the knowledge. ... Or who to. ... I swear. ... He probably thought I would use the break-in knowledge to get even with some of the other creeps. He didn't ask since he hates them as much as I do."

"I empathize with you more than you'll ever know. You were wronged. But my dilemma is, do two wrongs make a right. Before I decide that, I want to know more about Billy's association with Soltero and what Soltero might be holding over his head so I can make sure I have the whole picture. I talked to Billy, but  I think he's been holding back on me regarding Jimbo and Willard. Maybe now I can get him to fill in the blanks. And, yes, I know from experience that Al can be a pretty callous guy ... and he works for some pretty scary people."

Once again Suzzie said nothing.

"Where's Billy right now? At the disco?"

"No. I don't think so. When I left our room, he was sleeping it off in our cabin. He's been drinking all afternoon."

"Is that why Billy fell down the stairs that night, or did someone push him?"

"He didn't need any help, or maybe I should say he did need help. He was drunker than anyone thought that night. That's why I left when I did. He was disgusting me, and there was nothing I could do to get him to stop drinking. I'm pretty sure he fell down those steps all by himself. He fell again later in our room. It's a miracle he didn't really injure himself."

"You know how the old saying goes. The good lord looks after drunks and fools ... and children."

"That's my husband – a drunken fool who never grew up."

"Better hope he's sobered up tonight because we're all going to go back to your cabin right now. I want to ask Billy some questions, and if he's as honest as I think you've been with me, it'll help me to decide on what I do next. And maybe I can help him handle Al. I want to talk to him before he can debrief you. Will you go along with me on this? I think Betsy and I are on your side more than you can imagine. You've just got to give some good reasons to be."

Suzzie gave a resigned nod. She knew she had no choice.

# CHAPTER 43

"What deck is your stateroom on?" Betsy asked Suzzie. "You think Billy's still there?"

"The Caribe deck. C-502. Was when I left."

Betsy, Will, and Suzzie headed for the elevator and took it down to Caribe. When they got to the room, Suzzie put her key card in the lock and pushed open her door. Instead of opening all the way, the door bumped into an object on the dark floor.

Suzzie called out, "Billy, are you decent? I've got company with me."

There was no answer.

Will reached in and groped for the light switch. He found it and turned on the lights. Billy was lying on the floor face down in his underwear with his feet towards the door. Will pushed again, but Billy didn't budge. He assumed Billy had passed out there from drinking. He shoved on the door a second time, but Billy still didn't budge.

"Billy's on the floor. I think he's unconscious," Will called out. "Betsy, you're thinner than I am. See if you can squeeze in and move him over enough for me to get the door open all the way."

"Oh, my God," Suzzie uttered. "Is he hurt?"

Betsy managed to squeeze into the room and bend Billy's legs up enough for Will to finish opening the door, and then they all went in. Will kneeled down and shook Billy. He got no response. Then he turned Billy over. When he did, he saw an empty CVS isopropyl alcohol bottle next to him and noticed for the first time that Billy's skin looked blue-tinged.

Will held the bottle up for Suzzie and Betsy to see and said, "I think he may have alcohol poisoning."

"Oh, my God," Suzzie uttered for the second time. She immediately kneeled down next to Will and elbowed him aside. She interlocked her fingers and began to administer CPR by pumping rapidly on Billy's chest. She got no response. She opened his mouth and began to blow rescue breaths into him. Still nothing. By this time, Will had grabbed Billy's arm and began to see if he could feel a pulse.

"I don't feel anything. Betsy, call the room steward and tell him to get the ship's doctor up here asap. Tell 'em we have an emergency."

"What room is this again?"

"C-502," Suzzie gasped between breaths as she continued to try to administer CPR.

When a young Philippine doctor arrived, he probed Billy for vital signs and found none.

"I'm afraid we're too late," he finally said. "This man is dead. What happened?"

At this point, Suzzie collapsed and began to wail. Betsy reached out to comfort her, but Suzzie pushed her away. Will picked up the isopropyl alcohol bottle and presented it to the doctor.

"I think this might be the culprit."

The doctor felt Billy's temperature mumbled something about cardiac arrest.

"Does this belong to any of you?" the doctor asked Suzzie.

She nodded her assent.

The doctor immediately went to the stateroom phone and called for help. A stretcher arrived and they removed the body. The room steward stood silently in the background waiting for further instructions from the doctor. Will looked around the room for the first time and saw bloody vomit. The smell almost made him gag. He pointed this out to the doctor. The doctor told the steward to start cleaning it up.

Will got out the room's desk chair and led Suzzie over and sat her down on it. She continued to cry nonstop. Betsy whispered to Will not to try to talk to Suzzie but to let her cry herself out. When that finally happened, she quietly asked Suzzie, "Do you want us to stay here with you for the rest of the night?"

"I'm not spending the night in this room," Suzzie said.

"Then come to our stateroom."

"No. I want to be with Danny. He's a few rooms down on this deck C-509."

Will noted Danny's stateroom number and went down the hall to knock on his door. He left Suzzie's door ajar so he could get back in.

"Who's there? Go away," a grumpy Danny yelled out when Will rapped on his door.

"Danny. It's Will Black. We have an emergency with Suzzie. We need you right now."

After a short delay, Danny opened his door. It was obvious he had been asleep.

"Billy's dead. You need to come and support Suzzie. She asked me to come get you."

Danny was standing in his doorway in his underwear. Without changing or looking to see if anyone else was in the hall, he ran down it and burst into Suzzie's room. She jumped up, ran over, and began crying uncontrollably on Danny's shoulder. Once things seemed to be under control, Will and Betsy excused themselves and left Suzzie and Danny to be alone.

"If either of you need us, call us. Suzzie has our room number. I don't care what time it is, call," Betsy said as they left. "Suzzie, I know this is meaningless to you right now, but Will and I are so sorry. I wish we could have prevented it."

As they walked back to their stateroom, Will told Betsy, "So much for questioning Billy about Soltero. Do you think he or his bodyguard could have been involved with Billy's death, or do you think Billy's a victim of his own alcoholism?"

"At this point, I really don't know, and I'm too emotionally drained to think about it. It's probably a tossup as to which option could be the answer to your question."

# CHAPTER 44

Both Will and Betsy slept fitfully that night. While Suzzie Cobb's confession clarified some matters, Billy death raised new unanswered questions. And they still had no clue as to who had tried to kill them with a poisonous snake or why. Plus, now that Billy was dead, he wouldn't be able to shed any light on how or if Adolfo Soltero fit into all the misevents that had occurred on Will's reunion cruise. To top it off, all the bad cards Suzzie had drawn in her lifetime made them feel terrible and remorseful even though they were blameless. This misplaced guilt made them even more determined than ever to unravel this whole sordid mess.

Exhaustion finally prevailed sometime before dawn, and both Will and Betsy slept until midmorning. When they finally arose and while they were still in the privacy of their stateroom, Will aired his doubts with Betsy.

"I don't know what to do about Suzzie's confessions. I'm not accustomed to having to be both judge and jury."

"That makes two of us. How can we be sure we finally know all there is to know about what happened on that football trip so long ago?"

"There's probably still more. My gut tells me though that she was telling us the truth."

"But we don't know that."

"No, we don't, my dear, but can you ever be one hundred percent certain about anything?"

"I'm a hundred percent certain about you."

"But you weren't when that crazy cashier stalker who worked for me tried to convince you that she and I were having an affair."

"You're right, but should I remind you that I wasn't dealing with all the facts since you weren't being totally forthright with me?"

"I admit that I wasn't, but on the other hand, it appeared to me that you were acting irrationally because of that nutty cousin of yours."

"And I guess I was. Can you forgive me?"

"As far as I was concerned, there's nothing to forgive. We all have lapses in judgement from time to time."

"We both did, my darling. If you were perfect all the time, you wouldn't be human. I love you so much."

"Since you just reminded me that I haven't told you to remind me that I love you recently, that time is now. Out of all the women in the whole wide world, thank God that you were the one he chose to send for me to love and spend my life with. But back to Suzzie ..."

"Let's sit on it until we're sure. That girl has drawn some bad hands. She lost both her best friend and now her husband. And who knows what kind of cloud she might have to live under if some of Al's shenanigans with Billy become public knowledge."

"Not only bad hands but a bad leg as well since she said that's where her limp came from."

From that point both Will and Betsy were silent, each caught up in their own thoughts. The silence was broken by the ringing phone. Will answered it.

"Will? Jimbo. I hope I'm not interrupting anything, but I heard Billy's dead. Is it true?"

"I'm afraid so."

"What happened?"

"I'd rather not discuss it over the phone. Why don't you come by our stateroom, and then I'll tell you what we know."

"When?"

"Give me five minutes, so Betsy and I can put some clothes on. It's B-443 on the Baja deck. That's forward not aft."

"Heading your way."

Will hung up the phone.

"Let's get dressed. Jimbo's on his way up here. Maybe I haven't exhausted my last option in finding out how Soltero and Willard fit into this whole picture after all. I'm sure Jimbo probably knows pretty much as much as Billy did about all this since as Willard's lawyer and Billy's best friend, he was involved in introducing Willard to Al in the first place. I'm not going to let him off as easy as I did the last time. This time I'm going to put the squeeze on him to try to get the whole truth. And if you don't mind, let me put the hammer on him, and you just listen."

"Sure, my dear. Anything you want."

Ten minutes later, there was a knock on the door. Will let Jimbo into the room. Jimbo didn't waste time on small talk and got right down to business.

"So, tell me what happened. Were you there?"

"Betsy and I both were. We had accompanied Suzzie back to her cabin after we had had a discussion with her here. Billy was on the floor facedown when we got there. At first we thought he was just passed out drunk. Suzzie had told us that he had been hitting the bottle pretty heavy yesterday afternoon."

Jimbo sighed and said, "Billy and his bottle. He should have been in rehab or AA a long time ago."

"We couldn't stir him. Suzzie tried CPR, but it turns out he wasn't dead drunk but dead period. There was an empty bottle of rubbing alcohol on the carpet next to him. Betsy called the room steward and told him we needed the ship's doctor immediately. He pronounced Billy dead when he got there. That's about all there is to tell."

"So, Billy drank himself to death on rubbing alcohol? He was worse off than I thought."

"That's what it was made to appear, but anytime someone comes to a bad end who has had dealings with Al Soltero, I have to ask myself was Al somehow involved."

"Surely not. Billy was a sot."

"I've dealt will Al on too many occasions not to have my suspicions. That's one reason I didn't want to discuss this matter with you on the phone. Suzzie filled us in on and clarified a lot of things when she was down here yesterday. I tried talking to you once before about Billy's and Willard's involvement with Al, and you blew me off with your lawyer confidentiality crap.

"Now that Billy's dead, I expect you to fill in the blanks before you leave this stateroom. And I'm going to tell you right now, just like I told Suzzie, if you don't, I will go out of my way to make your life a living hell ... and do it in public. There's too much shit going down on this ship for it to all be coincidences. And don't forget, you yourself have been hurt in a mysterious accident, and Willard's been through two of them. The next time out neither of one of you might not get off so easy. You might end up dead like Billy. Don't forget. I know Al and his tactics extremely well."

Jimbo ran his open hand down his face and shook his head back and forth.

"I told you everything there was to tell."

"Wrong answer. I mentioned the fact that Suzzie clarified some things. One thing she described in graphic detail was the story about the rape scene after our junior year Corinth game. And ... she was very specific about the names of the people present and their roles in the assault. And ... I have the whole conversation recorded. Now, are you still sure that you don't have some disclosures to share with me a well. I'd hate for the wrong person or persons to hear what she had to say and have them draw their own conclusions."

Sweat broke out on Jimbo's brow, and his lips quivered. Will and Betsy remained silent, waiting for him to be the first to speak.

"I didn't assault either Misty or Suzzie that night."

"I didn't say you did, but according to Suzzie, you didn't do anything to stop it either."

"There wasn't much I could do. Things were too out of control. Did Suzzie tell you if she had told Billy about me being there?"

"She said she protected you since she didn't want to rupture y'all's friendship."

"I've done her some favors since then to try to make things up."

"They would have to be awfully big favors to make up for what y'all did to Misty and her that night."

"Believe me. They were. I guess I should thank her for her discretion. Billy never would have forgiven me. Though I guess it doesn't make much difference now since Billy's dead."

"I wondered why she seemed so uncomfortable about being around you that day the four of us were up on the deck together. Now, after what she told me, I'm beginning to understand."

"Yeah. Things were complicated."

Jimbo got up and walked over to the sliding glass door leading to Will and Betsy's outside deck. He stared silently at the sea. Finally, he spoke in a low, hesitant voice.

"I don't know where to begin telling you about Soltero."

"How about the beginning with Willard's airplane loans."

"OK, Will. You win. I guess you know Billy couldn't get in Ole Miss's law school because he had lousy grades and a low score on his LSAT. So, he went to Nova in Lauderdale. Pretty much anyone can get in there. It was when he was in south Florida that he first met Al. Billy's mama was a Florida Hispanic. Al used Billy as a mule to carry cocaine back and forth to Mississippi when Billy went to visit Suzzie or his folks. Billy could use the dough, and this was easy money. When Billy got out of school he came back to Greenville because Suzzie didn't want to live in Florida. That's when he and I tried to start a practice together, but it never really took off."

"But Willard was one of your clients."

"Right. He was our old teammate ... and friend. Plus, we figured he'd be an important client one day when he came into his inheritance. It was no secret that his dad was loaded."

"So far you haven't told me anything I don't already know or that Suzzie hasn't already filled me in on."

"Hey. You said you wanted the whole story and that's what I'm trying to give you. Now, do you want to hear it all or not?"

"I'm sorry to interrupt. Go ahead."

"Then the shit hit the fan with Willard's folks over Zelma. They didn't think she was good enough for either him or them. But Willard was determined to get his way, if for no other reason just to spite them and for once win. He never took his old man's threats to disinherit him seriously since he was an only child. But the more his dad badmouthed Zelma, the more Willard was determined to have his way, so he married her. I don't know if he really loved her or not, but he was determined to show his dad. Actually, I think part of it was that Zelma hoodwinked him into thinking she was pregnant when she wasn't."

"So, that's when he tried to start the flying service?"

"Right, but he didn't have any money. Do you know what a new Ag Cat costs? Even in those days, you're talking right at a million dollars. But it's only basically good for crop dusting. He needed the Cessna for other types of jobs. Now were talking another couple of hundred grand. So, Billy got Al to lend Willard the money, but Willard wasn't making enough money to pay Al back and still have enough money for him and Zelma to live off of."

"So, let me guess. Al made Willard start running drugs for him."

"Right, and other things as well like illegals."

"So, did Willard ever get Al paid off?"

"To tell you the truth, I really don't know. Willard was never a genius when it came to managing money. As you know, he did eventually inherit the plantation, and he did have ongoing money needs – like crop loans and he never seemed to put enough aside to pay his taxes."

"I heard a rumor to that effect. That he has had IRS miseries."

"Willard didn't file a tax return for five years. The service was on his ass like stink on shit."

"So, Al came back into his life."

"And stayed there."

"So, is Willard smuggling things for Al still?"

"I'm sure he is, but with a few losing crop years and his IRS problems, he just kept digging the hole with Soltero deeper and deeper. So Soltero came up with a solution."

"Which was?"

"He'd buy Willard out at a price of his choosing."

"And did Willard agree to do it?"

"That's when the trouble began. Willard turned Al down."

"And how do you fit into this whole picture?"

"Billy and I were supposed to talk Willard into it."

"I take it that Al has kept his tentacles in Billy all along."

"Oh, yeah. He got Billy the job in Tampa. And hell, he controls that law firm."

"And you? Does he have his hooks into you?"

"Unlike Billy, I don't owe Al anything. But Billy and I go way back. Al let me know if I didn't help Billy out that he would see that something really bad happened to him. I had to do whatever I could to keep that from happening. It wasn't fair to make Billy pay just because stupid Willard kept getting himself in fixes that he couldn't get himself out of. I guess you know that the stress of dealing with Al is one of the things that started Billy drinking. Since Al got him the job in Tampa, he's made Billy help him launder money and cover his trail with the Feds. Billy couldn't take the gravity of what Al kept asking him to do. And once Al had gotten his hooks in Billy ..."

"I'm very familiar with how Al does business. And I know how his requests are more than requests, but let's get back to Willard. So, that's what the meeting in Cartagena were all about? Al trying to force Willard off his place. And all the powwows you three have been having on the ship? Same thing?"

"Yes."

"And that's why Willard got mugged? To let him know how serious Al was? And the poisoned fruit? Another reminder from Al?"

"Probably, but I don't know that for sure. I guess you know that Al controls some members of the ship's crew. He most likely had one of them deliver the fruit basket to Willard's room."

*And maybe a poisonous snake to our room as well. But why us? I still don't understand.*

Betsy's look told him she was thinking the same thing.

"And your accident?"

"Al's bodyguard tripped me."

"And you've kept this to yourself?"

"He told me the first time was just a warning."

"Was Dickie-do part of all this?"

"Not to my knowledge. Dickie-do might have just imply ODed. I don't think we'll probably ever know for sure, but it's possible Paul may have had something to do with him. I guess you know that Paul's girlfriend was arrested once as a pusher, and she and Dickie-do at one time had dated. And Dickie-do had been hitting on Michelle from day one on the boat, and I'm pretty sure Paul was blind with rage. You know how he can get. Do you remember Tillie's Lounge?

"Of course. Out on the highway. Some of the toughest of the tough used to drink there. And more than one of them died there. I never had the guts to go in."

"That's the place. Paul almost killed a towboater there who was trying to screw over Michelle on a drug deal. Hit him in the head with a piece of pipe in the parking lot. Paul could be a very violent person if someone crossed him. Especially if Michelle was involved. He might've just hit the breaking point because he'd had enough of Dickie-do's flirting."

"I thought they were big buddies."

"Buddies don't hit on other buddies' ladies and stay buddies."

"I guess you have a point."

"And what light can you shed on Rusty getting a razor blade in his shoe?"

"That one I can't help you with. But you do now know that the inspiration for Rusty's bestseller 'The Rape' came from what happened that night in Corinth. And it made him a celebrity since it was not only a bestselling book but since it got also made into a movie. Rusty's been holding court all over the ship bragging about all his contacts in Hollywood and how much money it's all made for him. Plus, he's teaching classes about his book aboard the ship as if he's a goddamned celebrity.

"I'm sure you've seen people fawn all over him asking him to autograph books and take pictures with them. It really rubbed Danny the wrong way. He showed up at one of Rusty's signings, bought a book, and the tore it up in front of everybody there. He told people attending that they shouldn't buy books written by a criminal and them stomped off in a huff. I'm sure that other than Rusty I was the only person there who knew what Danny was referring to.

"And don't forget after all, Danny is a locksmith and could've gotten in Rusty's cabin whenever he wanted to."

"I get the drift. You've made some good points. I never would have connected the dots before Suzzie told us what she did."

"So, what are you going to do now? I guess you know that you could endanger both me and Suzzie if Al felt it necessary to shut us up to protect himself. And if that happened, you'd open up a whole new can of worms."

"Actually, I might be able to use what I now know to get Al off of both of y'all's backs once and for all."

"How's that?"

"A plan of action is forming in my head. For the moment, I'm just going to let it stay there. If it works, I'll tell both of you about it then. I promise. But before I do anything, I need to make sure I understand exactly what I'm dealing with. You made two statements that still need clarifying. One, you said you have done some things for Suzzie to try to make up for that night. And two, you said I could open some new cans of worms."

"I'm not so sure I should go behind Danny and Suzzie's backs without their permission and ..."

"Do you want to resolve matters with Al, or do you want to have his axe hanging over your head forever like it was with Billy?"

Jimbo began to pace and run his fingers nervously through his hair. He exhaled loudly as he debated what he should do next. Finally, he spoke hesitantly.

"I – I -- I -- guess you've left me no choice. Uh. Those two statements are related. There's still another person involved, and if something happened to her, I don't think I could live with myself."

He continued to rub his fingers through his hair and look at the floor. He finally spoke.

"Misty's alive and dependent on Suzzie, Danny, and me."

Will and Betsy gave each other a shocked look. Betsy, who had been trying to only be an observer and let Will conduct Jimbo's interrogation, finally spoke up.

"Alive! That can't be."

"I'm afraid so. You see, her last suicide attempt was unsuccessful, but it left her permanently brain damaged. I guess I wasn't being totally honest when I said Al doesn't have his fingernails in my hide. In return for favors, Al got Misty a complete set on new IDs, and she is sequestered in an asylum in Costa Rica that owes Al favors. That's one place he took Suzzie and Danny the day our ship was there. That's why Danny hasn't been able to move on with his life. His wife is still alive."

"But she was reported dead. Did Al get a fake death certificate too?"

"He didn't have to. She was never officially reported as dead. We just simply told people she was. She didn't have any family still alive so there were no complications on that front. When people asked Danny about a funeral, he just told them it had already happened, or that he'd decided against a service. He told them that she wanted to be cremated so he'd honored her wishes. You know he doesn't have a whole lot of close friends – in fact, Suzzie is probably about as close as anyone is to him – so everyone took what he said at face value. He never ran an obituary."

"So, how'd you get Misty to Costa Rica?"

"Oh, that was easy. Willard flew her there at Al's request."

"Good old Al has a way of requesting things. So, is Al paying to keep her there?"

"No. Danny, Billy, Suzzie and I share the cost. It's pretty reasonable since she's in a third world country. But if something happened to Suzzie and me now that would leave Danny to have to pay the freight all by himself, and I'm not sure how well he could afford it."

"Was Al using this as leverage in the Willard transaction?"

"Oh, yeah. He told Billy and me that if we didn't get Willard to sell to him, that he couldn't guarantee Misty's future. That was one reason Billy was staying drunk every day. You might say he was drowning his conscience. Now that Billy's gone, that just leaves the other three of us to keep a lid on Misty and pay her bills."

"You're probably guilty of kidnapping," Betsy uttered.

"I'm sure we are," Jimbo agreed, "but our motive was good."

"So, let's get back to Billy. Do you think Al had him killed to get your attention and force you to push on Willard harder?"

"Your guess is as good as mine, but I think there's a better than even chance Billy did it to himself. He just couldn't live with himself anymore. And Al was going to continue to make him an accomplice to his money laundering and tax evasion efforts."

"Until Billy lost his license," Will said, "which apparently was in danger of becoming a reality."

"And if that happened, Al wouldn't give shit. He'd view it as just a short-term setback, he'd just find a new gopher. Maybe me."

You've given us a lot to think about. Let me ask you another question. Suzzie never told Billy about your involvement that night. Did Misty tell Danny, or did she keep you out of it with him as well?"

"I honestly don't know. I don't know if Danny secretly hates me but feels like he has to maintain a cordial relationship due to the circumstances. As you know, he's a really strange introvert who seems to have a permanent mad-on with the whole world. I don't think anyone knows what goes on inside his head."

"Anything else you've forgotten to tell me?"

"Can't think of anything. I think you know it all now."

"Then I'm going to take the facts I have and run with them. I'll be back to you."

"Please, don't dump me in the creek with Soltero."

"Actually, I hope to finally drain that swamp once and for all and rid it of gators. Thanks for coming clean with me, Jimbo. Now I understand your reluctance to do so before now. And don't worry. I do have a plan. When I'm through with Señor Soltero, he going to think long and hard before he messes with any of you again going forward. Al is a pro when it comes to evaluating risk versus reward. It's one of his talents that's kept him alive all these years."

# CHAPTER 45

"So, do you really have a plan, Stan?" Betsy commented to Will when they were alone. "Or were you bluffing with Jimbo?"

"I may bluff on some things like having our conversation with Suzzie recorded, but there's some things I don't bluff about. Al Soltero and his associates are too dangerous for me to put my classmates in jeopardy unnecessarily by giving them a false sense of security."

"So, did you plan on sharing your plan with me or were you going to leave me dangling like you did with Jimbo like a joke with no punchline?"

"Would I do that? The analogy I had in mind was leaving you hanging like a severed limb."

"Oh, gross. Only you would think of that."

"Actually, the person I plan on bluffing is Al."

"You're not serious. Oh, bullshit artist, thou art my husband. Or should I say the bluff-shit artist? Explain."

"I'm dead serious. I'm going to make Al think that I have access to incriminating information on his affairs that will be made public if anything happens Jimbo, Suzzie, or Willard."

"That's brilliant, I think. You do have a death wish," Betsy said sarcastically. "So, instead of going after them, he'll go after us instead. Just what I always wanted to do. Look over my shoulder for the rest of my life."

"I don't think we'll have to. Not the way I have it planned. Trust me. By the way, do you know the ultimate definition of trust?"

"I assume I'm about to find out."

"Two cannibals giving each other blowjobs."

"Oh, please. No more. I guess you know that I trust you about as much as I trust an atom. Both of you blow stuff up."

"Or how about stairs? They're always up to something."

"Uncle. You win. I give. So, how do you plan on getting an audience with Al?"

"Good question. I haven't figured out that part of the plan yet. But if you don't mind, I think I'd rather make it mano a mano."

"I know this is totally contrary to how you like to do things, but why don't you just be honest with him and say you want to tell him about what happened to Billy since Billy has represented him from time to time in legal matters."

"Brilliant. And when I married you, I thought you were just a pretty face on a hot bod. Speaking of hot bods, why don't we ...."

"Down, tiger. Save that thought for later. Right now, you need save your hot thoughts for Al while the news on Billy is still hot off the press."

"I think I'll call him right now."

"Good think. And please don't come across too heavy-handed with Al. As you know, politeness and subtlety are the name of the game in dealing with him."

"I'll put on my most charming face so I can outcharm the snake charmer."

"I'm not sure that's possible. No one oils his way around the floor like Señor Slick."

Will called Al's room, and his bodyguard picked up the phone. When Al came on the line, Will explained that Billy Cobb had had a fatal accident and that he wanted to fill Al in on it and ask his advice. They decided to meet on the aft portion of Deck 16 since few people used it.

When Will arrived, Al and his bodyguard were waiting and had positioned two chairs near the stern of the ship facing forward so each of them could easily detect any other passengers who might wander within earshot. The bodyguard positioned himself so that he would always be in Al's range of vision and also be able to watch the stairs to detect any newcomers.

After a few preliminary pleasantries, Will told Al about how they had found Billy dead the night before. Will did not mention his meeting with Suzzie beforehand. Al did not interrupt him with questions but instead politely listened and took in what Will related to him before offering his condolences. Will noticed that Al did not make the usual offers of being available to help the widow going forward.

When he was sure Will had told him the whole story, Al said, "You mentioned that you wanted my advice on another matter."

"Yes. I guess you know that Billy Cobb was a troubled individual, which I'm sure was part of his alcohol problem. He also was the subject of a bar association investigation."

"Do you know why he was being investigated, or how far along that investigation had gotten?"

"No to both questions. While he and I have known each other since we were kids, we were in completely different industries, and he was in Tampa while Betsy and I live four hundred miles away from there in Key West. Until this cruise, we hadn't been in contact with each other much more than being friends on Facebook.

"That's why I was so surprised when I got a flash drive from him. The cover letter accompanying it stated that it detailed many of his dealings of the last few years and that it would explain much of what he was being investigated about."

"Have you looked at it?"

"No. The letter told me to just keep it safe in case something ever happened to him, but it's true purpose was to protect his widow and his best friends, Jimbo Littleton and Willard McFarley since he would not be here to do it himself. It said for me to use my own judgement, but if I deemed it necessary, I was to turn it over to the law enforcement agency that I deemed most appropriate. It seemed almost like he was anticipating his own demise."

"Sounds that way. But why was he concerned about them? I do know who they are. I have met each of them on occasion. He wished to protect them from what?"

"I can't answer any of those questions. This whole matter is a mystery to me. This came out of the blue."

"If your relationship is a distant one at best, why would he entrust this to you?"

"I asked myself the same question. The only answer I could come up with was that he considered me to be trustworthy because I'm accustomed to acting as a fiduciary and that I have connections to the banking community because of Betsy."

"And you're sure you don't know what this is all about?"

"I'm telling you. I don't have a clue. But there's one more thing I haven't brought up."

"And that is?"

"The note said there are failsafe copies that have been sent to someone else with instructions that if any harm were to ever come to any of the people I just mentioned that *they* were supposed to turn one flash drive over to the bar association and the other one over to the FBI."

"Do you know who this someone is?"

"Didn't say so I guess it could be anyone. It's like he didn't have enough faith in any one person to trust them exclusively. I guess you could say that it was his plan B. Or maybe I was the one who was his plan B."

"Sounds like it could be either one. So, what's your question to me?"

"If you were in my shoes, what would you do with it? Should I turn this over to someone right now?"

"If you did, it seems to me you'd negate Mr. Cobb's real purpose that apparently is to protect these three people from some potential future peril. Did he specify what kind of peril he might be worried about?"

"It just said for me to use my judgement. I guess it could be anything that endangers them in any way – financially or otherwise. I assume this means I'm going to have to maintain a much closer relationship with all three of these people going forward than I have in the past. I feel it's almost like I've become their guardian. I suppose I need to talk to each one of them and tell them that Billy wanted me to be their mentor or unpaid trustee without telling them everything. I wouldn't want to cause them unnecessary worry. I'll tell them to call me if they feel like there's some matter that I should intervene in."

"That's a heavy responsibility."

"Best idea I could come up with. I don't mind telling you that I'm not very comfortable with this role, but since Billy's not here for me to discuss the whole affair with, I guess I'm stuck having to do what he requests."

# CHAPTER 46

Will got the Regency Rapper out of their stateroom mailbox and brought it in.

"We got a flyer along with the Rapper saying that there'll be a memorial in the ship's chapel this morning to honor Billy and Dickie-do."

"Planning to go?"

"I think we should. I'll call the Petersons and see if they want to go with us. It's at ten."

Dick and Beth said sure. Will and Betsy went by their stateroom, and the four of them went down to Deck 6 shortly before ten.

The chapel was a small room off of the ship's atrium. It was approximately a 20 by 25-foot room in the middle of the ship and had no windows. There was a portable nondenominational podium at the front. The chairs were all padded folding chairs. There was a closet at one end large enough to store the chairs when they weren't being used. It was obvious that it had been designed as a multi-purpose room.

People were slowly drifting into the room and finding a place to sit. Al Soltero and his bodyguard sat apart from the other guests by the righthand wall near the back. Will and Betsy made eye contact and nodded at him. Al smiled and nodded back.

Will whispered to his wife, "Notice when Al smiles. His eyes aren't smiling."

"According to a BBC documentary a few years back, there are nineteen different kinds of smiles but only six of them denote happiness."

"A comforting fact. Let's sit somewhere other than beside him."

They found four contiguous seats and waited for the service to begin. Will's class president, Jamie Kingston, stood by the entrance and greeted people as they arrived. At ten he closed the door and walked to the podium at the other end of the room. Tom came in with his acoustic guitar and pulled up a chair beside Jamie. Blowups of Dickie-do and Billy's senior yearbook pictures sat on two easels.

Will whispered to Betsy, "In case you've forgotten, Jamie is a preacher."

Jamie donned his ministerial smile and raised his arms to head level with his palms held outward to get everyone's attention.

"Welcome on this the last day of our reunion cruise. I wish it could have been a more joyous gathering. My friends and fellow classmates, we gather here today to remember the little things that made William Cobb and Richard Dunne have a special place in our hearts. To remember those happier times when we all laughed together as well as those time when our hearts broke as one."

At that moment the back door reopened. Danny Pearce stumbled in with a drink in each hand. He almost dropped one of them trying to close the door. He had obviously been imbibing all morning long. Jamie paused, waiting for Danny to manage it all and find a seat.

Danny gave up and mumbled, "Fuck it" as he stumbled to an empty chair.

People turned around and looked. Willard, who was sitting near the back, got up and closed the door again. When it seemed that Danny was settled, Jamie continued.

"For who can put a price on memories."

"They're priceless alright for a reason, because that's all they're worth," Danny muttered.

"We gather to share the pain. To unabashedly and unashamedly hurt without presuming our level of pain is the same for each of us."

"You don't know what fucking pain is," Danny said loudly enough for most people around him to hear.

"To cry when we cry and not try to hide or avoid our tears."

"What shiiit!"

"For tears are memories in motion."

Danny let out a big burp followed by a fart.

"We gather to give the gift of grief to our lost classmates and honor them for touching our lives while we are still here together."

"For Suzzie's sake I'll cry for Billy, but I just want to make sure that fuck-face Dickie-do is gone once and for all. Adios, mother-fucker."

More people were starting to turn and give Danny disapproving glances.

At this point, Tom jumped in hoping to defuse the situation and began to sing "Wind Beneath My Wings."

*Did you know that you're my hero.*

When he got to the line saying, "I can fly higher than an eagle," Danny broke in with "I'm flying higher than a steeple."

Al silently nodded at his bodyguard who rose to put a stop to Danny's mockeries. Suzzie rose at the same time to do the same.

"Danny noticed Suzzie for the first time and rose to try to stumble up to where she was sitting. He turned over his own chair in the process and tripped and fell into Al's bodyguard who connected with a hard jab to Danny's stomach. Danny let go with a torrent of vomit that hit the bodyguard in the face and spattered everyone else within range including Al. As his drinks went flying through the air showering still other people. Danny's drink glasses launched straight up and shattered when they came back down and hit the floor. Al's bodyguard efficiently produced a police baton from seemingly nowhere and whacked Danny's right hand, breaking his fingers.

Panicky people began to rise. Someone accidentally hit the light switch, leaving the room in total darkness. As Suzzie rushed towards Danny in the dark her walking stick caught in the empty chair next to her and turned it over directly into Valerie's path. As Valerie fell, she caught Michelle's tube top from behind, tearing it off. As she continued to fall, she blindly grabbed at Michelle's breasts. Michelle let out a shriek and then thinking that Jerry's common-law wife, Judy, was the culprit, grabbed Judy's hair and began pulling. When the lights came back on, the two were on the floor swinging and gouging at each other, Michelle's naked, tattooed breasts swinging wildly back and forth as the two fought, taking Amanda down in the process. Somehow Amanda ended up plopped ass down, on Zelma's face, breaking her nose. She screamed when Zelma bit down hard on her inner thigh.

Tom stopped playing, jumped up to try to intervene. In the process, he tripped over an easel leg and careened into the pictures of Dickie-do and Billy, grinding both under his feet as he struggled to get back up. As he tried to right himself, his guitar neck hit Jamie squarely in the balls. Jamie gasped, momentarily thinking Tom had hit him on purpose. He snatched the guitar away from Tom and screamed "Jesus H. Christ." He backhanded Tom with his Bible and swung the guitar like an axe. The guitar's head shattered as it came down on Tom's head. Tom was dazed and remained on the floor.

Danny continued his mad rush towards the front of the room trying to get to Suzzie, screaming profanities as he held his broken hand. He slipped on the broken glass and fell into Jimbo. The hot coffee Jimbo had left on his chair covered the front of Al's white linen suit. Al responded by pepper spraying everyone near him. He then backhanded Danny as hard as he could. Danny let go with a second torrent of vomit, covering the class gossips who had sat together as a group. Each in turn puked into each other's hairdos. This caused further chain reaction vomiting that sprayed both the Petersons and the Blacks. Al's bodyguard picked Danny up and slammed him into the wall. Suzzie saw this and turned to try to make her way back to where the now sober Danny was lying groaning, throwing chairs out of her way as she went.

Jamie tried to regain control of the meeting by beginning to sing "Amazing Grace."

He was met with people yelling things back at him like, "Oh, Jamie, shut up. Enough already" as they limped from the room.

Jamie finally said in a non-ministerial way, "Fuck you too. All of you. "

# CHAPTER 47

"Well, my dear, let's look around the cabin one more time and make sure we're not leaving anything behind. This is the last time we'll ever see it."

The cabin phone rang. It was Cee Cee Craig. Betsy answered it.

"Betsy? Oh, I'm glad I caught you before we all start going our separate ways and make sure you have both of our phone numbers and our mailing address. DV and I have enjoyed getting to know you two *so* much. I still can't believe you've lived in Discovery Bay. We definitely want you to come down and stay with us sometime. And I promise you less drama than we've had on this cruise."

"Thanks, Cee Cee. We may just take you up on that. We don't need much of an excuse to go to Jamaica. And if you remember, I told you about our good friends Henry and Rose Davis who live on the same hill as you do? I'm going to call Rose as soon as we get home and arrange for y'all to get together for rum punch or tea. And maybe she'll fix you some of her delicious solomon gundy. I can tell right now that y'all are going to like each other. They are true blue friends, and as Henry says, 'Show mi yu friends, and mi see who yu are'."

"What's solomon gundy?"

"Oh, you'll find out. I'll let it be a surprise. Now, thanks for calling. We will definitely stay in touch, and I hope you know that you always have a place to stay in the Keys. Y'all have an irie trip home."

"Well, I guess that finalizes the voyage on a positive note. I was really starting to like them."

"I guess all good things have to come to an end," Betsy replied.

"Is your next trite-ism going to be to say that nothing lasts forever?"

"Nah., I thought I'd save that one for you."

"Mighty decent of you. By the way, do you know who first said all good things must come to an end?"

"I guess I will in about thirty seconds."

"A schoolteacher in early August. Yuk. Yuk. Yuk"

"Please. Enough already."

"I've gotta wonder what my desk at the office looks like. I bet you can't even see that sucker."

"Mine too, but we may be pleasantly surprised. After all, Barbara and Margaret do take pretty good care of us. Life at the office will probably be dull compared to what all has happened on this cruise. One thing that remains true about you, my darling, is you sure know how to treat a girl to a good time."

Betsy made one last pass through the bathroom and looked in the closet while Will went through the desk drawer and bedside tables. He noticed something that made him pause briefly and put it in his shirt pocket.

"All clear. Let's head for our assembly point in the Explorers Lounge and get some coffee and Danish while we wait to be called to disembark. By the way, Dick and Beth won't be there. The P's disembark well after the B's. This is one of those times I'm glad we're in the President's Club instead of disembarking with the herd."

"You got that right. No use staying up here. Still think we're doing the right thing not turning Suzzie in?"

"More convinced than ever. After all, she didn't kill anyone. She just framed some assholes and got even with them for past wrongs. And let's face it. They screwed her and Misty royally."

"Literally. You have such a way with words."

"Hell. I feel for her. She lost her best friend, and now she's lost her drunken husband as well. At least she'll have an income, however, since she does own her own business. And I think she's safe from Al. And who knows, Billy may have had some life insurance."

"And also, who knows what'll happen to Paul and Jerry. There's a good chance they'll be exonerated before all's said and done. But she's made sure they'll go through mucho hell before it happens."

"And have to spend a shit-pot-load on lawyers before they're done. And if it doesn't all come out in the wash, I think they deserve punishing anyway. It could easily work out that way. Tom's already got off on the shoplifting charge. Suzzie just made him sweat bullets for a little while."

"Yeah, shoplifting's one thing, but Paul's charges of being a national security risk and Jerry being called a pervert are a bit more serious than petty theft."

"But don't forget to put it in perspective. Their crime against Suzzie and Misty was more serious than Tom's. They were actual rapists. Tom was just an observer who did nothing to stop it."

"Not just an observer, but an accessory. All things considered, Suzzie let him off light, but my conscience makes me agree with you. I'm sure glad we got a chance to tell Suzzie that you're pretty sure you fixed things so that Al won't bother her further going forward."

"Me too. I wish I could have seen Jimbo again to tell him how things shook out with Al. He and Willard will be more in Al's spotlight than Suzzie is. Willard's got something Al wants. Maybe we'll see Jimbo before we disembark. If not, I'll call him as soon as we get home."

"I don't guess we'll ever know for sure what happened to Billy."

"My best guess is that both of Billy's accidents were self-inflicted. Booze killed Billy. I bet he fell down those steps all by himself. He was drunk as a skunk that night. And I'd be willing to bet he was going through the DT's and drank that rubbing alcohol too."

"You could be right, but there's always the Al factor."

"I don't see why Al would want to do Billy in. He needed him to be his gopher. And to try to whip Willard into line ... Unless he viewed Billy's drinking and the potential loss of Billy's license to be dangerous enough to turn him into a liability."

And what about Jimbo?"

"That's a different matter. Jimbo admitted that Al's bodyguard tripped him as a warning."

"And Dickie-do?"

"I'd probably have to assign that one to Paul. You don't know Paul like I do. He was a mean, damn lowlife redneck with a propensity for violence who knew how to play football, ... Don't forget. Paul came close to serving some time for almost killing another drunk redneck at Tillie's Lounge when he got cute with Michelle ... and as we saw, his pal Dickie-do had a history with Michelle and *was* hitting on her on the ship as well. I wouldn't doubt one little bit that she could have gone to the dickman's stateroom to provide him with drugs that night and he got out of line. And she then told Paul about it, and he went ballistic. In fact, he might've even been there while Dickie-do was acting up."

"Which is another reason that Suzzie's bagging him may have been justified. And Rusty's razor blade accident?"

"I'm thinking that was a Danny. Danny couldn't stand the fact that Rusty's book, "The Rape," the fictional retelling of Suzzie and Misty's rape actually made him a lot of money and turned him into a celebrity as well. And now Rusty was on this ship in effect throwing the whole affair in Danny's face by teaching classes about it and signing books. Don't forget, he did cause havoc at one of Rusty's book signings for what seemed at the time to be an inexplicable reason. I think Rusty's success was too much for him."

"So, Mr. I've-got-all-the-answers, how'd we end up in the middle of all this crap and get a poisonous snake sent to our room?"

"I wasn't been able to figure that one out until this morning when we were searching the room for the last time. Then it hit me."

"Mind sharing your thoughts with me?"

"Yep. Both of these handwritten notes were in the desk drawer. Note number one – 'Raise and Call'."

"OK. That's the note that we couldn't understand the meaning of that came with the snake basket."

"Right. Now note number two. 'Can't think of anyone else who is more deserving of an incredibly happy day. Happy birthday. Al'."

"I know. The note that came on your birthday with the Tortuga Rum Cake."

"Right again. Now, notice the handwriting. It's very distinctive and neat. See the similarities. Look at the capital C on both notes. Both of these notes were written by the same person."

"By God, you're right. They definitely are. But what does 'Raise and Call' mean?"

"At the time we got it, nothing, but after Jimbo came clean with me, and after I saw these cards side by side this morning, it suddenly meant a lot. I think a room steward under Al's control delivered the pot with the snake to our room by accident. 'Raise and Call' was a message to Willard that Al had run out of patience in their negotiations, and if necessary, he was going to get Willard's plantation out of his estate by dealing with Zelma. He was raising the price he was offering for the last time, and he was calling for Willard's to either put up or shut up. I think that snake was supposed to bite Willard not us. Either that or scare the shit out of him. I'd almost be willing to bet that Al was sending something nice to us, like maybe a bottle of wine or something, and the steward got the packages mixed up, and we ended up with Willard's package by mistake."

"Sherlock Holmes Black, I think you may be on to something. There is no doubt that these notes were written by the same person."

"Our big mistake all along, I think, is that we were viewing all of these mis-occurrences as being connected, and they weren't. We had four different situations occurring simultaneously. Some semi-related and some unrelated."

"If you're right, you've got to have one of the most dysfunctional graduating classes on earth. So, what do we do now?"

"Nothing. Not a damned thing. There's very little here that would stand up in court. I guess we just have to say that it's an imperfect world, and that justice isn't always absolute. But if you don't mind, let's continue this discussion later. I hear coffee and Danish calling me. They're saying 'Will, come get me.' Let's not disappoint them. I've got our carry-on."

"Do you realize that this is the first cruise we have ever taken that didn't wind up back at Port Everglades?"

"Yeh, I do. Kind of miss just going over to the parking garage and picking up our car and driving home down U.S. 1 instead of having to face airports and flights."

They caught the elevator down to Deck 6 and strolled down the hall to the Explorers Lounge. They found a table and Betsy held it while Will fetched their breakfast.

“I got you both an apple and a lemon Danish,” Will said when he returned.

“I like them both.”

About that time, they saw Jimbo enter.

“Oh, good. I was hoping we’d get lucky. I really wanted to talk to him in person rather than long distance from home.”

“Jimbo. Over here,” Will yelled and waved.

Jimbo waved back and came over.

I was hoping I’d see you before we left,” he said.

“Funny. I was just telling Betsy the same thing about you. Get your coffee and come back. I’ll watch your carry-on while you do it.”

“That was a helluva sendoff we gave Dickie-do and Billy yesterday wasn’t it.”

“After everything else that has happened on this cruise, I guess it was only fitting that we end it on a fiasco. Think we should do another cruise for our next reunion?”

“Are you brave enough to even have another reunion?”

“Maybe next time we’ll all go to Disney World.”

“I’m not sure they’d let this bunch in. They don’t have enough insurance. Space Mountain and Spaceship Earth might not ever recover.”

“But the Twilight Zone Tower would sure be fitting. Speaking of fitting, do you know what Cinderella asked her prince charming?”

“Tell me.”

“Wanna see if it fits?”

“With that, I’m going to get some breakfast.”

When Jimbo came back, Will said, “On a serious note, I think I’ve got your problem with Soltero solved.”

Jimbo glanced at Betsy and looked somewhat uncomfortable .

He asked, “Should we discuss that here?”

Will quickly added, “Don’t worry. Betsy knows all about what’s going on. She’s probably had more dealings with Al than either one of us has.”

Jimbo relaxed somewhat and said, “You didn’t threaten him, did you?”

“Didn’t have to. That’s not how you handle Al. You have to subtly outfox him with charm and guile. Here’s the deal. I have convinced Al that Billy assembled an entire dossier on their dealings together before he died and then gave it to me on a thumb drive with instructions that I am to turn it over to the authorities if anything should happen to Suzzie, Willard, or you. And I don’t just mean just your deaths. I mean economically as well as physically -- at my option.”

“What’s to keep him from just taking it away from you and destroying it and then killing you?”

“Because I told him it wouldn’t do him any damn good since Billy sent another copy to someone else and I don’t even know who that person is.”

“So, do you really have anything?”

“Hell, no. I was just making that shit up. But Al doesn’t know that.”

“I guess that explains why he got hold of Willard last night and told him that he had decided that Willard’s plantation was not a fit in his investment portfolio after all.”

Will looked at Betsy and gave her a high-five.

“I think we’ve won another round with Señor Slick Soltero. YES, this has been a good trip after all.”

Jimbo laughed.

“See you in ten years. Try to stay out of trouble until then. I wasn’t kidding when I said get it on your calendar.”

“Thank God its ten years off. Maybe by then I can recover from this reunion.”

"I've heard that every parting is a form of death, and that every reunion is a form of heaven."

Betsy and Jimbo looked at each other and both said together, "BULLFUCKNGSHIT."

❄ ❄ ❄

# About the Authors

David Beckwith is a three-generation native of Greenville, Mississippi, with a BBA and an MBA from Ole Miss. His parents owned an independent cash commodity trading firm which also cleared securities trades through Goodbody & Co. David spent 40 years in the securities business, the first half of his career with Bache & Co. and its successors, the second half with Morgan Stanley. He retired as a Senior Vice President with approximately $500 million in responsibilities. For 25 years he has served as an adjunct professor at five different universities.

His first book was a narrative nonfiction work published by the University of Alabama Press in 2009 entitled *A New Day In The Delta*. The Mississippi Institute of Arts and Letters chose it as the runner-up for nonfiction book of the year. The book is often compared to Pat Conroy's *The Water Is Wide*.

David's wife Nancy earned a doctorate in finance and was the largest commercial lender and underwriter for Florida National Bank/1st Union/Wachovia, a member of their President's Club, and a board member. Also, she served as the provost of the Brookley Campus for the University of South Alabama.

David and Nancy started writing the Will and Betsy Black Adventure Series in 2010. The protagonists of this series are a married couple somewhat reminiscent of Nick and Nora Charles of *The Thin Man* Series or Jonathan and Jennifer Hart of *Hart To Hart*. Their unique hook was that like the books' protagonists the authors were also a happily married couple.

Moving to Key West, the Beckwiths were tapped to write a book review column for the Key West *Citizen*, which David continues to produce on a weekly basis.

ABSOLUTELY AMAZING eBOOKS

AbsolutelyAmazingEbooks.com
or AA-eBooks.com

www.ingramcontent.com/pod-product-compliance
Lightning Source LLC
Chambersburg PA
CBHW060947030726
47503CB00003B/768
* 9 7 8 1 9 5 5 0 3 6 3 9 9 *